CR... OF BITTER THORN

ALSO BY KAY L MOODY

The Fae of Bitter Thorn
Heir of Bitter Thorn
Court of Bitter Thorn
Castle of Bitter Thorn
Crown of Bitter Thorn
Queen of Bitter Thorn

The Elements of Kamdaria
The Elements of the Crown
The Elements of the Gate
The Elements of the Storm

Truth Seer Trilogy
Truth Seer
Healer
Truth Changer

Visit kaylmoody.com/bitter to read the prequel novella,
Heir of Bitter Thorn, for free

CROWN

OF

BITTER

THORN

KAY L MOODY

THE FAE OF BITTER THORN

3

Crown of Bitter Thorn
The Fae of Bitter Thorn 3
By Kay L Moody

Published by Marten Press
3731 W 10400 S Ste 102, #205
South Jordan, UT 84009

www.MartenPress.com

Cover by Angel Leya
Edited by Deborah Spencer and Justin Greer

ISBN: 978-1-954335-01-1

CHAPTER

1

When her life flashed before her eyes, Elora wanted to forget it all.

The balance shard that had the power to turn her into a fae shattered into tiny pieces inside her heart. Its power spread all through her body. All reality ceased to exist as memories replayed in her mind. Along with each memory came a flood of the emotions associated with it. If everything positive had been heightened, the experience might not have been so bad.

Instead, the negative emotions were heightened far worse than she had ever borne during her lifetime.

Mistakes, fear, frustration... grief. All of them cluttered her memories. They brought pain, anxiety, even heartache. Since her birth, not a day had passed that didn't hold at least a sliver of negativity. And too many of them held more than just slivers.

Those moments hurt. They screamed and clawed. But… they filled her too. Filled her right up to the top of her head. At least she wasn't empty and alone.

Reliving every emotion of her lifetime all at once brought more pain than she could bear. Letting go would have been too easy. Too relieving. Her parents' deaths hurt most of all.

The pain hurt, but it didn't come alone. It brought meaning.

Each time a new negative moment sizzled in her mind, it almost left her stronger. Of course, the memories sliced and skewered her insides, but at least they had happened. At least she had lived.

At least she had loved.

When she'd plunged the balance shard deep into her chest, she knew the cost. She knew she might not survive.

She'd never expected to find peace in the process.

All that pain, all that heartache, it meant something. At some point in the process, swirling amid pain and change and memories, she found herself smiling.

At least she had lived.

While reliving the memories, her body seemed to float inside nothingness. She could not see, taste, hear, or smell. She could only feel.

After what must have been days of this, only one thing struck her as odd.

A sequence of emotions marched across her mind as potent as the others, but they had no memories attached.

She felt wonder, adventure, and magic. As with all her positive emotions, those flitted past quickly, barely a spark. Then the negative emotions came. Fear, anger, and eagerness to escape. The feelings boiled inside her just like all the others, but the part of her mind containing those memories was blank. Or maybe it was detached.

As the nothingness fell away around her, those blank spots in her memory wriggled under her skin. Where had they come from?

Now the sensation of floating began to be replaced with one of standing. It filled her, but her feet did not touch any surface. Gray mist closed in around her. She couldn't see, but maybe there was nothing *to* see.

One foot lifted and fell in a step. Nothing about it felt like walking. It felt more like floating, and the air had caught her foot where it wanted it to stop. She took another step forward.

The gray mist shifted into focus. It gained substance. A hazy light hung inside it, the exact same color as a dusky, Faerie night. Sparkles of every color burst all around. There was no up or down or inside or outside. There was just everything and nothing all at the same time.

No rain fell, but cool, minuscule droplets danced across Elora's skin from the mist. The air tasted clean, but it sizzled too. Echoes pranced across the space. Tinkling bells, trickling water, a light wind. The sounds came out so soft, they could have been a dream.

By the time she stepped again, a sweet scent drifted all around her. It smelled of wildflowers or maybe wild berries. Perhaps it was both.

With each new step, the space around her became more substantial. Her feet still didn't touch any kind of surface, but just ahead, she could see a path forming. Instead of dirt or rocks or even grass, the path seemed to be made of stars.

Moving across it felt like stepping over popping bubbles.

Faerie surrounded her, that much was clear, but not any location in particular. Maybe her imagination spun the idea, but it felt like she stood not just in Faerie but *inside* Faerie.

After that realization, the star path ahead diverged into two. She stood in a clearing just ahead of the fork in the starry road. She had a choice to make, a path to choose.

One path had stars and a dusky light. It smelled sweet. The same cool mist surrounded it. The path would be good to her, it could bring happiness.

But the other…

Sparkles showered the second path, bathing it in a rainbow of light. Its air crackled with energy, beckoning for her to choose it.

The balance shard had created these two paths. To become fae, she first had to sacrifice her mortal life. She had to say goodbye forever to the mortal life she might have had. She had to turn away from it. Take the other path.

If the second path had only sparkles and sizzling energy, the choice wouldn't have been a choice at all. But, of course, it had more to it than that.

Thundering footsteps from a distance tore down the second path toward her. An enormous creature with green skin and yellow teeth growled as it swung a curved axe. A troll.

The sight of it awakened the strange blank spot in her memory. It sparked like a light inside her, growing until a fight to the death with a troll didn't just seem like something she had to do now. It seemed like something she had *already* done before.

She stumbled backward as the troll sliced its blade toward her. Hair raised on the back of her neck as she went to grab her trusty sword. It wasn't there.

Why would it be? She clearly existed in some dream-like state while the balance shard worked through her.

A gurgling growl that had more spit than noise erupted from the troll's throat. The creature swung its axe a second time. Ducking into a roll, she got away just in time. A lock of her hair didn't have the same luck. The blade sliced through it, causing several pieces to float away into nothingness.

How could she choose the magical path when a troll kept her from it? Without a weapon, she'd never have a chance against the creature. Her heartbeat skittered as she attempted to find her feet again. Instead, she tripped over the strange nothingness.

Without meaning to, she took a few steps down the first path, the one with no magic. She didn't choose the path yet, but her feet certainly stood completely on that path and not the other.

It might have passed her notice completely, except the troll swung its blade toward her again. The swing came too fast to give her time to duck. Her first sight of the blade was only a moment before it split her head in two.

Except it didn't.

Just before the blade could touch her, it stopped midair, as if some unseen force held it in place. The troll let out another gurgling growl and pulled its arm back to swing its blade again. The creature's movements came without any restriction until the axe met the same exact spot as before. Once again, the weapon stopped just short of reaching her head.

She glanced down.

The path must have done it. She stood on the side that represented her mortal life, which acted as a barrier against the axe. When the troll attempted to use a fist on her instead, the path stopped that too. Danger could not get to her if she chose the mortal realm.

Her eyes flitted over to the magical path. But could she give up on the magic of Faerie just because it had a little danger attached to it?

Closing her eyes, she reached deep within herself to a place that possibly only existed in her dreams. Faerie had magic. Maybe that magic had limitations, but she refused to accept them. She refused to be bound by anything other than her own dreams.

The air around her buzzed. It recognized her plea, but it fought against her too. She fought back, unwilling to be shackled by any limitations. Soon, pops and sputters tickled the air. Her resolve deepened.

By the time she opened her eyes again, a leather-wrapped hilt appeared in her hands.

She had summoned her sword. Or perhaps she had conjured it. Either way, it looked and felt exactly like the sword she had faithfully used for years.

The distinction didn't matter because now she had a weapon.

Staying light on her feet, she darted away from the path representing her mortal life. The troll swiped its weapon toward her, but her speed outmatched the lumbering creature. It swung the axe at her several times. She always remained just one step ahead of it.

She jabbed and cut her own sword through the air, but it was mostly for show. A distraction. The two of them pranced and hopped around each other. They moved as if in a dance, except only she knew how it would end.

The fateful move came just moments later. Arching its arms high, the troll prepared to bring its axe down on her head. Little did it know, that action would be its undoing.

The moment its arms went up, her sword plunged. She jabbed it in the troll's one weak spot.

Her blade sank deep into the skin just under the creature's arm. Ice-cold blood trickled down her blade and onto her hands. When she yanked her sword out of the troll's body, the troll fell away into nothingness. Even its blood vanished as she turned toward the magical path once again.

Whatever danger magic brought, she'd defeat it. Just like she'd defeated the troll.

Only a few steps down the magical path, everything changed again. Light streamed in through the duskiness while a breeze fluttered through her hair. The far-off sound of tinkling bells rang closer than before.

A voice entered the space. It didn't come from any one place in particular. It simply came from everywhere. The voice was calm, peaceful. Assured.

"You are a puzzle, young one. Faerie faces a conflict so great it affects all six of its courts. In all the possible outcomes of this conflict, you were never even a player. And yet, here you are."

Elora craned her neck, trying to find the source of the voice. It sounded more female than male, but perhaps it was neither. "Who are you?"

"Not *who*."

Raising an eyebrow, Elora shifted on her feet. "Then *what* are you?"

"You already know."

Swallowing, Elora glanced upward. "Faerie itself?"

The voice went on, neither acknowledging nor denying her observation, but she still knew it to be true.

"Faerie is at a crossroads. Prince Brannick still has a chance to regain his rightful place as High King, but he cannot do it on his own. Sometimes help comes from the strangest of places."

Glancing down, Elora trailed a thumb over her leather hilt. "You mean like me. Because I am a mere mortal."

"You will not be mortal for long. You will soon have the power needed to right the wrongs of the past."

Discomfort twisted in Elora's gut. "Do you mean saving Faerie is my destiny or something?" She gave a hard swallow. "Am I the only one who can do it?"

Something like a laugh filled the space around her. The sparkles in the air gave off greater bursts. The mist grew thicker. "Of course you are not the only one who can save Faerie. You make it your destiny only because you will not stop until it is done. You alone control your fate."

Before Elora could speak again, the sparkles in the air glowed brighter. They drifted together until all of them combined right in front of her. They pulsed with energy. Every color glowed from them, but some colors became less concentrated. Though all colors moved through the clump, it mostly glowed with a purple hue.

Reaching out, her fingers stopped just short of touching the sparkles. "Is this my magic? The prince said when a mortal becomes a fae that Faerie itself provides the magic."

"You are correct. It has been arranged to match your essence."

Elora's eyes widened. She kept her hand elevated, nearly brushing the magic. She continued to reach but kept her fingers just shy of touching the magic. Something about it felt familiar.

Welcoming. It reminded her of when she got her wings. The magic felt like something that had always been a part of her; she just hadn't known it yet.

"What kind of magic will I get? King Huron had magic in bargains. Prince Brannick has magic in essence." Her shoulders nearly shuddered as she remembered the magic of another fae. Ansel had magic in blood, and he had used it to find out she was the daughter of Theobald. Brushing that thought to the side, she stared into the cluster of sparkles. "What magic will I have?"

"That is for you to discover."

The air thickened around her. Magic pulsed. *Burst.* In a shower, it enveloped her. Every pore in her skin stretched and tingled. Her senses sharpened. Suddenly, she could hear, see, and feel everything a hundred times greater than she had before. Her hair turned silky, growing a little longer too. Her ears prickled as they came to points.

Letting out a breath, her entire body tensed. It relaxed a moment later. The change came quickly, but it washed over her slowly, sinking in deeper with each breath.

Now she was fae.

Rays pierced the gray mist until nothing but a bright light flooded the space. All around her, the light glowed and shined. The voice spoke again, fading away more with each word.

"You are at the center of this crossroads now. If you had never come to Faerie, another fae would stand in your place. But you are here now. You have earned your place. Faerie is molding its history around you."

CHAPTER

2

Light folded into the creases of Elora's eyes. The nothingness faded away while substance formed all around her. At some point, her eyes had fluttered closed. The grip on her sword remained steadfast as her body lost the sensation of standing. Now, she was clearly lying on a bed with a plush blanket covering her limbs.

The scents of crisp rain and a lush, mossy forest drifted around her. She could almost taste the stone walls that formed her bedroom inside Bitter Thorn Castle.

After noticing the bed, she heard a delicate melody being plucked across harp strings. She didn't recognize the song but still appreciated its beauty. Even in her half-awake state, the complexity of the song was obvious. Only one person in her life could create such music. Her mother.

The thought spun in her mind while her chest tightened. But her mother was dead. Though that truth still stung her heart, at least she had finally accepted it. But if the music didn't come from her mother...

At last, Elora's eyelids snapped open. "Grace."

She sat up with a start, shooting her eyes toward the corner of the room where the music originated.

Her youngest sister dropped her hands from the harp and jerked her head toward Elora. Before either of them could speak, their middle sister jumped onto the bed next to Elora.

Chloe's blonde hair practically glowed under the light of the floating sprites up above. "You're awake." Her voice came out breathless. She pressed the back of her hand to Elora's forehead. "Your fever finally broke yesterday, but then you still didn't wake." Her voice dropped. "We were worried."

Grace had been moving across the mossy floor with tentative steps, but once her sister finished speaking, she jumped onto the bed to sit on Elora's other side.

Feeling her chin tremble, Elora pulled her sisters into a tight hug. "How did you get here? To Faerie?"

The two sisters snuggled in closer to their big sister. Soon, the three of them were nothing more than a bundle of arms and tears.

"Prince Brannick brought us here." Grace used her whole palm to wipe away the copious tears on her cheeks. She brushed them away right into the red hair framing her face.

Chloe gave a vigorous nod. "You had just barely left with the prince, and I was about to start copying one of my favorite poems from a book I had borrowed, but then the prince suddenly returned."

Brushing a knuckle across her nose, Grace sniffed. "Someone knocked on the door first. Don't forget about that."

17

"Yes." Chloe touched a hand to her collar. "Someone pounded on the door like the world might end if we didn't open it. And then Prince Brannick appeared and told us you were dying. We didn't believe him because you had just barely left only moments earlier."

Dropping her head on her oldest sister's shoulder, Grace gave the faintest shudder. "That's when the man at the door started shouting."

Now Chloe shuddered. "I didn't like the sound of his voice, but the prince hated it even more. His whole body went stiff, and he turned toward the door like it was a snake. Then he conjured this swirly portal tunnel thing and told us to hurry and step through it."

"The tunnel is called a door." Grace sat a little straighter, clearly assuming her oldest sister had never seen a Faerie door before.

Chloe dropped her voice to a whisper. "Maybe we shouldn't have been so trusting, but that voice at the door was scary. And *you* seemed to think the prince was okay, so we went with him. And then we found you here, dying, just like he said."

A smile twitched at the corners of Elora's mouth as she pulled her sisters closer. "He actually brought you here. For me."

Pulling herself away, Chloe brushed the hair away from her oldest sister's ear. "We saw your body glow and your ears got pointed. They told us you would change if you lived, but we didn't believe it."

Grace touched the tip of Elora's other pointed ear, only to let out a breathy chuckle. "How does it feel to be fae?"

Elora sucked in a deep breath, perhaps deeper than she ever had. She could feel every particle in the room, taste every speck of dust, and smell like she had never smelled before.

Letting out a slow breath, she finally released her sisters. "It feels magnificent."

They pulled away from her, supporting her elbows as she tried to stand. Despite their fears, she got to her feet without any trouble. Her room had changed.

The harp Quintus had made for her sat in the corner nearest to the door. A velvet-cushioned seat stood behind it with a metal music stand at its side. A wooden desk sat next to it that hadn't been there before. Piles of parchment and open books scattered the top of the desk. Some papers even littered the nearby floor.

Two new beds had been added to the room, one at the foot of Elora's bed and one at the head. They lined one wall of the room. Clay vases with geometric designs painted on the front held big bundles of purple wildflowers. At the foot of one bed, there sat a wooden bowl of berries.

A few dresses were strewn about the room. All along the ceiling, light purple ribbons were tied to the green vines that stretched over the stone walls. It gave off a much cozier feeling than it ever had when Elora had been alone there.

Once on her feet, she reached for the hilt that rested in her belt. Just as she realized the belt was *not* the magically invisible one Brannick had given her, her sister drew in a sharp breath.

"Your sword?" Chloe jumped from the bed. She poked the weapon on Elora's waist while her face scrunched up. "Kaia told us to keep it on the other side of the room by the bath. How did you get it?"

With a shrug, Elora wrapped her fingers tighter around the hilt. "I summoned it."

The two younger sisters glanced at each other with eyes narrowing.

"How?" Grace finally asked.

19

"I don't…" Elora shook her head while her insides tumbled with an energy she had never felt before. "I do not know."

Chloe poked the sword again. "Doesn't the iron bother you?"

Smiling, Elora rubbed a thumb over the hilt. "Not when I touch the leather instead of the metal." She bit her lip as she formed more words in her head. But were they true? As a fae, she wouldn't have the ability to lie anymore. Nodding to herself, she continued. "Anyway, the sword was with me when I changed. I think it has magic just like I do now."

The sword could be examined later. She had other things she wanted to check. Slipping her hand into one pocket, she felt for the light green crystal that contained Brannick's essence. It buzzed against her fingertips with the same energy it always did, but this time, she felt it all the way to the center of her heart.

Being fae must have made the sensation stronger than ever. While her lips twitched with a smile, another thought struck her. How else had her body changed since becoming fae? With only a thought, she pushed out her wings. They shimmered with a light purple hue as they burst from her back. Her two younger sisters gasped at the sight.

Grace tried to tuck a strand of red hair back into her bun. "Do all fae have wings?"

"No." Elora sent her wings flapping. Remembering what she had learned from her sprite friend about flying, she urged her muscles to relax and simply enjoy the sensation of rising into the air. It didn't strain her muscles much when she lifted off the ground. She still only flew as high as the tree in her room before she had to lower herself back to the ground again.

Being fae had definitely improved her flying, but she would still need practice to go higher or to go great distances.

By the time she reached the mossy stone floor, her sisters were looking at each other again. "We should send a message to Lyren," Grace said in a lowered voice.

Chloe responded with an eager nod. "She said she would tell us the news about Swiftsea once Elora awoke." Chloe pinched her bottom lip between two fingers. "We should send a message to Vesper too."

Grace's cheeks stretched wide with a smile. "He can tell Elora about the plan to overthrow the Fairfrost queen."

A snort sputtered from Chloe's lips. "What plan? They have no plan except that they plan to make a plan."

The words ate at Elora's insides. Others had been busy making plans while she lay useless on a bed in her room. Reaching for both her sisters, she tipped her eyebrows up. "You will not believe this, but Vesper is—"

"Our brother," Grace finished. Her mouth scrunched to the side. "Well, our fae brother. He told us how he married our great-great-great-great-grandmother, Cosette."

Elora's hands fell away from her sisters' arms. "How did you know?"

A sad smile etched across Chloe's features. "You've been asleep for a long time. Weeks probably."

Those words ate at Elora's insides more completely than the others had. Her eyes turned downward. "There is no time in Faerie."

Letting out a chuckle, Chloe shook her head. "You're talking like a fae already." Her body spun as she surveyed the room. "Now, what can I use as an offering to send a message? The sprites just need something that is personal to me. Do you think those berries will work?" She gestured toward the bowl

21

at the foot of her bed. "I was supposed to eat them, but I didn't because they're too sour. Do you think that counts as personal?"

Grace shrugged as she glanced back toward the harp.

After a few steps toward the bowl, Chloe spun around to face her older sister again. "You'll have to change your clothes first. That dress is so dark."

With all the other things in the room to notice, Elora hadn't bothered to look at her own clothes. A black dress with delicate sleeves and a full skirt covered her. She recognized the green and silver geometric embroidery at hem of the dress. Brannick had conjured this dress for her after Ansel had used blood to discover her identity. It was after she had accidentally killed the fae that attacked her.

She swallowed hard at the sight of it.

"We put you in black because…" Grace trailed off as she clasped her hands behind her back. Her voice came out quieter when she finally spoke again. "We thought you would never wake up."

They all held their breaths until Chloe finally pranced across the room, her blonde hair bouncing. "What about this dress?"

She held up a simple lilac-colored dress that had been draped over the empty stone bath at the other end of the room. The pointed hem landed just below the knee with fringe coming off it. Intricate silver beading adorned the edges.

Elora frowned at the dress before throwing a wistful glance around the room. "I had a skirt from Mother that—"

"Oh, I cut that up and turned it into ribbons," Chloe said with a flippant hand wave.

Jerking her head toward her sister, Elora blinked. "You what?"

"Look." Grace's young eyes turned alight as she gestured toward the purple ribbons tied to the vines across the ceiling. "Now Mother is all around us."

Elora blinked again. It took another moment for the shock to wear off and then another to appreciate the gesture. But soon, the knot in her stomach untied. She had clung to her mother's skirt while in Faerie. It was one of her only connections to the mortal realm. But now her sisters were here, and they wanted to remember their mother too. How better to do it then to be surrounded by pieces of her skirt?

Gripping her sword hilt, Elora gave a gentle nod. "I like it."

The crease between Chloe's eyebrows faded as she let out a sigh of relief. "Oh, good. Hurry and put this dress on and then we can send a message to the others."

The lilac fabric felt as thick as wool but as luxurious as silk. Elora glanced toward her sisters. "You said Vesper wanted to make a plan to overthrow Queen Alessandra?"

Chloe tipped her head to the side. "Well, she's High Queen Alessandra now, but yes."

While fastening the belt for her sword around her waist, Elora glanced toward the door. "And what about Brannick? Have you seen him?"

She managed to keep the next questions inside, but even unspoken, they still bubbled in her throat. *Has he come to see me? Has he worried?*

Their silence offered no reassurance. She turned to give a pointed glance toward her sisters. They looked at each other instead, sharing some memory Elora didn't share. Even as a fae, she couldn't possibly decipher the meaning of the look.

While unspoken words hung around them, the door to the room yawned open. With a hopeful flutter in her chest, Elora

23

glanced toward it. Her heart dropped a little when she saw the emerald hair of Kaia.

The dryad held a stone cup in her hands. The moment she laid eyes on Elora the cup tumbled to the ground. Its contents spilled over the mossy stone with a great splash.

"You are awake." Kaia's brown and green eyes pulsed as her jaw dropped.

Elora offered a smile in return. "Yes. And I want to know more about the plan to overthrow Queen Alessandra."

CHAPTER 3

The leather under Elora's fingertips coursed with energy. Or maybe her fingertips held the energy. She gripped her sword hilt, but it did nothing to stop tension from filling the air. It floated through the room, pricking at every corner. She had no idea *why* it was there, but she did know *who* it came from, at least.

Kaia dropped to her knees while her light brown dress fluttered around her. Her limbs shook as she reached out to grab the stone cup she had dropped. Her shoulders shivered hard enough to cause her waist-length emerald hair to shake. When she tried to stand, she stumbled and dropped the cup again.

"I did not think you would awake." Her voice quaked over every word.

Lending a hand to the dryad, Elora helped her to her feet. "You say that almost like you are upset about it."

"Of course not." Kaia's brown and green eyes grew wide as the cup tumbled out of her hands onto the ground again. She pressed a hand to her forehead before waving it off. When she turned back to face Elora, heaviness weighed her eyes down. "My child, I have a confession to make."

Throwing a hand to her chest, Elora tried not to gasp. "Is it Brannick? Did something happen to him?"

Both of Kaia's green and brown eyes narrowed. "No."

Elora closed her eyes for a brief moment before opening them again. "It's the bargain then. Is he still bound to Queen Alessandra?"

Shaking her head, Kaia touched a hand to her forehead. "No. You sacrificed your mortal life for him, which broke his side of the bargain with *High* Queen Alessandra. Actually, it broke the entire bargain. He no longer has to follow her orders. He is completely free."

A soft huff left Elora's nostrils. "Then what is your confession about?"

The light dulled from Kaia's eyes as she tucked a strand of emerald hair behind one ear. "It is about you."

Tension curled in Elora's chest at the sound of those words.

Averting her eyes, the dryad gestured toward one bed. "You should sit down, my child." Her eyes drifted to Chloe and Grace, who looked as pale as fresh milk. "You should all sit down."

Stomping across the stone floor eased some of the tension in Elora's chest. But when her sisters sat on either side of her wearing grim expressions, even more tension returned. She glanced toward her youngest sister. "Do you know what this is about?"

Darkness may have clouded Grace's dark eyes, but she still straightened her back. She was always desperate to appear older than her actual age of twelve. "No." At least her voice didn't quiver when she spoke.

Elora turned to her middle sister, who sat on her other side.

Chloe gazed at the desk on the other side of the room. Her eyes focused on the papers and books atop it. She bit her bottom lip. "I don't know either, but I've read enough poems to know it's not going to be good."

The dryad clenched her jaw while conjuring a simple wicker chair. Even once she settled down on top of it, she seemed to have difficulty raising her gaze to Elora's. "Prince Brannick brought you to Faerie to help with the testing, but you had been here once before." Her gaze fell to her lap. "I brought you here." She gulped. "To Fairfrost, in fact."

All three of the sisters gave a collective gasp, but Chloe's was the most fervent. She folded her arms over her chest as she looked toward her older sister. "You never told us? I read poems about Faerie and adventures all the time. You never thought to confide in me?" Her voice cracked as it lowered. "I would have believed you."

Waving off her sister's words, Elora rolled her eyes. "Kaia is lying."

Chloe tightened the grip of her arms over her chest. "Fae can't lie. Everyone who studies Faerie knows that."

Elora let out a sigh. "I have only been to Fairfrost twice, and Vesper brought me there both times." Her eyebrow raised. "I am fae now too. How could I tell you all that if it isn't true?"

"Because you honestly believe it to be true." Kaia cleared her voice before speaking again. "But it is not."

The tightness in Elora's chest twisted. Now *she* gulped.

Kaia stared at her hands while they rested in her lap. "I did bring you to Fairfrost."

"Why?" With so many thoughts spinning in her head, that was all Elora could think to ask.

Words left the dryad's lips, but they seemed reluctant to come out. "You killed a troll." Her lips dropped to a frown, which stretched the dark brown skin around them. "You had no choice, really. The troll wanted to kill you."

"I killed a troll?" Elora reached for a small section of her hair to play with while she turned the words over in her mind. Doing so caused her to remember how the shard had worked through her body.

The magic of the shard caused her to relive every emotion in her life. But there had been one section of emotions that burned as bright as the rest, except they had no memories attached.

She reached for her hand, rubbing a thumb over the lopsided scar in between her thumb and forefinger. Opening her mouth, she muttered under her breath. "Brannick told me this looked like a troll bite." Her eyes shot upward toward the dryad again. "Is that where my dagger went? I had a dagger that went missing a few weeks before Brannick found me in the mortal realm."

"*Prince* Brannick." Kaia winced when she spoke again. "The dagger may have been yours, but it bore your father's symbol. His shield and chevron symbol with the star inside is well known in Faerie."

Elora sat up so straight, she almost jumped off the bed entirely. "Queen Alessandra knows the symbol too. She showed it to me when she had my sword." Churning writhed inside her stomach as she sank back onto the bed. "She said

28

my father killed a troll and left his dagger inside it. She knew it was him who killed the troll because of the symbol."

On either side of Elora, her two sisters leaned forward to shoot each other questioning looks. Those were followed with shrugs.

Kaia's chin had dropped to her chest. She wrung her hands in her lap, pursing her lips as she moved.

Aches dug deep into Elora's throat as she touched a hand to her chest. "*I* killed the troll?" Tears pricked at her eyes. "Queen Alessandra killed my parents because of that troll, but it wasn't even my father who did it." Now her eyes pierced the dryad in front of her. "Was it?"

Slumping her shoulders forward, Kaia's chin began to quiver. "I did not know she got revenge. I did not think she would ever find out."

Grace's young hand shook as she brought it to her lips. "High Queen Alessandra killed our parents?"

"It is my fault." Kaia's entire delicate body shivered. "I accept responsibility for it. I should have given you a different weapon to fight with. I should have realized. I thought you would be safe, but I had forgotten about the symbol on your father's weapons."

With the memory of their burned cottage still fresh in Elora's mind, she curled her fingers up tight. It took effort to force words from her mouth. "Why did you bring me to Fairfrost? What was so important about killing that troll?"

Kaia's emerald hair shivered as she shook her head back and forth. She did not answer.

Elora sat forward on the bed. "Was the troll just a byproduct? Was I there for a different reason?"

The dryad pressed her lips together, still shaking her head back and forth.

29

Closing her eyes, Elora searched the emotions she had felt that had missing memories. It only took a moment before she had a guess. "I helped Brannick escape Fairfrost. Didn't I?"

Chloe's blonde hair glowed in the light of the floating sprites up above. "Prince Brannick was stuck in Fairfrost?"

Ignoring the question, Elora leaned forward. She reached both hands out expectantly. Pleading. "Why do I not remember?"

Kaia curled her arms over her stomach. Her eyes turned downward as she spoke. "Some things are best kept untold."

Elora refused to be satisfied by that answer. Maybe her memories were blank, but that didn't stop her from remembering the emotions that had gone with them. She turned them over in her mind, checking them against what she already knew. Her head tilted to the side as she pieced everything together. "Someone gave Queen Alessandra a memory elixir that made her forget Brannick." Elora's eyes turned straight to the dryad now. "But I must have taken a memory elixir too."

Brown and green eyes flashed upward to Elora for a brief moment before Kaia looked down again. She remained silent.

Elora narrowed her eyes and set her jaw. "Am I right?"

One last shudder shook through Kaia's whole body. "My lack of judgment has gravely hurt you and your sisters." She gulped. "I caused the death of your parents. I vow to—"

"No." Elora raised a hand to prevent any further words. "I do not want whatever retribution you think will make this right."

Kaia frowned. "That is the way things are done in Faerie. We use vows to ease our consciences."

The words only barely drifted into Elora's ears. "Does Brannick remember?"

"No." The dryad jumped out of her chair, knocking it to the ground in the process. She touched a hand to her chest while trying to calm her sudden heavy breaths. After a deep breath out, her face hardened, as if made of stone. "You must never speak of this to Prince Brannick. Not ever."

Elora glanced at both of her sisters before she responded. "Why not?"

Chloe and Grace shrugged, but the tears in their eyes suggested they were only half listening to the conversation now.

Still breathing deeply, the dryad righted her wicker chair and sat in it once again. Weight lined the words that left her lips. "His essence suffers enough as it is. Escaping Fairfrost is the only victory he has. He cannot find out he had help escaping, or it will be his undoing."

"Your hair is turning into leaves." Grace showed her true age when she pointed with a dropped jaw toward the dryad.

The dryad's emerald hair had indeed turned stringy with leaves forming toward the bottom. Even her soft brown skin had turned rough. Now dark striations appeared across it, looking exactly like the bark from a tree.

Not willing to make eye contact with the dryad, Elora looked at her youngest sister instead. "That is what happens when she has been away from her tree for too long."

"It also happens when she is greatly distressed." Chloe's voice came out as soft as a squeak.

Everyone in the room turned toward the middle sister.

Chloe turned up one corner of her mouth in a smile. "I have always been fascinated by dryads. They were my favorite fae creature."

A beat of silence filled the room before Kaia stood. She left the wicker chair and glanced toward the door. "I must hurry back to my tree." She gave a pointed look toward Elora now. "But before I go, I vow to—"

"No." Elora stood from the bed, cutting off the dryad once again. "I want my memories back. That is the only thing you should offer as retribution."

Kaia shrank at the words. "I cannot make such a vow."

"Why not?"

She reached for her emerald hair, which now looked like a tangle of branches, moss, and leaves. "It might not be possible."

Elora pressed her lips together. "Then I might not be able to keep myself from telling Brannick."

The look of sheer horror that passed over the dryad's face was enough to keep Elora from saying anything to Brannick. But she wasn't about to admit that she'd keep quiet. She glanced back at the bed toward her sisters. "You two stay here. I am going to find the prince."

32

CHAPTER

4

Every creak and whisper that trailed through the hallways of Bitter Thorn Castle stood out to Elora like never before. She could hear intricacies in the sounds that she never would have thought to imagine. As a mortal, she didn't have the ability to appreciate such things. But now as a fae, she could bask in the wonder of it.

Every step resounded all around her, allowing her to both hear and *feel* them. She could hear conversations between fae even when they weren't in the same hallway as her. Their whispers drifted over to her easily.

When she neared the council room, her ears attuned even more. She was still a hallway away, but she heard two distinct voices in the council room.

"Quintus is waiting for us in his home." Prince Brannick sounded broodier than usual. His voice held a weight like each breath cost him.

When a shimmery sound followed his words, Elora knew he had just opened a door.

Now came the voice of her fae brother. Vesper spoke slowly, as if afraid of how the sentence would be received. "I will meet you there."

Someone's boot crunched over thorns. "Do you have something more important to do?" A sharp edge formed around Brannick's words.

When Vesper spoke again, it came out softer than before. "I wanted to check on Elora."

Silence followed. She could hear bodies shifting, but even her fae senses couldn't guess what facial expressions crossed between the two fae. She began to run toward the council room. If they were going to Quintus's home, she wanted to accompany them.

Vesper cleared his throat. "I will check on her after our visit with Quintus. I know how important it is to see…"

Her feet picked up speed as Vesper trailed off. If she didn't hurry, she'd miss them. Even with the noise of her boots slapping against the stone, she could still hear Brannick and Vesper shuffling across the council room floor.

By the time she finally made it inside, it was too late. Brannick's swirling door vanished just as she got close enough to see it.

She let out a grunt, but the situation didn't stop her for long. Her lips curled into a smirk as she raised her hand high above her head. After she clicked her tongue three times, a glowing green sprite zoomed down from the ceiling to land on her palm.

34

The sprite had bright yellow-green hair. It poked out at haphazard angles. He wore a brown coat and green pants that had been ripped to be knee-length. Sparkling yellow-green eyes blinked at Elora expectantly.

A thread from her lilac dress would have to be her offering. Hopefully it was good enough. The sprite spent a moment examining the thread before he tucked it into his magical pocket.

Her lips turned into a smile. "I need you to send a message to Lyren of Swiftsea from me, Elora of..." The words caught in her throat for a moment. They buzzed and tumbled while she considered. Indecision only lasted for a moment. "Elora of Bitter Thorn." Her spine straightened at the sound of those words. She was not of the mortal realm anymore. "Tell Lyren that I request her presence in the Bitter Thorn council room."

The sprite zoomed off without any fanfare. Maybe he saw nothing remarkable in that moment, but it didn't matter. Elora let out a sigh that felt more like a sparkle. Her body flopped into the nearest chair while a grin stretched wide across her face.

Elora of Bitter Thorn. It had a nice ring to it.

She could only bask in the moment for half a breath before a swirling tunnel appeared at her side. The foamy white and bright blue waves along the edges smelled of salt and sand. When Lyren stepped through it into the room, she had blue-painted fingernails pressed against her lips.

The brown in her eyes was bright; the silver in them burst with light. Her dark brown skin radiated with life as she pranced across the council room floor. "It *is* you. I thought the sprite was playing a trick on me, but they never do such things. Still, I did not believe..." Her voice caught as she swallowed down a gulp. "You are alive."

Her brown skin stood out perfectly against her bright blue nails as she reached forward tentatively. She poked Elora in the shoulder. Next, she brushed Elora's hair back until she could see the pointed tip of her ear. "You changed."

When Lyren lowered her hand, Elora clasped her own hands behind her back. "How did you know?"

Lyren scoffed. "Prince Brannick sent a message to everyone he could think of to help you wake." A devious smirk passed over her lips. "He owes me a debt now." Her eyebrows pinched together. "But you were asleep for so long. We all lost hope."

Not knowing how to respond, Elora merely shrugged. "I suppose I had a lot of memories to get through." Leaning forward, her voice took on a more serious quality. "Brannick and Vesper went to Quintus's home in Bitter Thorn. I think they are trying to find something."

"Ah, yes." Lyren gave a nod as she narrowed one eye. "Quintus did say his home might be a good place to see the... creatures."

Sucking in a short breath, Elora tried to stand up straighter. "Will you take me there? I want to help them." It didn't seem necessary to mention that she was also desperate to see Brannick.

After only a moment of thought, Lyren waved her hand and her white and blue door reappeared. "Prince Brannick and Vesper had an invitation and we do not. It will take more effort for us to get to the home."

Despite her words, Lyren gestured that they should go forward.

On the other side of the door, they landed on a mossy forest path. Lush green trees surrounded them with soft light filtering through the leaves. The path stretched through two clumps of trees. At the end of it sat a house made of trees. *Living* trees. The branches had been carefully bent and tied together to form walls and a roof. Clay and moss filled the spaces between the trunks and branches. Little birds landed on the roof as if it were no different from the other trees in the forest. The door was made of wood and painted bright green.

"Getting there will not be as simple as it looks." A warning laced Lyren's words.

When Elora turned to look at her friend, she let out a gasp. "Your flower."

The white sea flower that was tucked behind Lyren's ear amidst her tight black curls had turned dusty. It crumbled like ash.

Clicking her tongue, Lyren pulled it from behind her ear. "Not another one." She let out a sigh as she began walking down the path. With the wave of her hand, a shimmer of light passed through the flower, starting at the center and moving all the way through the edges. The light caused the petals to freshen until they looked as new as ever. She tucked it behind her ear once again.

With her boots crunching over a clump of black thorns, Elora raised an eyebrow. "Did you just glamour that flower? Or did you actually bring it back to life?"

Lyren glanced around the forest with eyes narrowed before she began walking forward once again. "Here in Bitter Thorn, I can bring it back to life. In Swiftsea, I would have found another flower."

More black thorns and briars twisted over the path with each step forward. They jumped out like reaching fingers attempting to trip them both. "What does that mean?" Elora's voice lowered as she asked.

It took a moment for Lyren to answer because she was glancing over her shoulder. "Bitter Thorn has magic the rest of the courts do not have." When her words were met with silence, she continued. "Faerie began in Bitter Thorn. It holds creation magic within it at all times. That is why Queen Noelani of Swiftsea believes Prince Brannick must become High King. Bitter Thorn was always meant to be the High Court. Without that ruling power and authority, it cannot spread its magic to the other courts the way it is supposed to."

Thorns covered the path now. Whatever trace of moss that was once visible was now swallowed up by the black, twisting vines. It took effort to balance while stomping over them. Elora glared at the thorns. "Why is Swiftsea the only court with the decay then? Why not the other courts?"

Lyren winced as she nearly tripped over a patch of thorns. "We do not know, but we may have a hint. We finally discovered—"

The sound of snapping claws rang in the air around them. A shriek that almost sounded like the wind cut through the air as well. Even without turning around, Elora could tell something flapped in the air right behind her. The hair on the back of her neck stood on end as she gulped.

Did she want to turn around?

Jerking her head to look behind, Lyren let out a scream. She threw her hands over her head and dropped until she crouched among the thorns.

The decision had been made. Elora definitely had to turn around, but she'd draw her sword as she did it. After turning, her feet settled deep in the thorns while she pointed her blade high.

An enormous creature hovered in the air before her. Its wings flapped hard. Its obsidian eyes sparked with sharp edges.

Instead of sending a strike toward the creature, Elora could only stare at it. The shape of it looked like a cross between a dragon and a tiger. It boasted large fangs and pointed ears. It also had a long tail and a full body.

But those things didn't keep her staring. It had no fur, no scales. In fact, it didn't even have a heart or stomach or innards of any kind. The entire creature was made of thorns. Twisting, creaking, black, sharp thorns.

Another shriek erupted from its lips. Again, it sounded like a whistling wind that tore through too tight a space. The creature swiped its claws at her. They were formed from the sharpest thorns.

Now her sword sliced toward it. The creature flew backward just in time, which didn't make any sense. The wings had too much space between all the thorns to actually lift the creature off the ground. So then how did it fly? Was it magic?

She sent her sword swinging yet again, this time aiming for a wing. With no innards to cut through, the wings seemed like the best thing to eliminate.

As her sword swung the second time, Lyren grabbed Elora's arm. The sea fae's fingers gripped tight as she spoke through her teeth. "That will make things worse."

Elora pulled her arm free. She managed to strike the creature, cutting off a portion of one foot. The other thorns forming it just twisted and rearranged until another foot appeared in its place.

Lyren grabbed her again. "The demorogs are not natural creatures. They are part of the curse on Bitter Thorn. It will only go away if you show fear, and even that only works sometimes."

"Fear?" Elora stabbed the creature's chest. As she suspected, it had no effect. "I thought fae were not supposed to have emotions."

When the creature flapped down toward them, Lyren threw her arms over her head again and dropped to the ground. "It is an insult to the fae of Bitter Thorn. The portal to the mortal realm is strongest here. And because High Queen Winola created the portal, fae must show their mortal weakness to be free of the demorogs."

By now, the thorn creature had gotten a few strikes in. Blood trickled down Elora's wrist. She scrunched up her face, almost unwilling to show fear just on principle. She was not one to cower.

But when the demorog dug its thorns into her shoulder, she finally let out a half-hearted scream. Her eyes rolled upward when she crouched to the ground and covered her face. The creature didn't seem to recognize her sarcasm.

With one last wind-howling shriek, the demorog started to fly away.

Lyren grabbed Elora's wrist and yanked her closer to the house. "Hurry. If more of those decide to bother us, we will be in real trouble." She had to practically drag Elora up the path.

Elora tucked her sword back into her belt. She had the strength of a fae now. She probably could have destroyed that creature if she had tried harder. Still scowling, she glanced toward her friend. "You said you might know more about the decay in Swiftsea?"

Gulping, Lyren glanced over her shoulder again. Her voice came out breathless. "Yes. High Queen Alessandra might be responsible after all, but it is not in the way we thought. And she may not even know exactly what she has done. Waverly and I have discovered…"

Something caught in her throat then. Was she nervous or sad perhaps?

But the words affected Elora too. She thought back to the final phase of High King Romany's testing. She had beaten Ansel in a sword fight only to have him kidnap her and bring her to his home in Mistmount. While there, she had found Lyren's mermaid friend, Waverly.

The mermaid had been anxious and frightened. Elora didn't want to even consider what might have happened to her while in Ansel's house. She turned back to her friend. "Is Waverly okay?" A shiver trickled down her spine. "I worry about what happened to her in..." She swallowed. "In Mistmount."

They had finally reached the bright green door of the home. Thorns curled and twisted around their feet. Lyren shot one last glance over her shoulder. "We should go inside before I explain. Prince Brannick needs to hear this too."

CHAPTER 5

Elora stood back as Lyren knocked on the door to Quintus's home. With each strike of her fist, magical energy came off her hand in waves. The crackling blue energy skittered over the surface of the door, crawling around it until it moved inside the home.

When Elora raised an eyebrow at the magic, Lyren tipped her head toward it. "That will tell Quintus who is at his door."

Elora didn't even have a moment to bemoan the fact that she was fae yet had no idea how to perform such magic. The door to the house flew open almost immediately. Quintus's light brown skin and combed hair looked as bright as ever.

"Lyren." His face was somber, but it had measure of happiness attached to it at seeing his friend. "We were just talking about you. We wondered…"

He trailed off as his eyes moved from Lyren over to Elora. His mouth hung open at the sight of her. He didn't even blink as he stood there.

"What is it?" Brannick's voice came out hurried as he rushed toward the door. But when his eyes met Elora's, his body froze even more than Quintus's had. Not even a hair on his head fluttered in the wind.

She offered a smile, but it did nothing to melt his frozen expression.

From inside the house, someone shuffled across the floor. Vesper's voice accompanied the sound. "I thought it wasn't safe to keep the door open. Why are you all standing there like—"

His voice cut short as he pushed past the other two. His jaw dropped, but it snapped closed a moment later. He shook his head while a light filled his blue and gray eyes. "Elora." His arms opened wide as he pulled her into a stiff hug. "I knew you would awake."

Creaking thorns crawled across the path at Elora's feet toward the house. The noise pulled the others out of their trances.

Glancing over her shoulder, Lyren pushed everyone inside. Quintus slammed the door shut. He shook out his hand afterward.

Brannick's mouth had closed, but he continued to stare at Elora without a word. The intensity of his stare probably wouldn't have mattered to her if there weren't so many people around to see it. He reached toward her but immediately pulled his hand back.

Maybe he refused to touch her still, but his wolf had other ideas. Blaz padded across the floor to nuzzle against Elora's leg. She patted his head and ran her fingers through his soft, black fur. Even when they all started walking deeper into the room, Blaz stayed right at her side. Her fae senses made his fur feel more luxurious than ever.

The interior of the house had wooden chairs and a smooth wooden table. A bright green rug covered the floor, almost giving off the same appearance as moss. Clay dishes with intricate geometric patterns painted across their surfaces sat on the table. Carved stone cups littered a nearby counter.

Everything looked earthy and lush the way Bitter Thorn did, but it felt cozy too. And it still gave off a sense of luxuriousness.

While she admired the home, everyone continued to stare at her. She cleared her throat as she turned to the prince. "I heard you and Vesper were here to see something."

Brannick narrowed his eyes, which looked duller than usual. "Where did you hear that?"

She couldn't help the smirk that played on her lips. "I heard it myself. I was in the hallway on my way to the council room when you and Vesper left."

Vesper had plucked a stone cup from off the table, and he almost dropped it now. "You heard us talking from the hallway outside the council room?"

Her smirk grew. "I am fae now. I have the same extreme hearing the rest of you have."

Something very close to a snort burst from Lyren's lips. "Yes, but..." She glanced toward the others. They all shared a look before Lyren let out a soft snicker.

The sound of it caused Elora's hands to curl into fists. Quintus shot her a look that made it clear he did not believe her abilities were as extraordinary as she claimed. Vesper tilted his head and offered her a smile. It was probably meant to appear kind, but it just looked condescending.

Brannick stared at her with no expression at all. His face could have been made of clay and it would have been no different from the one staring at her now.

Now her mouth bunched up.

Nudging the prince, Vesper threw him a look. "We must have been talking louder than we thought."

Though Brannick nodded, his face continued to betray no expression.

It seemed like a good moment to sigh. Or huff maybe. Elora could do neither because a crack sounded through the room. Reaching one hand toward her sword, Elora used the other arm to shield her head.

Part of the roof caved in, just above their heads. When clay and moss fell inward, they both transformed into heavy stone. Sucking in a breath, Elora stepped away just in time to miss being crushed by one of them.

The others jumped away just in time, but then, another stone fell right above Quintus's head. He gasped as the stone dropped. At the last moment, it almost seemed to change directions. The stone fell close enough to scrape his skin but not close enough to injure it.

His combed hair whipped as he jerked his body away from the stone. At least no more of the roof was collapsing now. Taking a deep breath, Quintus reached into his soft green coat. He pulled out a white feather and let out a sigh of relief.

The sight of it caused Elora to reach for the feather tied in her own hair. She had two. Brannick gave her one before the first phase of testing that helped enhance her natural abilities. It had been useful when she played the harp for High King Romany. The other feather had come from Soren. He gave it to her as retribution for not calling her by her name.

Running a finger over the feather, she remembered its purpose. To protect her from accidental injury. Would the stone that just missed her have fallen right on top of her if she had not had the feather? Was Quintus's feather similar?

Shaking his head, Quintus stuffed the feather back into his coat. He lifted a large stone from the ground, which looked far too heavy for anyone to lift. He probably used magic of some sort. When it was high above his head, Brannick waved his hands and the stone turned into the clay and moss it had been before.

After the transformation, Lyren and Vesper used their magic to put the clay and moss back into the ceiling where it had been. Quintus and Brannick turned toward another stone to repeat the process.

Elora rubbed a hand over her arm. She watched them work for another moment before stepping forward. "I can help too."

Lyren and Quintus laughed and continued like she had said nothing. When she tried to lift a stone from the ground, Vesper lowered his eyebrows over his blue and gray eyes. His expression of pity sent daggers through her heart.

"I *can* help. I am fae now. Just tell me how to use my magic."

No one rebuked her words, but they didn't respond to them either. By the time they had finished repairing the ceiling, her mood soured.

Quintus rubbed his forehead before turning to the prince. "As I said, the curse is getting worse. You can see how it is affecting my house."

"That happened because of the curse?" Elora pointed toward the ceiling. Vesper offered a nod that bounced the brown curls on his head. Everyone else ignored her.

Seeming to sense her distress, Blaz nuzzled closer to her body. Usually, he would have gone back to the prince by now, but she didn't mind his company. In fact, feeling his soft fur beneath her fingertips brought an almost-smile to her lips.

Running a finger over the interior wall, Brannick frowned. "It is easier to control things closer to the castle. We have not had a demorog or a collapse since I returned from Fairfrost."

Quintus responded with an eager nod. "Once you returned, everything got better. Soren's feathers that protect us from accidental injury were necessary while you were gone, but we did not need them once you returned."

Brannick pinched the bridge of his nose before he answered. "But it is different now that High Queen Alessandra has taken charge?"

"Yes." Quintus's face fell.

It had nothing on the way Brannick's shoulders slumped forward. Whatever weight he felt at ruling a court with a curse only he could control seemed to strain even heavier on his muscles now. His eyes shimmered, but not with the multitudinous colors they usually did. Even the copper undertones in his light brown skin looked sallow.

The curse was getting worse—and so was Brannick's essence.

Elora had to pull her hand away from Blaz's fur because otherwise she might have unintentionally ripped it out. The wolf continued to stand at her side, but her hands curled into fists.

Things were supposed to be better now, not worse. But Queen Alessandra was High Queen of Faerie. What did Elora expect?

Gritting her teeth together, Elora stood up straighter. "My sisters told me you are planning to overthrow Queen Alessandra."

Brannick was the first to look her way, but no trace of emotion filled his features.

Vesper rolled his eyes as he shook his head. "It is *High Queen Alessandra.*"

With his entire palm on the wall of the house, Brannick took in a long, deep breath. When he breathed out, shimmers of silver and green threaded through the branches creating the wall. The thorns that had been peeking into the house now receded. Clay and moss filled in the gaps the thorns had made. With a glittery noise, the silver and green shimmers faded away.

Whatever color had been in his eyes before completely vanished now. They looked dull and weary, even worse than a mortal's eyes.

"I know High Queen Alessandra's plan." Lyren gulped as everyone jerked their heads toward her. "Some of it at least."

No words left his lips, but Brannick gestured that she should continue.

Elora leaned forward, eager to catch every word.

Taking a deep breath, Lyren continued. "We all know Ansel magicks in blood. He kidnapped my mermaid friend, Waverly. Ansel can tell many things from tasting or smelling blood, but he can draw power from it too. Fae blood has the most power, but the magic inside it can fight back when he tries to draw power from it."

Quintus reached inside his coat to run a finger over his feather. "That is why Ansel has so many mortal pets. He can draw power from their blood, but there is no magic inside it to stop him."

"Exactly." Vesper picked at the liquid inside his stone cup. He didn't lift his eyes as he spoke. "That is also why he prefers mortals who have fae blood in them. He gets a trace of the power fae blood has, but the mortal blood has no magic to fight back."

Brannick folded his arms over his chest as he tapped one foot. "We know this already. What does this have to do with High Queen Alessandra?"

Lyren touched a hand to the sea flower tucked among her black curls before she continued. "Ansel did experiments on Waverly while she was at his home. He *and* High Queen Alessandra."

With eyes open wide, Brannick dropped his hands to his sides.

Elora could feel that her jaw had dropped, but she was more focused on how her heart pounded hard in her chest. No experiment like that could have led to anything good. For no reason at all, she reached for the light green crystal in her pocket. The energy around it pulsed as it always did.

Lyren tugged on one of her black curls before she continued. "High Queen Alessandra is skilled at manipulating emotions to get others to do what she wants. She does not even have to use magic to do it, though her magic is even more effective. But both of those methods require her to be in the presence of anyone she wants to manipulate."

The pounding in Elora's heart threatened to break through her ribcage. She leaned forward. "She's trying to find a way to manipulate emotions even from a great distance?"

Heaviness seeped into Lyren's eyes before she answered. "That is what we believe, yes."

Vesper held his stone cup with two hands. His eyebrows pinched together so tight a crease had formed. "How would blood help with that?"

Some of the weight in Lyren's eyes lifted. "I do not know, but according to Waverly, Ansel and High Queen Alessandra do not know either. At least not yet." She gulped. "But High Queen Alessandra placed a talisman in Swiftsea that poisoned our air with iron. When Waverly was in Ansel's home, they poisoned the air with iron again."

Quintus glanced toward the roof of his home. A few black thorns were peeking through again. "Maybe the iron is unrelated."

"Maybe" Lyren shrugged.

Brannick scowled at the thorns in the ceiling before lowering his eyes to the ground. "Even if it is unrelated, it does not bode well."

Before anyone could respond, a crack sounded through the roof again. More of the ceiling caved in, turning to stone as it fell. As before, everyone just barely missed being hit by the large boulders.

But this time, more than just a damaged roof plagued them. At least two demorogs, possibly more, shrieked from outside the home. Their thorns clashed against each other as they tried to push their way through the hole in the roof. Their fighting prevented any of them from getting inside so far, but how long would it take before that changed?

Just as Elora had that thought, more of the ceiling collapsed above them.

Waving a hand, Brannick opened a swirling door. "We must return to the castle at once."

Everyone leapt toward the door, except for Quintus. He frowned as he eyed his crumbling walls. "But... my home."

As if on cue, one of the demorogs finally made it inside the house. It flapped forward with its claws out.

No one bothered to say another word. They all jumped through the door as quickly as they could.

CHAPTER
6

Landing with a thud on a patch of mossy stone, Elora grunted. A bruise was already forming on one arm where she landed. As a fae, she felt the force of the fall more acutely than she would have as a mortal. Still, she couldn't linger and bemoan her pain.

She leapt to the side to avoid Vesper and then Lyren as they jumped through the door into Bitter Thorn Castle. When Quintus came next, a scowl adorned his face. Perhaps it was the green light of the sprites above, but his neatly parted black hair looked dustier than usual.

Elora rubbed a hand over the bruise in her arm. Though receiving it had hurt more than she was used to, she could already feel it healing too. Blood and energy vibrated in and around the bruise. It went from throbbing to lightly prickling before she had even pulled herself to her feet.

Brannick came through the door last. At his side, Blaz snapped his teeth and a low growl hissed in his mouth. The prince kept both hands raised while he waved and pushed them. The reason wasn't obvious until a pair of thorny black wings began to materialize through the door.

Clenching his teeth together, Brannick shoved his hands forward. The swirling tunnel disappeared, but one of the wings managed to make it through the door. Creaking filled the air as the thorns twisted and curled around each other. They shifted until they formed an entirely new, albeit smaller, demorog.

The creature swooped down, attempting to slash its thorn-claws deep into Elora's neck. Her fingers twitched on her sword hilt, already drawing it out.

Before she could use it, Brannick shot his hand toward the demorog. When his fingers curled into a fist, the thorns hissed and let out wafts of steam. The creaking grew louder while they turned from black to a dusty gray. Soon, pieces drifted to the ground like ash.

They formed a small pile in the center of the castle hallway until nothing of the demorog remained.

A vein in the prince's jaw pulsed as he opened his door again. With the wave of one hand, the pile of ash swept into the door. By the time the door closed, all trace of the demorog was gone.

He let out a slow breath, keeping his back turned away from everyone. His body remained steady, but the trembling in his knees made it seem like the effort had cost him more than he wanted to let on. Blaz collapsed to his belly, letting out heavy pants.

Vesper, Lyren, and Quintus all eyed each other and then they eyed Elora. She hardly noticed with her eyes still on the prince.

Letting out a small cough, Vesper side stepped until he caught the prince's eye. "We are not in the council room." It was more a question than a statement.

"I need to think." Brannick squared his shoulders, but still, he did not turn around. "I will send for all of you when I am ready to speak of our plan again."

He turned a corner without another word. Blaz continued to pant heavily as he followed after him.

Elora had to press a hand over her lips to stop herself from screaming. Were the others as frustrated by his sudden disappearance?

One look confirmed they were.

Lyren rolled her eyes back before she opened her own door, probably back to Swiftsea. Vesper and Quintus gave each other a look that might have meant more if Elora had stayed to examine it.

Instead, she tore down the hallway, around the corner Brannick had just disappeared behind. Even with her new fae speed, it still took a few hallways before she caught up with him.

"Brannick." She called after him when she saw the ends of his long black hair whip around a corner just in front of her.

Her acute hearing made it possible to hear how he increased his speed. Taking a deep breath, she stomped after him even faster than before.

Twisting and creaking thorns spilled down the stone walls of the castle. More appeared with each step she took. Soon, they entered a hallway she knew well. It led to the throne room. Thorns infested the hallway like never before. Full briars and twisting vines of thorns covered every bit of stone. Her boots crunched over the thorns. At least the thorns had slowed Brannick down. She could see him easily now.

He ran so fast he nearly trampled a rabbit-sized creature with floppy ears.

Coming to a halt, the prince touched a hand to the top of the brownie's head. Fifer. It was the brownie who took care of the castle wing with Elora's bedroom. Brannick swallowed before he addressed the creature. "I should not have done that. I should have been more careful."

"I am uninjured." Fifer's voice came out as squeaky as ever, but a weight lined it that had never been there before. He glanced toward Elora as he scurried over the thorn-laden hallway. "The rumors were true, I see." Now he offered a smile that brightened his large eyes. "It is good to see you awake."

She offered her own smile in return, but her gaze turned to the prince's before she could think of anything to say. The brownie must have felt the tension between them because he scurried away immediately.

Jerking away from her, Brannick began moving down the hallway once again. Now he stood directly in front of the closed doors that led to the throne room.

"Brannick."

He kept walking.

"Do you even care that I'm alive?" Her voice broke. If he bothered looking at her, he'd instantly see that tears welled in her eyes as well.

But he didn't turn. He didn't step forward either. He stood still, frozen in place.

After another moment, Blaz turned and carefully walked over the thorns until he stood at Elora's side. He snapped his fangs together.

Finally, the prince began to turn around. He did it slowly, almost as if some excruciating pain kept him from his usual agility. He caught her eye for only a moment before his hair fell forward and blocked eye contact yet again.

"You sacrificed your mortal life for me."

Elora folded her arms over her chest. "I know."

Even without seeing his face, she could feel how tension radiated off him. At his side, he held one hand in a fist tight enough to whiten his knuckles.

Her heart skittered as she reached a hand to her collar. "Did it not work? Are you still bound by the bargain?"

"It worked." Brannick's voice came out huskier than before. "High Queen Alessandra tried giving me orders, but the bargain had no hold over me once you plunged the shard into your heart." He swallowed and dipped his head downward. When he spoke again, the words came out softer. "I carried you into your room, so I can touch you as well."

Frustrated by the hair that still covered his face, Elora took several steps to close the gap between them. "Then what is it? Why won't you look at me?"

He turned to face her fully and the sight made her heart stop.

His eyes looked empty. Dull. Nothing magical lingered in them as he clenched his jaw.

Needles pricked at her skin as she tried to maintain eye contact with the grim eyes. Her stomach churned at the sight, forcing her to look away. "You do not know how to thank me? Is that it?"

Every feature on the prince's face hardened as he took a step toward her.

She forced herself to look into his eyes again, which immediately made her swallow. Shaking her head, she turned toward his wolf, who still stood at her side. "I do not care about some stupid fae gift. You do not even have to say *thank you*, just—"

"I am *not* thankful." If his words had even a touch more steel, they would have sliced her in two.

She glared at him before glancing away. "What do you mean?"

He took a step toward her. Waves of energy thickened the air around him. Their presence twisted her chest into a knot that somehow felt fiery as well.

When he spoke, hot breath left his lips and landed on her skin like burning embers. "I have never been angrier in my life."

Scoffing, she angled her body away from him. "You are *angry* that I saved you from Queen Alessandra?"

He took another step toward her, raising himself up until he towered above. Despite his bravado, his voice came out tight. "You could have died. You *should* have died." He touched a hand to his forehead. The slightest crack in his stoic mask formed when he sucked in a shuddering breath. "And you never even considered if I could handle it or not."

His shoulders slumped forward then. Rapid breaths erupted from his nose while his head shook back and forth slowly. When he spoke again, his voice came out quiet. It was so soft that she probably couldn't have heard it with mortal ears.

"I told you it would break me."

Her throat ached, a lump forming. If he had just been angry or belligerent, she could have handled it, but this? Tears stung in her eyes while she tried to steady her breaths.

He shot her a piercing glare as he gestured toward the thorny walls. "Do you see what is happening to my court? I must use my magic constantly to keep the thorns and the demorogs at bay. I have to fight to keep homes and roofs from spontaneously collapsing." Even as he spoke, his eyes turned more lifeless. "I am fae. I am not supposed to have so much worry inside me. I do not know how to handle it."

Reaching one hand out, he hovered it just next to her cheek, not quite touching it. His jaw clenched tight, but she could still see how he struggled to keep his chin from trembling.

She forced herself to look into his eyes, no matter how much it killed her to see how dull they were. "Even if I *had* died, at least you would be free from the bargain. Are you not grateful for that?"

His hand dropped to his side like a weight as he took a step back. "Grateful that I almost lost my beloved?" He scoffed, turning his eyes downward. "Are you grateful your parents died in that fire? Their deaths led you to Faerie, in a way. You never would have been so desperate for wings if they had not died. By your own logic, you should grateful, correct? Are you not overjoyed that they are dead?"

Bile burned through her throat as she curled her arms over her stomach. "That's not the same." She glanced away. "They did not die in order to save my life."

Brannick tilted his head until she looked straight at him. His eyes were *so* dull. They looked more like ash than eyes. A scowl hardened his features. "It is close enough. And trust me, it would be worse if they *had* died to save your life."

His hair whipped as he jerked around. When he attempted to stomp away, Blaz leapt across the thorns. The wolf clamped his fangs down on the prince's pant leg, stopping him in place. Brannick simply huffed and ripped his pant leg from the wolf's teeth.

Before he could take another step, the wolf jumped in front of Brannick. Blaz's fangs glinted in the light as a growl roiled at the back of his throat. They stared at each other for a long moment. Sizzling tension sparked in the hallway. New growths of thorns appeared along the walls.

Finally, Brannick let out a heavy sigh. He turned and moved toward Elora with more of the agility he usually had. He wouldn't make eye contact, but the tiniest spark of life pulsed in his eyes.

Taking a deep breath, he reached for her hand. For several moments, he let it hover near hers, still not quite touching it. In those few moments, her heart went from a steady pulse to a rapid beating that made her stomach do flips.

But nothing compared to when he finally touched her. His skin was warm like a crackling winter fire. He had no calluses like her father had, but his fingers weren't satiny either. They felt strong and sure.

He curled his fingers around hers while they both took a moment to appreciate what they had been denied for so long.

It was only a simple touch, but it seemed to simultaneously stop and start every operation inside her body at the same time. It was only through deliberate reminders that she stopped herself from holding her breath.

He pulled her hand closer to him now. Pressing her knuckles against his lips, he gave them a soft kiss. Both of his eyelids closed while he took in a deep breath. "I am glad you are alive."

Dropping her hand only slightly, he finally opened his eyes and gazed into hers.

Colors burst in his eyes, stifling her desire to think or speak or even breathe. They pulsed with a mesmerizing array of sparks until they dimmed ever so slightly. But at least they weren't completely lifeless now.

He squeezed her hand gently before releasing it. When he turned to leave, Blaz did not stop him this time. Brannick's hair looked glossier as he disappeared around the corner.

The knot in Elora's chest finally untied.

She breathed slowly as she touched her fingers to her cheek. They were still warm from the prince's touch. Her stomach flipped at the thought.

Now her cheeks filled with heat. She might have stayed there for hours just enjoying the memory of his touch, but time didn't exist in Faerie. All she knew was she didn't stay there long enough.

Eventually, she turned and made her way back to her own room in the castle.

If she had to wait until later to talk to the prince, she might as well see how her sisters were adjusting to Faerie.

CHAPTER 7

No hint of harp music colored the air until Elora stepped inside her room in Bitter Thorn Castle. Once inside, her youngest sister's melodic song danced everywhere. Up above, the sprites twisted and floated in rhythm with the music.

Narrowing one eye, Elora glanced at the hallway before closing the door behind her. "Why can I not hear Grace's music in the hall?"

Chloe sat straight backed on the chair at the desk. Her finger ran across a piece of parchment while her lips moved, probably saying the words on the page.

"It's an enchantment." Grace offered a grin that brightened her cheeks as her fingers plucked the harp strings.

With her eyes still on the parchment, Chloe gave a nod that tousled her blonde hair. "The enchantment keeps all sound inside the room. Plus, no one can find the room unless they have been here before. There are other enchantments too, but I don't remember them."

Each of her words got quieter until she was barely whispering. The moment she finished speaking, she went back to mouthing other words. Elora stared for a moment, expecting more attention be given to her, but her sisters just continued on with their activities.

Apparently, they had adjusted a little too well to Faerie. Considering all the wonders it offered, she couldn't blame them.

It took a deliberate clearing of the throat before her sisters dropped their hands and turned toward her again. She reached for her sword hilt, hoping it might offer a fragment of courage. Even still, her throat still trembled. "Do you want to go home?"

Chloe winced as she jerked her head downward. "Our home is gone. It has been for weeks."

The grip on the sword hilt still wasn't enough to empower Elora, but she kept strangling it all the same. "I know, but do you want to go back to the mortal realm?" She swallowed. "You could have dresses, jewelry, money. I am sure we could buy you a nice home to live in."

Grace's fingers curled on her lap while her eyebrows lowered ever so slightly. "But you'll stay here?"

Letting out a sigh, Elora dropped her hands to her sides. "I am fae. This is my home now."

Her two younger sisters looked at each other for only a brief moment before Grace swept a hand over her red skirt. "Then Faerie is our home now too."

Elora touched a hand to her heart. How could they give up everything they had known just for her? But as she swallowed,

61

a darker realization hit her. Maybe they simply didn't understand what they were giving up.

She bit her bottom lip before forcing herself to speak. "There is nothing for you to do here, not as mortals."

Chloe snorted before she turned back to the parchment in her lap. "How is that any different from our lives in the mortal realm?"

Even though Elora opened her mouth to speak, her blonde-haired sister barreled on. Apparently, she would hear none of it.

"We were never more than pretty faces anyway." Chloe lifted the parchment from her lap. "I still get to study poems here. Grace still gets to play the harp. We have food and shelter and family. What more do we need?"

If her sister hadn't worn such a genuine face, Elora probably would have huffed. Still, she planted both hands on her hips and shot her middle sister a poignant stare. "All you have ever wanted is to fall in love."

Chloe responded with a wide smile. "Have you seen the fae here?" Now she started fanning herself. "Trust me, that will not be difficult."

A fit of giggles erupted from Grace's mouth.

Elora's eyes went wide. She dropped her head into one hand and shook it back and forth. "Oh no." She shook her head harder. "I do not like this."

When her sisters only responded with more giggles, Elora slammed her hands back onto her hips. "The fae are dangerous. All of Faerie can be dangerous."

The smile on Chloe's face never faltered as she shrugged. "We have ward necklaces, two each. Prince Brannick *and* Vesper gave each of us one."

Sitting up eagerly, Grace bounced her head up and down. "And we have other protections. We have stones in our pockets that will glamour us to be invisible whenever we touch them. And they will automatically make us invisible if a certain fae named Hansel or Anson or something is nearby."

"Ansel." Chloe gave a nod like that ended the argument. But then she covered half her mouth with one hand and whispered loudly across the room. "I think Prince Brannick is a little bit afraid of that fae."

Both of the younger sisters looked ready to giggle again. The shiver that shook through Elora's entire frame stopped them.

Elora gave a slow nod. "That is good. That was a clever glamour that will certainly keep you safer." Her shoulders gave one last shudder before she stood tall again. "But I need to make sure you realize everything you would give up before you decide you want to stay here forever."

With a haughty chuckle, Chloe sat back in her chair. "What exactly would we give up? We were nobody in the mortal realm and we're nobody here. It seems like things are the same as they've ever been."

Elora knew she should probably dim the excitement in her own eyes, but she didn't know how. Instead, she leaned against the tree growing in the middle of her room while a wild delight was surely sparkling on her face. "Faerie is not like the mortal realm. You can be more than just a pretty face here. You can be…" She trailed off, trying to find the perfect word.

"Special?" Grace suggested from atop her harp stool.

Elora reached for her sword hilt while her shoulder continued to press into the tree trunk. "What do you want to be?" She glanced back and forth between her sisters. "In the mortal realm, we were never allowed to dream of such things." Her eyes opened wide. "But now we can."

A childish wonder sparked across Grace's features. She looked toward her oldest sister and then her gaze moved upward to the leaves and branches above. When she spoke, it was in a whisper, like someone might chastise her for what she was about to say. "I want to climb a tree."

Warmth blossomed inside Elora's chest. "Okay. You can do that."

Grace bounced in her chair. "And learn how to cook."

That wouldn't have topped Elora's list of things she wanted to learn, but there was no reason to deny her youngest sister of it now.

In the stillness of the room, Chloe stood from her chair. The parchment that had been in her lap drifted to the ground. "I want to help overthrow High Queen Alessandra."

Tension bristled across Elora's lips before she could speak. It wasn't her fault that her voice came out patronizing. "Chloe."

Her sister stomped a foot, which sent her blonde hair up in a bounce. "Don't *Chloe* me. You just said we could do what we wanted." Her eyebrows knitted together. "She killed our parents." Her chin began trembling, but it stopped immediately when she clenched her jaw and pointed her nose toward the ceiling. "I'm smart. Maybe I'm not the smartest in the realm, but given the proper study materials, I can figure out a lot of things. I don't want to join any battles, but can't I help with research?"

The surety in her sister's voice is what cracked at Elora's insides. Her middle sister had always been sweet and quiet. The picture of elegance. She could be feisty at times, but only on rare occasions. For so long, Elora had thought *she* was the only one who felt held back by the rules of the mortal realm.

But her sister had jumped at the chance to do something meaningful *and* difficult. Maybe her sister had been just as frustrated by the mortal realm as she had.

Elora stepped away from the tree, giving her sister the same respect she'd give to an equal. "I cannot make a decision for the prince." Her sister scowled, but Elora just leaned forward. "But I will ask if there is anything you can do to help."

A small frown adorned Chloe's face as she dropped back into the chair.

More words leapt from Elora's mouth before she could stop them. "I wonder if you could discover—" Her mouth snapped shut as she jerked her head away.

"What?" Light sparkled in Chloe's eyes.

Waving a hand, Elora shook her head. "No, it is too difficult, I'm sure."

Chloe stood from her chair a second time and folded her arms over her chest. "What's too difficult?"

Elora reached for a lock of her hair. She pinched it before whirling it around one finger. "I want my memories back."

Chloe tipped her head to the side. "The ones Kaia took from you?"

"Yes." Elora wrapped the hair around her finger so tight that it pulsed. "But she said it might not be possible to restore them, and fae cannot lie. It *could* be impossible."

Plucking a light purple ribbon from the desk, Chloe gave a smirk. "I'll have to speak to Kaia when Grace and I go down to the forest to find an offering for Fifer this evening."

Despite all the protections her sisters had spoken of, a knot still twisted in Elora's chest. She swallowed hard. "I don't think it is safe for you to go into the forest."

Rolling her eyes, Chloe bent to retrieve her parchment from the ground. "We always go with an escort."

Grace nodded as she brushed a finger over the harp strings. "Sometimes Vesper takes us."

"But usually, it's a gnome from Prince Brannick's army." Chloe sat down, reading the parchment once again.

"Soren?" Elora asked as she glanced toward the ceiling.

Stifled giggles burst from Grace's mouth.

Even Chloe let out a few snickers. "Soren took us a few times, but I think we frightened him off with our cheerfulness. Another gnome takes us now."

Keeping her eyes upward, Elora responded with her mind only half on the conversation. "I don't know what else Kaia will tell you. She did not seem especially forthcoming earlier."

With a loud scoff, Chloe placed a hand to her chest. "I am an expert at extracting information from people." Now her grin turned devious. "And I am a mortal in Faerie. I plan to take full advantage of my ability to lie. Kaia won't even know she's helping us."

Grace plucked three harp strings with a delicate touch before she glanced toward her oldest sister. "What are *you* going to do? Did you find out the plan to overthrow High Queen Alessandra?"

It took every bit of Elora's self-control to keep from scowling. Her jaunt outside the castle hadn't gone well at all. She let out a huff before speaking again. "No. As usual, the prince is too busy brooding to tell me anything useful. But I will drag it out of him soon enough." Her eyes flicked upward once again. "In the meantime, there is one other thing I need to do."

As if they knew her intention, the sprites above gave off an even brighter glow. Glittery sounds trickled across the air. Of course they knew what she intended. They desired it too.

Elora took a deep breath, ignoring how her heart squeezed at the lack of a pink sparkle among the sprites above. "I made a vow, and I intend to keep it."

CHAPTER

8

Clusters of pain tightened Elora's throat, but she forced herself to speak anyway. "How do I rescue Tansy from Fairfrost?"

Grace's red hair bobbed as she whipped her head toward her oldest sister. "Who's Tansy?"

"She's my friend." Elora glanced up at the ceiling again, focused on the sprites hovering near it. "She said you had a plan."

Setting the piece of parchment into her lap, Chloe narrowed one eye. "Who are you talking to?"

"The sprites." Elora nearly rolled her eyes as she answered. If Chloe claimed to be so smart, she probably could have figured that out on her own.

But the lowered eyebrows on Chloe's face suggested she was still confused. "Sprites don't talk to anyone except when delivering messages."

Instead of responding, Elora just let out a huffy chuckle. Her eyes turned upward once again, eyeing the floating lights above. "I know you have a plan. I want to help."

Wind fluttered through the leaves above Elora's head, but no other sound filled the room.

After another moment, Chloe cleared her throat. "I don't think they are—"

Elora drew her sword with a great flourish, stopping her sister mid-sentence. With the sword tight in her grip, she yanked herself up the tree until she was high enough to reach the ceiling. "One of you fly over to me now, or I might cut you to pieces."

Grace let out a loud gasp as she pressed both of her hands to her lips. Chloe's jaw hung open. Elora ignored them both and jabbed her sword toward the nearest sprite.

Before the sword could touch him, a little sprite with sparkling yellow-green eyes zoomed forward until he hovered right in front of Elora's nose. She recognized him because of the haphazard yellow hair that poked out at all angles. His brown coat and green pants looked even brighter than when she had sent him to give a message to Lyren. He crossed his arms with a glare.

The sprite seemed to realize Elora's threat wasn't serious, otherwise he probably would have just flown away. It was true that Elora never would have actually injured one of the sprites, but at least the show had gotten a reaction.

Tucking the sword back into her belt, Elora raised an eyebrow. "I cannot help you if you do not speak to me."

The sprite's entire face scrunched up like he wanted to spit something foul from his mouth.

Elora pressed her back against the tree trunk as she got into a more comfortable position on the branch. It had been much easier than usual to climb the tree. Her fae characteristics must have helped. "I made a vow to rescue Tansy."

The sprite raised a forest green eyebrow. "A vow means nothing when spoken by a mortal."

"I am fae."

"You were not fae when you spoke that vow." The sprite continued to hover in front of Elora, but his sparkling eyes flicked upward at the other sprites nearby.

A loud whisper drifted up from the ground when Chloe spoke to her youngest sister. "She's talking to one of them. I didn't know anyone could do that."

Wrinkling her nose, Elora sat up straighter. "You want a vow from a fae? Fine. I vow that I will rescue Tansy from Fairfrost." The air around her crackled with energy while her chest tightened with an all-new heaviness. Something told her that the tightness in her chest would not dissipate until her vow had been completed.

The sprite only laughed and began slowly flying closer to the ceiling.

"Why do you laugh?" Elora pressed both of her eyebrows tight together. "I am fae, am I not?"

"Only slightly." The sprite let out a snicker.

"What does that mean?"

Rather than answer, the sprite moved even nearer to the ceiling and away from Elora.

It seemed like a good moment to let out a huff. Pulling herself up to her feet, Elora spoke to all the sprites again. "Do you have a plan?"

The sprite's yellow hair shook as he jerked his head toward the others. Glittery noises that sounded like a cross between wind and pebbles hitting the frozen ground tittered across the air. After several moments, the sprite finally began floating closer to Elora once again. "We need you to steal spears from the Bitter Thorn armory."

Elora had to grab the tree trunk to keep herself from falling down in surprise. "Brannick needs those spears in case Queen Alessandra attacks."

Turning his nose toward the ceiling, the sprite folded his arms over his chest. "Do you want to help or not?"

No answer came. Elora considered the action, and she considered the consequences. She had gotten into trouble in the past for doing before thinking. Moving her feet over the mossy bark, she began climbing down the tree.

The sprite followed after her, proving his desperation despite the act that he didn't care. Once at the bottom of the tree, the tightness in Elora's chest grew. She had a vow, and Faerie itself forced her to complete it.

Truthfully, she had little choice in the matter. Perhaps she could get away with only taking a few spears. Surely, a few spears wouldn't be missed. Taking a deep breath, Elora glanced toward the sprite. "I will only help if you promise to explain your plan."

"Promise?" The sprite narrowed both of his eyes. "Fae cannot break a promise."

Elora smirked. "Good. Do you promise to explain your plan?"

Though both his forest green eyebrows were drawn together so tightly a crease had formed, a hint of amusement still peeked through the sprite's eyes. "You do think like a fae."

"I *am* fae."

71

The sprite let out a laugh that grated Elora's nerves. "I promise I will explain *some* things on the way to the armory."

That was probably as good as she'd get. With a nod, Elora stomped toward the door of her bedroom. She glanced back at her sisters before leaving. "You two be safe." She gave a soft smile when turning toward her youngest sister. "Grace, you can start climbing that tree whenever you like, though I suggest you try wearing pants instead of a dress."

Chloe settled herself in at the desk. "And I'll start learning everything I can about lost memories."

Once in the hallway, the sprite landed on Elora's shoulder.

"Do you have a name?" Elora didn't really expect an answer, but the sprite gave one.

"Thisbe."

The moment the word left his lips, the sprite turned invisible.

Elora cocked her head to one side. "Now everyone will think I am talking to myself."

"What a shame." The words couldn't have been spoken with more indifference. "For you, I mean."

Shaking her head, Elora turned the nearest corner. "Explain this plan."

Even in an empty hallway, Thisbe's voice lowered to a whisper. "As you know, any sprite who enters Fairfrost is brought by magic to Fairfrost Palace."

Elora nodded. "Yes, and Queen Alessandra captures them once they get there."

A little tap on the shoulder indicated the sprite had sat down. "*High* Queen Alessandra has a room full of sprites. The magic forces them inside a bubble of enchantment."

When they rounded the next corner, they were no longer alone. A group of three fae glanced toward Elora with eyes narrowed to tiny slits.

With a little wave toward them, Elora stood taller. They continued to stare at her as she moved down the hallway. It made her heart pound. But at least she attempted to step forward like she wasn't up to anything suspicious. It was hard when the fae continued to stare after.

Once they entered a new hallway, Elora could finally breathe like normal again. She glanced toward her shoulder, which appeared empty but actually held the invisible sprite. "I thought sprites could get past fae enchantments. Tansy has helped me get past a few."

"We can. But once we get past the enchantment, the magic in Fairfrost forces us back inside the bubble as soon as we leave it."

"That does make things difficult, I suppose." With a frown, Elora reached to open the door that led to the armory. Her frown only grew when she found the door would not budge. Her eyes narrowed. This door had never been locked before. Why would it be locked now?

Rather than consider an answer, she simply gripped the leather strap tighter and yanked even harder than before. The door continued to stay in place, which caused the tightness in her chest to writhe in waves.

"The enchantment bubble in Fairfrost is not a barrier enchantment anyway." Thisbe spoke as if he were musing and not watching Elora struggle with the door. He continued nonchalantly. "We had another fae who is a friend to the sprites who tried to help us, but he is not in Fairfrost anymore."

It seemed like a good idea to draw her sword and use it as leverage to force the door open, but that didn't help either.

73

Only then did a new idea strike her. Tucking her sword away, she glanced toward her shoulder again. "You have magic to open this, right?"

"Yes." Thisbe answered without hesitation.

Elora kept the groan inside her mouth, but she still rolled her eyes. "Well, can you open it then?"

A glittery sound trickled into the air. When Elora tried the door again, it opened without resistance. Shaking her head, she addressed the sprite again. "If it is not a barrier enchantment, then what kind of enchantment is it? And who is this friend of the sprites?" She slid the door closed slowly before moving across the floor.

Thisbe shifted on Elora's shoulder, becoming visible once again. "You do not know the friend. Do not worry about him. High Queen Alessandra's greatest magic is in emotion. She learned early on how to create an enchantment that can draw all emotion out of an object."

At first, Elora could only consider the oddity that objects could hold emotion at all. But just as suddenly as the thought came, she remembered another type of object that held emotion. "Are you talking about tokens? An object whose essence has been altered by an experience so much that it holds that emotion inside it?"

Her own sword had become a token during her time in Faerie, but so had her mother's skirt, and the red ribbon Chloe had given her. Scrunching up her mouth, she spoke again. "If a token goes through the bubble enchantment, the emotion is taken out of it and it stops being a token?"

"Yes."

Nodding to herself, Elora yanked on the vine that would open the wall to the armory beyond it. Despite the yank,

74

absolutely nothing changed. With a frown, she examined the vines to be certain she had pulled the correct one.

Once sure it was right, she glanced toward the sprite. "Can you open this one too?"

A wince passed over Thisbe's features, but he waved a tiny hand at the vine anyway. The door opened easily when Elora tugged the vine again.

The stone door began sliding open, and a whiff of decay drifted forward immediately. Vines still hung all around the ceiling, but thorns twisted around each one. Briars gathered in every space of the octagonal room where the floor met the wall. Bits of stone crumbled from the ceiling, making it look ready to collapse at any moment.

Elora had to swallow over a lump in her throat before she stepped forward. Her feet moved cautiously, but every movement still seemed like it would crack the room apart. She spoke again, but her voice came out strained. "Why would Queen Alessandra put that kind of enchantment around the sprites?"

"We are not given sustenance while in Fairfrost."

For a moment, Elora forgot to move carefully. Her head jerked toward the sprite fast enough to make her hair swing. His response hadn't answered her question at all, but it horrified her too much to say anything about it. "None at all? You are not given food? Nothing to drink?"

The sprite puffed out his chest, but that did not change how his yellow-green eyes darkened. "We are the only fae creatures that can conjure our own food, but we can only do it if we have enough strength."

A thick lump settled deep in Elora's throat. It ached with each new word. She tried to swallow over it, but of course that did nothing. "Is that why sprites lose their essence while in

75

Fairfrost? They have to draw on their essence to conjure sustenance and that weakens them?"

Thisbe's head dropped to his chest, ruffling his already tousled hair. "Yes, but being imprisoned weakens the essence as well."

Cracks twisted through the lump in Elora's throat. She grabbed a handful of spears from the nearest clay pot. Each of them boasted a sharp stone tip at the end. Leather strings tied feathers to the spears at different heights.

Her breath hitched as she counted the spears. Eleven. Surely, Brannick's army could afford to lose only eleven spears. Hopefully. She held them tighter, turning toward the sprite. "Why do you need these? How will they help you?"

But Thisbe had glamoured himself to be invisible again.

Before Elora could question why, the stone door to the armory slid open once again. Feet moved across the floor with a characteristic stomp. Soren was already grumbling, which sent his white beard to bounce against his chest.

The gnome's all-black eyes shimmered. He gave a sharp glare. "What are you doing with those?"

CHAPTER 9

With the spears clutched in one hand, Elora donned her most innocent smile. It did nothing to affect the gnome standing in front of her. Even worse, he looked grumpier than usual. Plus, one of his eyebrows was twitching. He gave off prickling energy that put her even more on edge. But surely Soren knew she would never do anything to hurt Bitter Thorn.

The gnome took two stomps forward as he ground his teeth together. "I *said*, what are you doing with those spears?"

She glanced down at them, as if to examine. "I was just looking at them." The last word caught in her throat, which sent a hacking cough through her lips. But each cough seemed to cut off her air supply even more. They stole her breath until her eyes welled with tears.

Instinctively, she knew what to do, but actually doing it was another matter altogether. Sucking in a shallow breath, she forced a new set of words from her mouth. "I was going to steal them."

That at least sent a small twinkle into Soren's eyes. He let out the smallest chuckle before hardening his features yet again. "Now that you have lost your ability to lie, it is clear you have no idea how to deceive. Not like a true fae does."

She raised both eyebrows while lifting her chin. "Would you rather I *had* deceived you?"

That small twinkle vanished as quickly as it had come. Soren crossed his arms, grinding his teeth once again. "I would rather you tell me what you wanted to do with these spears after you stole them."

With a great flourish, she dropped the spears back into the tall clay pot that had been holding them. She still didn't know what the sprites wanted them for, but maybe it didn't matter. She wouldn't do anything to hurt Bitter Thorn. The sprites would just have to think of a different way to rescue the sprites in Fairfrost.

Despite the gesture, the gnome grumbled under his breath. She took it as a good sign that he was starting to act like himself. She leaned toward him. "How did you get here right when I was about to take the spears?"

A bemused grin fell over his face. "Showing your mortal side again, are you?"

Her stomach dropped. "You put an enchantment on the room to alert you if someone entered it?"

Chuckling, he shook his head while turning back toward the exit. "If you were a true fae, you would already know the answer to that."

"But I am a true fae."

He chortled, which was easily the freest laughter she had ever heard from him. If he hadn't been laughing at *her*, she might have appreciated it more.

Gesturing toward the exit, he waited until she left the armory and the outer room leading to it.

Though she moved at his direction, she still kept her chin high. "If I am not a true fae, then explain how I got through the enchantments protecting this room."

Once they both stood in the hallway, he slammed the door shut and waved his hand to create another enchantment. His answer came as an afterthought. "You had help."

It was true, but it still hurt. She might have thought of a retort except a crack sounded through the hallway. All along the ceiling, even above the floating sprites, a dark gray cloud churned.

Elora's jaw dropped involuntarily. No matter how long she had been in Faerie, it never ceased to amaze her. Clouds could form *inside* of buildings? Bitter Thorn Castle boasted large windows and stone walls that had moss and leafy vines growing over them. Trees grew from the stone in many of the rooms. Gentle breezes and the scent of wet bark always made the castle feel more like a forest than a building. Still, she never expected to see clouds *inside*.

A sense of wonder skittered along her nerves. It might have sparked into pure bliss, except then she caught sight of Soren's face. Color drained from his cheeks. His bug-like eyes turned dull. He reached for his chest, as if to clutch it, but then his fingers got tangled up in his beard.

That couldn't be good.

When she glanced up at the ceiling again, she knew why. Large snowflakes drifted down from above. Snowflakes could have only come from one court.

Fairfrost. Queen Alessandra's court.

One snowflake landed on the skin of Elora's arm, which immediately sent a needle-like pain through the spot. The pain carved into her until it settled in her heart. On her next breath, the pain blossomed into an icy slice that clenched her chest.

She gasped. Clutching the collar of her dress, she tried to breathe. To stand.

The iciness had thawed, but it left behind a little gift.

Anger.

The emotion had no conceivable root, but it spun inside her all the same. Her fingers curled into fists. Punching someone, or something, would be the only way to relieve any of the tension. Another snowflake landed, on her cheek this time. The needling pain got to her heart even faster.

Anger boiled inside her, threatening to rip apart her nerves.

With a deep breath, she retreated deep into her mind. The balance shard that turned her fae had done the same thing to her, except then, anger was only one of the many emotions she'd been forced to bear.

She urged herself to take steady breaths. Each one acknowledged the anger inside. She felt it, welcomed it even. Ignoring the feeling would only make it hurt worse later on. She had learned that the hard way.

After letting the anger bubble and boil and churn, she took another deep breath and...

She let it go.

The iciness that had sliced through her before, thawed to a small chill. After another deep breath, she was back to normal again.

More snowflakes landed, but when they tried to pierce her heart, they were met with calm resistance. No anger could take hold of her now.

Snapping her eyes open, she glanced to the side. Her companion had no such power.

Above his white beard, Soren's cheeks turned to a deep crimson. A vein pulsed in his jaw so hard she could see it through his beard. He clenched his fists tight enough that white spotted the knuckles.

Letting out a grunt, he swung a heavy fist toward her.

She jumped backward just in time to miss the hit. "Soren."

He swung another fist. His teeth were probably in danger of cracking due to how hard he clenched his jaw. When words left his mouth, he didn't speak. He growled. "How *dare* you break into the armory. How dare you disrespect my title as captain of the guard."

Her feet danced as she leapt to avoid every swing of his fist. He huffed at his inability to hit her and then reached into a pocket. From it, he drew a spear with a black, sharpened tip.

She gulped.

The sight of it probably should have caused more fear in her gut, but her mind was too focused on the pocket Soren had drawn the spear from. The spear was even taller than Soren. A mortal pocket could never hold something so long, and yet, every fae seemed to have a similar pocket that could hold anything regardless of size.

So, why didn't she have one?

His feet fell heavy on the stone floor as he barreled toward her with the spear. She was still thinking about the pocket when she absently blocked the blow with her sword.

A guttural scream erupted from his mouth as he slammed his foot against the ground several times. His anger might crack the stone floor if he wasn't careful.

Maybe logic would calm some of his anger. Hopefully.

"Soren, it's me, Elora. I would never do anything to hurt Bitter Thorn. You know I wouldn't."

More snowflakes drifted down from the ceiling. Each one that hit the gnome caused his face to grow even redder. He charged her again with his spear pointed high.

Jumping to the side, she only barely blocked the blow.

"I need to find Brannick."

She mostly spoke the words to herself, but the sound of his prince's name caused Soren to freeze in place.

"Prince Brannick?" He blinked a few times until another snowflake melted onto his arm. His fists clenched tight again. "Yes." He let out a huff. "He brought this curse upon us. I will make him pay."

His knuckles turned white as he tightened his grip on the spear. He glanced over one shoulder, as if he expected Prince Brannick to be standing there. A scowl painted his features when he found the hallway empty behind him.

Keeping her sword drawn, she stepped to the gnome's side. "I thought his mother brought the curse upon Bitter Thorn." She shook her head. "Actually, I thought High King Romany and the other rulers cursed Bitter Thorn."

Some of the crimson left Soren's cheeks as he blinked. "That is correct." He lowered his spear, still blinking faster than normal. "I..."

Her hand shot forward, catching a snowflake that would have landed on the gnome.

His eyes pulsed with an understanding that hadn't been there a moment ago.

She caught another snowflake before it landed on him. "Can you conjure a barrier or something that will protect you from these snowflakes?"

"I…" He shook his head, as if trying to force something out of it. "It will take everything out of me." His expression still looked blanker than usual, but he conjured a shimmery, silvery enchantment over his head. The snowflakes sizzled into steam when they met it.

Maybe leaving him while he was still only barely lucid was a bad idea, but she didn't care. If the cloud and snowflakes had appeared in this part of the castle, they had certainly appeared in other places as well.

Elora tucked her sword into her belt but immediately drew it once again. It would be better to be prepared as she moved through the castle. As she walked down the hallway, she glanced back at Soren. "Stay under that enchantment until the snowflakes stop falling."

Once the gnome nodded, she broke into a run.

Screams met her ears before she saw anyone else. After a few turns, she ran into a cluster of fae who were using various weapons against each other. There were spears and bows and arrows, but they also used fists and even teeth.

Did she have time to try and help? Or would finding Brannick be the most useful thing she could do? The prince would have enough magic to stop this, but not if he was filled with anger like everyone else. She'd just have to find him and calm him down and then he could take care of the snowflakes.

She'd go to the prince first and ignore the fighting fae for now.

In that moment of hesitation, loud cracks sounded through the air. When she glanced upward, she expected to find more clouds or faster falling snowflakes.

But the crack hadn't come from magic this time.

The castle ceiling and walls broke apart at several angles. Showers of black thorns and briars spilled in through the cracks. Even more cracks formed when more thorns forced their way inside the castle.

A broken castle and black thorns were bad enough, but of course it didn't end there. The thorns gathered together in clumps and then began forming into winged creatures.

Demorogs.

Inside Bitter Thorn Castle itself.

Her shoulders slumped at the sight of them. This was the last thing she needed.

While she stared upward, the fae around her had apparently finally noticed her presence. They pointed and spit at her. "This is *your* fault."

"Uh." Half a dozen fae stumbled toward her, each wielding a weapon she'd rather avoid. She couldn't fight them all, especially when their actions were fueled by insatiable anger. But maybe their anger could be directed toward something other than herself.

Her own face twisted as she jabbed her hand toward the newly formed thorn creatures. "The demorogs did this."

The other fae gave her blank stares.

She snarled even more than before and did her best to fill her face with red-hot rage. "Look at what the demorogs have done to our castle." She gestured around the room. "Look at what they have done to our court."

The change came slow at first, but eventually the other fae turned their anger. Now they pointed and spat at the demorogs. One of them snatched a crumbled bit of stone from the ground and chucked it at the nearest creature.

"Get the demorogs!" she shouted. She even began running toward the creatures with the other fae.

Of course, the fight would be futile. The demorogs had no innards, which meant no weapon could harm them. But at least it would distract the fae while she searched for Brannick.

She turned on her heel, even more desperate than ever. In hallway after hallway, she had to convince angry fae to channel their anger toward anything but her. It was hard enough without cracks and thorns impeding her progress at every turn.

When she entered the hallway that led to the throne room, she had to climb over huge briars and thorns that pierced her with every step.

But she was so close to Brannick's room now. He could fix this once she got to him.

Despite the sharp thorns and the shouts resounding from nearby hallways, she was filled with a sense of hope. She was almost there.

As soon as the thought struck her, it was ripped away.

Thorns gathered together, forming a demorog that hovered only an arm's length away from her. This one wouldn't let her get away unscathed.

CHAPTER

10

Black thorns twisted over the wall and floor. They formed briars and bundles of sharp vines that choked the life out of any green still visible in the hallway. With each twist, they let out creaks and whines. Mountains of the thorns bunched together in tight clumps. The smell of decay wafted away from the thorns. The more they twisted, the stronger the scent.

When the demorog in front of Elora flapped its wings, no wind fluttered away from it. There was enough space in between the thorns forming it that air simply passed through the wings like branches on a dead tree.

Shouts sounded through the walls of the castle, but none of them bothered her until she heard a scream she recognized. It was more like a groan than anything. It came from Brannick. In the next moment, his wolf howled.

Her heart tensed. Her fingers itched to reach for her sword, but she wouldn't let them. She had to get to Brannick as fast as she could, which meant she needed to think things through first. Getting past the demorog didn't have to be difficult. Not if she was smart about it.

Clutching her chest, Elora let out a gasp that shivered her entire body. She cowered, dropping herself among the mounds of thorns at her feet. When the demorog flew only slightly toward her, she shrieked and covered her head with her arms.

It was probably the most fear she had ever willingly shown in her life.

But the demorog was unmoved. The creature beat its wings faster, which didn't affect its flying at all. Still, the creature floated toward her. Its claws swiped, ready to pierce her skin.

She attempted one last shriek, but even as she did it, she knew it was a lost cause. The demorog continued to close in on her. Its thorns were just about to sink into her skin when she jumped up and slashed her sword across the creature.

A wind-like howl screamed from the demorog's insides. Its arms fell to the ground in a heap, but another pair of arms formed from its remaining thorns a moment later. While the new limbs rearranged, another slice of her sword tore off one of the demorog's wings.

As she had previously suspected, the lost wing had no effect on the creature's ability to fly. She scowled and sent another strike through the thorns in front of her.

The absence of innards made the strike useless for killing. But that strike hadn't been intended to kill. With her sword still deep inside the creature, she yanked her arms to the side. With the sword inside it, the demorog also got yanked to the side.

Her heart leapt as she began moving forward. She didn't have to defeat the demorog, she merely had to get past it so she could get to the prince.

She only managed a few steps before the thorns at her feet rose up to form a thick wall. Not expecting it, she crashed right into the thorns. Dozens of them sank deep into her skin. Her feet stumbled backward, only to be met by the thorny claws of the demorog.

Perhaps she *did* need to defeat the demorog after all.

The piercing thorns had hurt, but she could already feel her body repairing the damage. The wounds prickled into soft reminders of the pain inflicted only moments ago. It didn't matter what Soren or Thisbe, the sprite, said. She *was* a true fae. And if she was fae, she had magic.

Maybe she hadn't discovered her magic yet. Maybe she had no idea how to use it.

But it was in there. Somewhere.

She gave a few careless swipes of her sword to force the demorog back, but really, she just wanted to ground herself. Once the creature hovered an arm's length away from herself, she took a deep breath. Then she waved her hand just like she had seen fae do a hundred times.

The hand wave did nothing.

And now the demorog crashed toward her again. She sent a slash, a strike. Soon, the demorog moved back. The reprieve would only last a moment. She had to act.

Clenching her stomach muscles, she searched for the magic inside of herself. It was there. She had seen Faerie itself give it to her. And if it was there, there had to be a way to access it.

Her stomach continued to tighten as she focused on magic and what it might feel like to wield it. Then she waved her hand again. She imagined a golden blast shooting out of her fingertips and crushing the demorog.

But it was just a thought. No such blast erupted from anywhere. The creature merely swooped down and sliced her arm with a long, thorny claw.

The thorns at her feet began crawling up her boots. They twisted over her feet and then her ankles and then right around her bare legs. The sharp points dug into her skin, clawing at the resolve she sought to feed.

More thorns crept across the hallway. They reached out from the walls and curled around her arms and waist. At first, she thrashed her sword, desperate to cut away the vines that attached the thorns to each other. She sliced them away until they weren't touching her skin anymore. But new thorns followed. They followed faster than she could stop.

They punctured her bare skin. They cut through her clothing and dug into the skin beneath it. The demorog landed on her head, cutting lines down her cheeks and neck with its claws.

Pain stung throughout her body, but hopelessness ground through her insides. She was fae. She could heal faster now. Surely, these thorns couldn't kill her.

Could they?

When one of the thorns dug so deep that it scraped against her bone, the question answered itself. Of course they could. The smell of decay curdled in her nostrils. It pressed in on her from all sides.

The shouts in the rest of the castle got louder too. She tried to ignore them, which wasn't difficult considering the enormous amount of pain that distracted her.

But then, she heard the same grunted scream from before. A wolf's howl immediately followed it.

Maybe she would die, but it seemed Brannick might be close to death too. That thought hurt more than the thorns. More than her own death. More than the thought of losing her sisters.

For the first time since the thorns began to envelop her, she took a steady breath. Thorns may have scraped and sliced over every part of her, but she forced herself to be calm. To remember.

Yes, Faerie itself had given her magic. Her body had glowed with it.

But her sword had glowed too. If there was one thing she trusted, it was her sword.

She couldn't seem to access the magic inside of herself, but maybe she could access the magic inside of her sword. The weapon had been there for her through many painful years. It had never failed her. While in Faerie, the weapon had even become a token. More recently, it had been given magic by Faerie itself.

The demorogs and the thorns had no innards, so they could not be defeated with conventional weapons. They had to be defeated with magic.

Curling her hand over her leather sword hilt, she reached deep within herself. She breathed slowly, ignoring the trickles of blood that slipped down her skin. Her mind focused on the sword, trusting it to save her the way it always had.

A spark ignited inside her chest. In the same moment, sparks erupted from the blade of her sword. A purple glow emanated from the weapon while showers of sparks burst out of it.

Taking another deep breath to ground herself, she raised her sword. The showers of sparks followed the weapon, putting crackling energy into the air. She aimed above her head where the demorog sat. With a jab, she plunged her weapon into what she hoped was the body of the creature.

A high-pitched shriek filled the entire hallway, shaking the stone walls. She jabbed it again. The thorns around her head and neck released. Not waiting to find out more, she sliced her glowing sword through the thorns crawling up her limbs.

Everywhere her sword touched, the thorns withered in on themselves. They turned a sickly gray before bursting apart. They looked exactly like the thorns at Quintus's house when Brannick had used his magic against them.

Any thorns that hadn't been cut now twisted back into the piles of thorns on the ground. The demorog still hovered in the air, but it did so in jerky movements.

One last swipe of her sword reduced the demorog to a pile of ash.

The victory felt empty as she scurried toward the prince's room. If he hadn't been screaming so desperately, maybe she could have enjoyed it. But now, her heart clenched as she ran. Afraid of what she would find.

CHAPTER

11

The demorog had been beaten, but snowflakes continued to fall from the clouds hovering beneath the ceiling. She had almost forgotten them during her fight. Now each icy prick against her skin mingled with the blood that trickled there.

Her resolve tightened as she threw open the door to Brannick's room. Her eyes scanned quickly, trying to ignore everything but the prince. She refused to look at the overturned chairs and the branches torn off a tree at the corner of his bed. But even if she didn't look carefully, she had still seen them.

Her gut wrenched when she finally saw him. He stood in the center of his room, bruises peppering his arms and chest. This wasn't the time to consider where he had gotten them, but her gut still twisted at the sight.

The bearskin rug that usually lay on his stone floor was in his hands. He tried to tear fur out of the rug, but it didn't work.

With a snarl, he tried using his teeth to rip the fur off the bear skin rug instead. That didn't work either.

Clenching the rug in one fist, he waved a hand and conjured a clump of purple wildflowers that grew from the stone floor. The moment they finished forming, he crushed them with his heel.

While he moved, thorns crawled up his legs and dug into his skin, but he didn't seem to notice them. Or maybe the anger from Queen Alessandra's snowflakes had simply rendered him too far out of his mind to recognize pain anymore.

Elora heard panting. The sound indicated Blaz was nearby, but she couldn't see him. He was probably using his glamour that made people look anywhere but at him. Good. That had probably helped him during Brannick's fit of rage.

Raising her sword high, she began cutting through the thorns that crept up the prince's legs. Any thorns that threatened to come near her got sliced as well. When the last of Brannick's thorns withered and turned to ash, he finally noticed her presence.

A tiny snowflake landed on the prince's nose. His face twisted as he gathered a fistful of Elora's dress and yanked her close. With his breath hot on her cheeks, his nose twitched. "I *hate* you."

She tried to throw even the tiniest bit of nonchalance into her voice. "At least nothing has changed."

The anger in Brannick's face multiplied ten times. He pulled his hand back, perhaps preparing to punch something, her probably. But before he could do anything, a furry body pushed itself between her and the prince, knocking Brannick to the ground.

Blaz's black ears came into view right as he let out a long howl. Spit shot from the prince's mouth as he huffed. His fist went flying, and this time, it did hit its mark.

The wolf's body flew backward until it slammed against the side of the prince's bed. He let out a quiet whimper.

An all-new anger carved into Elora's heart, but the small whimper seemed to affect Brannick even more.

Every bit of anger got wiped from his face as his eyes grew wide. He stared down at his fist and quickly looked back at his wolf in horror.

Good. Things would be much easier while Brannick was at least somewhat aware of his surroundings. She stepped in front of him, forcing the prince to look her way. "Create an enchantment that will stop these snowflakes from landing on you."

He didn't move. Even his fist remained curled up tight. "When did you get here?"

Her hand lunged forward, stopping a snowflake before it landed on his arm. He continued to wear a blank expression while he got to his feet.

Now she had to stand on her tiptoes to keep a different snowflake from landing on his shoulder. But then, another snowflake was falling straight for the top of his head. She wasn't tall enough to reach it, and she didn't want to risk the chance the Brannick might try to stop her.

Pushing the wings from her back, she urged them to lift her off the floor. Now a little higher, she could more easily prevent the snowflakes from reaching the prince.

Her muscles ached after so much effort, plus her skin still bled in several places. After a few moments above the ground, she was already out of breath. She nudged the prince's shoulder with her knee. "The snowflakes!"

He cocked his head to the side.

She grunted. "They're hurting you."

He blinked twice before slowly glancing up at the ceiling. When he saw the cloud above, he took a small step back. His head shook. Now his gaze turned back toward her.

She had to swoop in an awkward flying motion to prevent the latest snowflake from reaching him. At least she didn't have to fly very high. Any higher and her flying skills would have failed her. This was a good reminder that she still needed to practice.

The prince cocked his head again. He glanced at the cloud and waved a hand through the air.

Effortlessly.

Even while he was barely aware of the world, he could still wield his magic. This was probably a stupid time to be jealous.

Shoving the thought away, she glanced toward the ceiling. But he hadn't created an enchantment. "You..." She let out a tiny gasp as she fluttered back down to the ground. "The cloud is gone."

"It did not belong in Bitter Thorn. I sent the magic back to its own court." His voice sounded faraway, like he was recounting a distant memory and not responding to something in that very moment.

Her feet hit the stone, and she pulled her wings back into her back. "You can do that?"

His eyes had trailed away from the ceiling and onto the crumpled bearskin rug on the floor. Then he glanced at her.

She shook her head and turned away from him. He was still out of it. There was no sense trying to have a conversation now. Instead, she moved over to Blaz.

Panting breaths escaped from the wolf's snout, but he didn't appear too injured. Just tired. He pressed his body against hers as soon as she knelt down at his side. He nuzzled against her leg before resting his head her lap.

Her fingers wandered through his black fur while she glanced toward the prince.

He was staring at her. Again. And then he glanced back at the bearskin rug.

Suddenly, a spark lit inside her chest. A memory that had been insignificant a moment ago now tugged at her insides.

The prince had gotten that bearskin rug when he escaped Fairfrost. He had disguised himself as a dancing bear for some unknown reason. What had he said about that dance?

I was dancing with someone, a servant from the palace I think, but I do not remember why.

What if it hadn't been a servant after all? Her breath hitched. What if it had been *her?* Kaia admitted that Elora had aided the prince in his escape from Fairfrost. What if a dance with a bear had been one of the memories taken from her?

Her fingers stilled to a stop while she cleared her throat. "Are you remembering something?"

Brannick tore his gaze away from the rug and shook his head hard. He came toward her but refused to allow any sort of eye contact. Instead, he knelt directly in front of his wolf.

The two of them stared at each other for a very long time. Were they communicating?

If so, the prince's facial expression suggested he was giving an apology. Or perhaps he was healing the wolf's injury. Or maybe both.

Silence continued to stretch between them, but their expressions changed. Both Brannick's and the wolf's. Could she ask about his memory again? He certainly seemed more like himself than before. Or maybe it would be best to start with a less dangerous question. Maybe she'd just ask him why he kept looking at his bearskin rug.

Swallowing, she glanced toward him. "Brannick."

"How did you get in here?" He didn't look at her. His gaze had turned toward the floor.

She cocked her head to the side, hoping it might draw his attention. It didn't. "I have been to your room several times."

"That is not what I meant."

Her fingers tightened over her sword hilt. It wasn't intentional, but her voice came out softer than before. "I had to battle a demorog in the hallway, but—"

"Why did the snow not affect you?" He finally glanced at her for the first time.

"Oh." She had to ignore how dull his eyes were, especially because a few sparks were lighting in them little by little. "I don't know."

He lifted an eyebrow.

The hairs on the back of her neck prickled as she shrugged. "I think it's because of what I went through when I became fae. I have better control over my emotions now. Or I guess *control* is the wrong word."

It would have been easier to speak if he hadn't been staring at her so intensely. His gaze pinned her down, making it difficult to swallow let alone form words. Of course, her stomach decided that was the perfect moment to do flips.

She glanced away. "I can't decide how I feel, but the emotion doesn't take over me either. I can recognize it and feel it but still be okay. If that makes sense."

His eyes narrowed, which somehow caught her gaze again. This time, she couldn't look away. He gave a slow nod, still trapping her with his eyes. "It is beginning to make sense, but I still have more to learn."

One hand crept forward as he spoke. By the end of his words, his fingers were close enough to softly stroke her cheek.

She would have leaned into his touch, but he immediately got to his feet and began pacing across the room.

Only now did she notice how much of his furniture had been destroyed. One of the wool blankets from his bed had been ripped completely in half. Stone rubble near the hanging wall of vines in one corner of his room suggested his bath had been destroyed.

He sucked in a deep breath through his nose as he marched across the floor. "The clouds are still present throughout the rest of the castle, but my essence is too drained to send them all away."

His shoulders jerked as he turned toward the window. "I believe the castle alone was targeted since there are no other clouds outside. There never were." His chin dropped. "It was the last thing I noticed before I lost myself to the magic."

Scurrying to her feet, she positioned herself directly behind the prince. When he turned to pace again, he nearly toppled over her.

His jaw flexed as he caught himself just in time.

She attempted a smile, but it was probably nothing to the heat warming her cheeks. Looking up at him through her eyelashes, she bit her bottom lip.

He held his breath for a moment, captivated. At least she hoped that's what it was.

But then he jerked his head away. "I am still angry with you."

She lifted one shoulder in a shrug. "Can't you be angry but still in love?"

"Yes." He gulped. "Unfortunately, yes."

Her lips turned upward as he reached for her again. At the last moment, his fingers curled into a fist. He turned his body away from her. "Do not tempt me right now. The others in the castle are still suffering."

A faraway scream reiterated his point.

He stuffed his hands into his pockets as he moved toward his bedroom door. Blaz gave her a nudge that suggested he wanted her to follow before he fell into step at the prince's side. At the last moment, Brannick's hand emerged from his pocket. With a simple hand wave, he conjured a silver enchantment above his head just like the one Soren had conjured that protected him from the snowflakes.

She let out a little huff, only *slightly* annoyed. Why did he assume she wanted to *tempt* him? She hadn't been trying to tempt him at all. It did feel nice to be treated as something so intensely desirable, however. Still, she only wanted to help him with his essence, perhaps strengthen it a little before he took care of the rest of the clouds.

Maybe it was silly to believe her love could help him. She reached into her pocket for the green crystal. It had helped him during the tournament. Maybe it could help him now. Then again, during the tournament, it only kept Queen Alessandra from manipulating his emotions. It might not help with his essence at all. But could Elora's love for him really help with that either?

When she stepped into the hallway outside his room, he glanced back from only a few steps ahead. His eyes shimmered with a burst of colors.

Then again, maybe her love had been exactly what his essence needed.

Either way, there was much to do.

CHAPTER

12

The scent of decay drifted around every corner of the castle. More thorns meant more of the rancid smell. Elora tucked her nose into one elbow while her other hand gripped tight around her sword hilt.

As during her previous travel through the castle, fights had broken out everywhere. Stone walls were cracked. Fists were held high. Weapons were drawn. Every fae shouted and snarled around her, but they didn't react to her presence any more than they reacted to the prince's.

Brannick walked several paces in front of her with Blaz at his side. Perhaps he had put a glamour over the three of them that made them appear invisible. Or perhaps the fae around them were too lost to their anger to notice anyone traipsing by.

The prince stomped over the ground, moving with purpose. She couldn't see his face, but it was likely as hardened as the twisting thorns all around.

Other demorogs had gotten into the castle, but there seemed to be fewer of them than before. Each time he saw one, Brannick raised one hand into the air and curled it into a fist. At the same moment, the demorog would curl in on itself until it withered to ash.

At last, they reached the front entrance to the castle. The prince turned around fast enough to shake his glossy black hair. His eyes fluttered closed as he raised both hands high. His lips parted as he muttered, but the words he spoke were too quiet for anyone to hear, even with the extreme hearing fae boasted.

While he muttered, blasts of silver enchantments shot from his fingertips. The shimmery magic floated through the air until it settled just beneath the clouds. Soon, every cloud within sight had been blocked by the enchantment. The snowflakes could no longer reach the ground. Still, enchantments continued to stream from the prince's hands.

It would probably take a while before he created enough enchantments to protect the entire castle. As he worked, the colors in his eyes dulled to a grayish slop. Sooner than she expected, he dropped his hands to his sides.

She tipped her head toward the ceiling, glancing at the silver enchantment he had created. "That was easy."

He did not meet her eyes when his chin dropped. "It will not last." A gulp went through him before he spoke again. "But now I can think of something that will take care of the problem for good."

Turning on his heel, he pushed open the castle doors and stepped into the forest.

Blaz glanced back at her with eyes bright and ears twitching before he followed after the prince.

She narrowed her eyes before hurrying to catch up. "Where are you going? Everyone in the castle still needs you."

Brannick whipped his head toward her. His jaw was clenched, his shoulders rigid. But nothing compared to the pure rage burning in his eyes.

Her mouth went dry. "I suppose you already know that."

He didn't spare her another look. He just huffed loudly and stomped deeper into the forest. The moss beneath his feet was a brilliant green compared to the destruction they had just seen in the castle.

She followed with more tentative steps now. Her hands clasped behind her back as she met his eyes for only a moment before looking away. "Will you make a new enchantment then? One that is permanent?"

His nostrils flared as he stuffed his hands into his pockets. "It is not that easy."

It took a few more stomping steps, but he finally stopped in front of a tree with a lovely brown trunk and such brilliant moss it was almost emerald green. He traced a finger over the side of the trunk.

Elora recognized the tree right away. It was the dryad's tree. She expected the tree trunk to start blinking with Kaia's brown and green eyes, but it didn't. Kaia must have been somewhere else.

Brannick's shoulders jerked as he glared at the tree. "I need…" His hair jumped as he shook his head. "Never mind. It never helps enough anyway."

Taking a step to the side, Elora gestured toward a large tree with wet bark and regular-colored moss. "You could try climbing a tree again."

An airy pant escaped from Blaz's snout that almost sounded like a laugh. He padded over to the tree and settled onto the ground by its base.

The prince sneered at the sight of it. Then he looked into Elora's eyes and sneered even harder. "A tree? Why would I climb a tree?"

Her shoulder lifted in a shrug. "It helped with your essence last time."

Now the prince's eyes narrowed, cutting off the few colors bursting inside them. "You assume I need help with my essence just because I came to see Kaia?"

She folded her arms over her chest. "I know I'm right."

He scowled at her for another moment before throwing his hands into the air. Despite his actions, the lack of protest spoke louder than anything.

Gesturing toward the tree again, she attempted a gentle voice. "Up you go. This tree here looks nice, and it should give you a fantastic view of the forest."

His mouth twisted into a knot while his nose twitched, but he stomped toward the tree all the same. Once he began climbing, she reached for a branch and followed after him.

After a single glance backward, he climbed with even more vigor. "You believe your presence will somehow improve my climbing experience?"

"Yes."

He glanced back with wide eyes. How could he be startled by her quick retorts? Hadn't he experienced them enough?

His head jerked back to the tree as he continued to climb. "Well, that is just—"

"Absolutely true? I know. Hurry up."

A noise escaped his throat. It was probably intended to be a huff or grunt, but it sounded more like a chuckle. Once he

103

neared the top of the tree, he settled himself back onto one of the branches. His eyes lowered. He glanced at his wolf still at the base of the tree before he finally relaxed and pressed his back into the trunk.

She found a nice branch near his where they would be close enough to touch, but only just. Her eyes also found Blaz. He seemed content resting on the mossy ground. Buzzing filled the air, probably from the sprites above. It smelled of crisp rain and wild berries. The scent of decay had been left behind in the castle.

Her spirits already lifted just from glancing around a little of the lush forest. But Brannick's attention focused on the castle.

Cracks stretched through almost every castle wall they could see. Both large and small chinks broke through the black exterior. With her eyes on the castle, the smell of decay seemed more prominent. Black thorns crawled up the walls, forcing their way into any cracks they could find. Even some of the moss that grew up the sides of the castle or along stairs had darkened to a moldy black.

Her eyes danced over to the prince's. His face had gone slack. The magic in his eyes was nonexistent. Even his shoulders slumped forward in despair. "I do not know how to permanently remove High Queen Alessandra's magic from my castle." His voice came out quiet, almost a whisper.

Swallowing, Elora attempted to move herself closer. The branches weren't close enough for it, but at least the movement had caught Brannick's eye. She dipped her head toward him. "Can I help?"

He rolled his eyes as a snort burst from his lips.

The urge to move closer vanished immediately. She pulled her knees up to her chest and pushed herself against the tree trunk at her back. "Why does everyone keep doing that? I *am* fae. I have magic inside me."

"But you do not know how to wield it." His focus turned back on the castle again.

A light breeze ruffled through her dress. She pulled her knees even closer to her chest. "I just need someone to teach me how. I taught you how to use a sword. Can you not teach me how to use magic?"

The softest bit of pity tugged at the corners of his eyes. "That is not how magic works."

She sat up a little straighter. "Is it like flying? The way to do it is just to do it?"

He gave a noncommittal shrug. "I do not know how to fly."

With a nod, she settled back against the trunk again. Her fingers found the fringed hem of her dress where silver beads adorned the edge. Her thoughts turned to the black dress Brannick had conjured for her. "How do *you* access magic?"

He was staring at the castle again. "I cannot answer that question for you. Only you can know how to access your own magic."

She huffed before dropping her legs down onto the branch. "Let me guess. I will not be able to answer that question until after I've already figured it out."

Dipping his head only slightly, he spoke with disinterested words. "That is most likely."

Maybe he had been right after all. Maybe climbing a tree could not help his essence this time. He kept staring at his breaking castle, which only made his shoulders slump more by the moment.

He needed something bigger than that to help with his essence.

It took a steady breath and several reassurances, but she finally convinced her limbs to move. Swallowing over the dryness in her throat, she reached out.

Despite the reassurances, it still scared her. For so long, her mere touch could have ended the prince's life. Her hand trembled across the entire distance.

Once her fingers met with his hair, a spark in her chest lit her entire body on fire. She had been aiming for his cheek. But the ability to touch him was so new, she lost courage at the last moment. Now her fingers slipped through the glossy black strands of his hair, which were even softer than she imagined.

The look he pierced her with sent a buzz all through her skin. Now the colors in his eyes returned. They swirled and pulsed and mesmerized her like they always had.

Her lips twitched in the faintest smile as she allowed her hand to brush across his pointed ear.

His eyes closed as he took in a deep breath. But then they snapped open right away. "What are you doing?" His voice came out husky. His shoulders tensed like he wanted to resist. Wanted to, but couldn't, mostly because she wouldn't allow it.

She allowed her smile to grow as he brought her hand against his cheek. The colors in his eyes spun even faster than they ever had before. Her heart pounded as she leaned forward. After a swallow, her gaze turned toward the prize she sought.

His lips.

He must have seen her staring at them, but with her gaze unwavering, she couldn't see his eyes to know for sure. All she knew was that she had to keep moving forward. Just a little closer. Maybe it wouldn't fully repair his essence. Maybe it wouldn't even help. But what better way to find out than by trying?

She was close enough to feel the prince's breath on her cheeks. She moved forward slowly, unable to overcome the fear that this might hurt him. But she had been touching his hair and face for several moments now. And she had used the shard and sacrificed her mortal life. She *could* touch him. Maybe that alone terrified her enough to slow her movements.

Apparently, Brannick had no patience for her fears. He wrapped an arm around her waist and tugged her close until her body met his chest. His lips were the ones searching now. They pressed against hers as hot as fire. The air around them crackled. His arm around her waist somehow pulled her closer but with the gentlest touch.

As the kiss deepened, another crackle of energy went through the air. It was louder this time. Or… maybe it wasn't because of the kiss after all.

Both of them seemed to notice the change in energy because they pulled away from each other just enough to glance to the side.

Nothing obvious met their sight. But then, a wild shriek sounded all around them.

Brannick kept his arm around her waist, but he angled his head to get a better look at the castle. His arm dropped away as he let out a gasp.

She could see it now. The same sight that had caused the prince's gasp. At the foot of the tree, Blaz jumped to his feet with his ears perked up.

Demorogs.

An entire swarm of them had nearly reached the castle. They shrieked again with that strange sound that was almost like wind whistling through a tight space. But it was louder. And it set Elora's nerves on fire.

Without a word, Brannick leapt from his branch and jumped straight down to the mossy forest floor. His fae strength must have caught the brunt of the fall because he immediately began running toward the castle. Blaz immediately followed after him.

Elora called the wings out of her back and then took her own leap from the tree. With her wings beating, it only took a moment to catch up to the prince. Soon, her feet met the ground. She pulled her wings back inside while running at his side.

One hand already gripped her sword hilt tight. If she could fly high enough, she could use her magic sword to destroy some of the demorogs.

But the prince worked too fast. He raised both hands high above his head and pulled them into fists. Then he brought his fists together. With a burst of silver all around them, the demorogs began withering away.

She still had one hand on her sword as she glanced upward. "You did it. You destroyed the entire swarm in one go."

But once her gaze turned back to her side, she found that Brannick had collapsed. He clutched his chest while trying to catch his breath.

Her knees bent immediately, dropping to his side. She lifted her hands but wasn't sure what to do with them. She had to help. She had to do *something*. But what could she do?

A hard grunt left Brannick's lips as he collapsed even more. Now he was lying on his back with his arms stretched out. "Everyone must leave."

"What?" She brushed a lock of hair away from his face.

He took in a breath before he answered. Even then, his voice came out tight, like he didn't have enough air. "Everyone has to get out of the castle."

"Why?"

He turned away from her before he closed his eyes. "I cannot protect it."

She placed a hand on his upper arm, which was thicker than she anticipated. "But... I thought the castle was the safest place in Bitter Thorn."

"It was." He shoved both hands over his face before continuing. "Do you not see? This destruction is *my* fault. The demorogs only came because I succumbed to the anger from the snowflakes. The castle only fell apart because I did. If had I had been stronger." His entire body flinched. "If I had done my duty as prince—"

"Stop it." She reached for his hand and held it in her lap before she opened her mouth again. "This is not your fault. Queen Alessandra did this."

Though tension seemed to rock through his whole body, the hand in hers at least felt relaxed. His eyes remained closed as he shook his head. "It does not matter now. She will continue to attack the castle. She thinks I would never abandon it. I will put my protection magic into a different part of Bitter Thorn instead. A nearby village could work. Everyone will have to hide there."

"But what if..." The words trailed off as Elora considered what she was about to say. It didn't matter. Even if she learned how to use her magic, it wouldn't be enough. If the prince of Bitter Thorn couldn't protect his castle, of course a brand new fae like her couldn't either. He was right. Nothing more could be done.

With several grunts, he forced himself to his feet. Blaz pressed into his leg, perhaps giving him strength of some sort. Or maybe it was only to show support. Once Brannick placed a hand on top of the wolf's head. He glanced toward her.

His eyes turned dull again, gray and sludgy and nothing like they should have looked. His entire face was fallen. "Go to your sisters. The enchantments in their room should have kept them safe from this attack. You all need to get some rest. I will you call you to the council room when I am ready to make a plan."

He probably needed more rest than anyone. But at this point, coming up with a plan might lift his spirits better than anything. She'd go to her sisters now. But then she'd help him find a way to stop Queen Alessandra for good.

CHAPTER

13

Fissures and chinks marred every stone wall that Elora passed. Thorns twisted and creaked with renewed energy. They didn't just sway in the gentle breeze. They closed in on the castle walls, as if trying to squeeze the life out of them. The moss on the floor and along the walls was turning a moldy black. Decayed scents struck from every side.

And it was quiet. Much too quiet. The bustle of the castle never seemed to make much noise, but the absence of that noise hit hard. Nearly everyone must have been gone by now.

As Brannick had predicted, the enchantments on Elora's room had kept her sisters safe during the attack. The walls still cracked, and the moss still decayed, but at least they hadn't been subjected to the snowflakes like everyone else in the castle.

It was difficult to sleep that night, but all three of them eventually managed it. They huddled together for most of the next day until Elora finally received a message that called her to the council room. Her sisters were not enthusiastic about her leaving their room. The shouts and cracks had scared them enough.

But there was work to be done.

The thickening scent of decay caused her stomach to writhe. By the time she made it to the council room, she wished for a bucket. Just in case.

What sight met her eyes? Two long emerald braids sat against a gauzy light brown dress. Kaia's brown skin looked smooth and bright, so she had probably just come from her tree. She stood near the wall, walking on her tiptoes. Her head turned slightly. When she noticed Elora standing nearby, the dryad jumped.

After touching a hand to her chest and taking a breath, the dryad shoved a hand into her pocket. She blinked her brown and green eyes as she brought out a flower crown made of purple flowers. Her hand stretched forward. "This is imbued with—"

"Will it bring my memories back?" Elora thought it best to interrupt the dryad before she could make a vow Elora did not want.

Kaia's eyes dimmed as she pushed the flower crown forward again. "It has magical properties that can protect—"

"Will it bring my memories back?" Elora laced her words with more insistence this time.

The dryad continued to hold the crown out hopefully. "No."

Elora turned away from it. "Then I do not want it."

A head of glossy black hair appeared in the doorway. Brannick's eyes were narrowed when he peered around the corner. "What are you two talking about?"

In an instant, Elora's throat went dry. If Kaia was right, the prince's essence would suffer even more if he found out Elora had helped him escape Fairfrost. Maybe he could handle the truth in other circumstances, but Elora had no desire to damage his essence anymore, especially not after the attack on his castle.

The word *nothing* very nearly left her mouth, but then she remembered what had happened the last time she tried to lie. Distraction would have to work instead.

She gestured around the castle with the most interested face she could muster. "Have all the other fae left yet?"

As her hand made a sweeping motion toward the castle, her eyes drifted upward. The glowing sprites who usually hovered just under the ceiling had disappeared. She had expected that, but she hadn't expected to see Brannick's silver enchantment nearly bursting, full of heavy snow up above.

It looked ready to rip apart at any moment.

"Most have." Brannick's own eyes trailed upward, which immediately made him flinch. He turned around and moved back farther into the council room. "The brownies are not cooperating."

Elora's mouth twisted to the side as she followed the prince into the room. "The brownies? But Bitter Thorn Castle is their home. They can't leave. They have stronger magic when they are here."

The prince flinched again. This time, the sight of his throne that merged stone and tree together had probably done it. Thorns choked the entire thing so tight that the branches had started to sag. Sitting in it would not be an option.

Brannick took the chair to the right of it instead. "I know, but it is not safe here anymore. The brownies need to find new homes."

At that exact moment, Fifer appeared on top of the table directly in front of Brannick. The prince jumped at the sight of him. Fifer's big eyes grew even bigger. He clasped his spindly fingers in front of his chest while his flappy ears bounced with his words. "I still want to stay, my prince. The snowflakes did not affect me once I used my brownie magic. I will be safe from them after your enchantment fails."

He gestured toward the ceiling. The silver enchantment beneath the ceiling probably wouldn't bear the weight of the snowflakes much longer. It might make it until night fell, but surely not any longer.

Brannick pinched the bridge of his nose. "What about the thorns? What about the demorogs? The castle is being torn apart as we speak."

As if Faerie itself wanted to emphasize the point, a chunk of stone fell away from a castle wall and crumbled onto the ground. Brannick tensed.

Fifer merely stood taller. "I will stay. Bitter Thorn Castle is my home. Who else will look after it while you are gone?"

The prince had dropped his head into one hand now. He let out a long sigh, which sounded eerily like a groan. "I will not force you to leave, but it would be much safer if you did."

Sniffing through his squat nose, Fifer gave a tiny bow. "It is settled then. I will stay." He disappeared without a word.

From behind them, a new voice appeared. "This is…"

Elora glanced around to see Lyren clutching one of her black curls. Her dark brown skin looked dry under the silver enchantment. It was probably just a trick of the light, but it didn't help that her eyes were so wide. "You explained in the message, but I never thought it would be *this* devastating."

Vesper and Quintus arrived a moment later. No jokes or epic stories passed between them. Vesper only managed a small nod in Elora's direction before he collapsed onto a chair at the council table. Soren stomped into the room and didn't grumble once. He kept his eyes staring at the spear in his hands.

Brannick stood from the table, ready to speak. But the sound of shoes scraping against stone stopped him.

Someone stood just outside the room. But who? No one else should have been in the castle.

"Show yourself." The command came out booming, proving that Brannick could be frightening when he chose to be.

Chloe ducked into the room, fiddling with a light purple ribbon tied around her wrist. "Are we really leaving the castle?"

Elora began to rise from her wooden chair. "Yes, I told you we must."

Chloe's eyes darted to the prince. "But you told everyone else you would stay. I heard them talking about it. You said High Queen Alessandra could never drive you out of your own castle."

A long breath escaped the prince's nose before he spoke again. "She has spies in my court and so do the other rulers. I had to tell the others I would stay. I do not want anyone else aside from those in this room to know I plan on leaving the castle."

"Oh, but…" Chloe shoved her thumbnail into her mouth to chew on it. "Can we take the library?"

Brannick blinked twice. He cocked his head to the side while one eye narrowed. "Can we take the *library?*"

Lowering herself back into her chair, Elora raised her eyebrows. She didn't even know Bitter Thorn Castle *had* a library. Now she wished she had discovered it earlier, though it was no surprise Chloe had found it first.

Chloe threw her hands into the air. "I don't know. You have magic, don't you? I thought maybe you could take the library with us?"

"We cannot take the library." Brannick glanced toward Elora for the smallest moment. Though his face remained mostly unreadable, a hint of a smirk lingered there.

Stomping one foot, Chloe let out a huff. "Fine. Then I need to gather some books before we leave." She turned to exit the room but immediately turned back toward the others again. "And Grace needs her harp."

It was Quintus who responded now. He raised one eyebrow. "We are going to be staying in my home, which was built to comfortably fit two fae, not the seven who will be staying there. We do not have room for a harp."

Chloe waved a flippant hand. "A little one then. You can craft one, can't you?"

The blue in Vesper's eyes brightened as he sent a smirk toward Chloe. "Have you always been this bossy?"

She sent him a glare. "Oh hush, *brother*. Unless you want me to tell everyone about your little escapade the other night."

Vesper's cheeks immediately turned bright red. "Goodbye, Chloe." He jumped up from his chair to shoo her out of the room. "Go gather your books while the rest of us talk."

While she stomped away, Elora turned to the prince. "Only seven of us are going?" Her gaze turned toward Kaia and then toward Soren.

Kaia's lips turned downward as she stroked one of her emerald braids. "I cannot go, of course. I must stay close to my

116

tree." She swallowed. "But it will protect me from any future attacks."

Soren gripped his spear even tighter and kept his eyes averted. His voice came out gruff. "I will stay as well. Prince Brannick added magic to my protection enchantment." He gestured toward the silver enchantment that still floated over his head. "That will make it last indefinitely. I must prepare an army, and that requires that I travel to and from the castle regularly."

Now Elora's gaze turned back to the prince. "You cannot create an enchantment for the rest of us?"

His whole face fell. Gray choked out the colors in his eyes as he dropped his chin to his chest.

She waved off the words. "Never mind." If he could have saved everyone, he would have done it already. "What are we going to do to overthrow Queen Alessandra?"

Quintus nearly jumped out of his chair. He sat up straight, his eyes intense. He had probably been waiting for this exact moment just to say what he was about to say. "We could close the portal to the mortal realm."

With a hand on the white sea flower in her hair, Lyren gave a tiny nod. "There are fae in my court who have suggested the same thing."

Vesper was sitting again, but nothing about it looked comfortable. A shiver passed through his shoulders. His mouth dropped into a deep frown.

Brannick sat wearing a passive expression, but at his side, Blaz's body shuddered uncomfortably.

Elora glanced over everyone again before speaking. "High Queen Winola, Brannick's mother, opened the portal to the mortal realm."

Quintus folded his arms over his chest. "And when she did, it allowed mortal emotion to seep into Faerie." His eyes narrowed. "Emotions like anger."

Sitting forward in her chair, Lyren wrapped one of her curls around one finger. "Closing the portal would cut everyone off from mortal emotion. High Queen Alessandra could no longer wield it as a weapon against us."

"But emotions exist in Faerie now." Elora shook her head, anxious to properly form the words. "Even if you closed the portal, surely the emotion that is here would still be here. Queen Alessandra could still wield it."

When her remark was met with silence, she glanced toward Brannick. At his side, Blaz covered his snout with two paws.

The prince's face remained passive. "The emotion would linger, but it would not stay forever."

Churning surged in Elora's gut at that thought. Without emotion, she wouldn't feel... anything. Her kiss with Brannick the day before would have felt the same as throwing a stone or eating a mushroom. She glanced toward the prince, but he would not meet her eye.

Instead, her gaze turned toward Vesper. If the portal was closed, he would never reunite with his beloved in the mortal realm. Even worse, without emotion, she wouldn't even be his beloved anymore. He wouldn't even care that he'd never see her again.

But as Elora had learned before she became fae, feeling nothing was worse than feeling pain.

She glared at Vesper, pleading with him to say something.

It only took a moment until he did. "We have found a good balance with the emotions we have in Faerie. If we cut it off completely, it would cause chaos. Everyone would have to find a new balance."

Stroking one finger over the silver chain of her seashell necklace, Lyren nodded thoughtfully. "I agree that closing the portal is not the only way to stop High Queen Alessandra. Even if we did, she could still wield the power for a while before all emotion faded away."

Quintus steepled his fingers under his chin. "Then there is only one other way to overthrow her." He raised one eyebrow. "With a crown."

Elora jerked her head toward him.

His neatly parted hair was more tousled than usual. He raised his eyebrow even higher. "We must do what the rulers did when they overthrew High Queen Winola."

Now Elora turned toward Brannick. "I thought they killed High Queen Winola. Did she not die when they overthrew her?"

While her gaze remained on the prince's stoic face, she could tell the others had turned to look at him too.

The prince swallowed and dropped his hand onto his wolf's head. He held her gaze before looking down at the table. "Rulers in Faerie have two rights that give them power. The first power comes from Faerie itself. The second power comes from the fae who swear fealty to that ruler. Since she had both powers, High Queen Winola was the truest High Ruler Faerie has ever known."

A bit of thread at the end her belt provided the perfect thing to fiddle with while Elora mulled over these words. "So, did the other fae take away their fealty then? They stopped acknowledging her rule, and that's how they overthrew her?"

Brannick glanced down at his wolf before he answered. "It is not that simple."

Of course. She should have known.

He continued. "Fealty once given cannot be rescinded."

119

From across the table, Vesper shoved a hand through the brown curls on his head. "Plus, High Queen Winola had great power, which Faerie itself gave to her. To choose a new High Ruler, they needed someone who had even more power than that."

Lyren strummed her blue fingernails on the council table. "But no fae had such power."

Still steepling his fingers, Quintus nodded. "Instead, the other rulers had to give it to him. The rulers of Mistmount, Swiftsea, Dustdune, Fairfrost, and Rarerose, as Noble Rose used to be called, all came together and put great magic into King Romany's crown. The crown a Faerie ruler wears gives him power to rule. After all the other rulers imbued King Romany's crown with added power, he then had a crown even more powerful than High Queen Winola's. Only then could they take the title away from her."

Brannick picked at one his fingernails, still unable to lift his eyes. "Once they swore fealty to High King Romany, they stripped my mother of her title and demoted her to princess, and then they cursed this court."

The words bubbled as she turned them over, but Elora still didn't fully understand. "But how did she die? Fae are immortal unless they are killed, so something must have killed her."

Everyone at the table seemed suddenly interested in their hands or the grain of wood in the table. No one would meet her eye. No one would answer her question.

When the silence continued, Quintus finally broke it with his quietest voice. "She made a choice and suffered for it."

The words had barely left his lips when Brannick stood from his chair. He glanced toward the ceiling and flinched. But then he spoke in a regal tone. "We will need to gain support from the other courts. High Queen Alessandra rules over

Fairfrost *and* Noble Rose now. That means we only have Swiftsea, Mistmount, and Dustdune to help us. We will need all the power we can get if we want to succeed at overthrowing High Queen Alessandra."

When he glanced up a second time, he flinched again. The reason was obvious once Elora also looked up. The silver enchantment full of snow was even closer to bursting than before.

Brannick swallowed before speaking again. "For now, we must go."

CHAPTER

14

Elora could not open her own Faerie door. She waved her hand and dug deep within herself the same way she had when she got her sword to do magic. It wasn't enough. No matter how she willed magic to dance along her fingertips, it never listened.

Brannick had gone ahead to Quintus's home to rid it of demorogs and thorns before the rest of them would follow. Chloe had finally finished gathering the stacks of books she apparently couldn't live without. Even Grace had packed a large sack full of clothes and harp music she couldn't be parted from.

Chloe gathered the ribbons made from Elora's old skirt and divided them equally between the three sisters. Now they all had ribbons tied around their belts. Elora braided hers through the leather of her belt. It was nice having the fabric of her mother's dress close to the sword from her father. Still, neither of them helped her open a door.

From the edge of the council room, Lyren traced a finger over the silver chain of the seashell necklace she had gained for her courage during the fight against King Huron. The other seashell necklace sat a little higher on her neck. She kept herself from snickering, but Elora could tell the fae found her attempts at using magic amusing.

Squaring her shoulders, Elora tried again. Embarrassment would only prolong her ability to use magic. It was better to keep trying, even if her attempts were laughable.

Eventually, Brannick returned. Everyone stepped through his door, straight into Quintus's house. They left Bitter Thorn Castle behind with no idea when they would return.

Though Brannick declared Quintus's home safe, it was hardly livable. Shards of clay pots scattered all over the room. Woven rugs of brown and black had been shredded to pieces. The bright green rug that once looked like moss now had mud caked deep in its fibers.

Moist dirt and crumbling ash littered the ground.

Quintus reached a hand over his stomach at the sight of it. His light brown face lost color. When he noticed a wooden table that had been split in half, his lips turned downward.

Watching him, Brannick's face fell. He jerked himself away from the others and marched toward the front door. "I need to place a few final enchantments around the home. Everyone stay inside. It is not safe outdoors."

Lyren stood tall and started giving everyone assignments.

Before Elora could be given her own assignment, she trailed over to the door. With it open a crack, she could see the prince waving his arms. Magic streamed all around him, but his eyes looked lifeless. His face looked sunken.

"Leave him."

Elora jumped at the sound of Vesper's voice. She turned around to meet his eye.

Vesper glanced out through the door, but then let out a sigh. "Prince Brannick will draw strength from knowing the fae of his court are safe. Let him work in peace until he is done."

The words came out with such fervor, following them seemed like the best action. Still, Elora spared one last glance toward the prince before she fully closed the door. Vesper gestured toward a front room in the house. He also carried a broom and a large sack, probably for the shards of clay and other debris everywhere.

Elora waited until they moved deep into the room before she spoke again. Vesper swept debris into one corner and then she held the sack against the ground while he swept the debris pile inside. Once finished, he set to work sweeping another portion of the room.

Lowering her voice to a near whisper, she stepped toward him. "You will not let them close the portal, right? You would never get to see your wife, Cosette, again."

His shoulders twitched before he indicated that his newest pile was ready for the sack. "We are far from needing to take that route. Using a crown to overthrow High Queen Alessandra will be more effective anyway."

His words didn't temper her anxiety in the least.

What else could she say? Of any fae, he probably wanted to close the portal the least. If he wasn't concerned about it, maybe she didn't need to be either.

They finished sweeping in silence. Vesper's blue and gray eyes went back and forth between clear and gloomy. Perhaps he was more worried than he wanted to let on.

When they moved to another room, most of the debris had already been cleaned away. It had a large stone basin for bathing, a wardrobe, and even a long wooden table with all sorts of crafting materials on top. The broken remains of a bed had been shoved to one corner.

"Quintus said this is where you, your sisters, and I will all be sleeping," Vesper said. "Lyren will return to Swiftsea each night. Quintus and the prince will sleep in the other bedroom." Vesper ducked a head into the hallway only to nod and grab items from outside it. "Prince Brannick has already conjured sleeping mats and blankets for us."

He dropped a handful of thick, woven mats into Elora's arms. When he left the room again, it was to retrieve the blankets.

She placed them neatly on one side of the room. Once Vesper returned with the blankets, she raised an eyebrow in his direction. "*You* are going to sleep in the same room as my sisters and me?"

Flipping his brown curls back, he shrugged. "I am your brother. Your mortal sense of propriety should not be bothered by me sleeping in the same room as you."

Her eyes narrowed as she took a blanket from off the pile in his arms. "True, but I feel like there's something you are not telling me."

He gulped again, which only added to her suspicions. Letting out a sigh, he dropped the pile of blankets onto the ground. "Oh fine, I will tell you. Prince Brannick wanted someone with magic in your room to protect you if… just in case anything happens."

The words should have brought comfort. Instead, her fingers tightened as she spread a blanket over the next sleeping mat. "If I could just figure out how to use my own magic it wouldn't be necessary for you to stay in our room."

Her brother donned a pitying look that only frustrated her more.

Huffs billowed from her nose as she slammed the last blanket over its sleeping mat. Vesper must have decided that was the perfect time to leave because he slipped out of the room without a noise.

Yanking the broom from its place against the wall, she forced the last bit of dust and debris into the corner with the broken bed. Her movements came jerky and hostile. If she had magic, maybe her movements would have been smoother.

She huffed again.

While sweeping around the long table, the end of the broom found a sketchbook hidden underneath it. She plucked it from the ground and brushed off a thick layer of dust. Quintus often carried sketchbooks with him. This must have been one of his old ones.

She made a place for it on the table but flipped through a few pages first. Apparently, he often sketched items he intended to craft, but he sketched other things too. The drawings on the pages varied from scrawled, rough sketches to detailed drawings filled in with smudges of color.

When she turned another page, her fingers froze in place. Taking in a shallow breath, she traced a finger over the intricate drawing. A chandelier.

She had seen the same chandelier before. It hung in a hidden room of Bitter Thorn Castle. She remembered well the story Brannick had told her about it. The man who crafted the chandelier was an apprentice. His master promised him freedom once the chandelier was finished, but the promise was taken away as soon the time came. High Queen Winola had killed the master and brought the apprentice to Bitter Thorn, where he then lived out his mortal days.

Even seeing a drawing of the chandelier made Elora's insides skip. Holding her place in the sketchbook, she ventured into the hallway. The others were sweeping, dusting, and organizing. She stomped past them until she cornered Quintus.

He stood in the other, much smaller, bedroom, trying to smooth a wrinkle from one of two sleeping mats.

Elora held the sketchbook out to him, pointing to the drawing of the chandelier.

Though he had glanced toward her as soon as she entered the room, he quickly went back to his work. But he couldn't ignore her once she put the book under his nose.

Brushing dust away from his leather coat, he finally got to his feet. "You found one of my old sketchbooks."

She jabbed a finger at the drawing. "Did Brannick's father craft this chandelier?"

The only answer she received was a twitch along Quintus's eyebrow.

Her eyes narrowed. "I know the prince's father was mortal."

Now Quintus turned away. "I know what information you truly desire. I cannot give it to you."

Her feet trailed across the floor until she was looking him in the eye. "Then tell me what you can. Tell me anything."

He rubbed a hand across his forehead before he responded. "Help me clear the mud out of my bath." He gestured across the room at a large stone basin that was in even worse condition than most of the house. Most of the twigs and branches had been cleared away, but mud and dirt still caked the stone.

Nodding, she moved straight for the water-filled wooden bucket sitting next to the basin. She grabbed a rag from inside the bucket and held it above the stone. "I will help, and you will talk." She spoke the last part as a command.

Quintus let out a sigh as he took the second rag. While he squeezed water over a splotch of mud, he began talking. "You are correct. Prince Brannick's father crafted that chandelier. I was a craftsman even before High Queen Winola opened the portal to the mortal realm. I did my best, but she always found my skills to be lacking. I did not understand why until she opened the portal and brought back Martin, Prince Brannick's father."

With a hand scrubbing a mud spot, Elora snapped her head up. "Did he teach you how to craft better?"

The smallest light sparked in Quintus's eye. "Yes, but that was not the only change he brought. Before the portal opened, High Queen Winola was cruel and cunning. With Martin around, she inexplicably became kind as well. Her personality did not change exactly. It just grew. It did for all of us. She often ventured into the mortal realm to collect mortals. Fae who had mortals around adjusted more easily to the sudden appearance of emotions in Faerie."

Elora dunked her rag into the water and did her best to wash away most of the mud on it. Her thoughts circled back to her fae brother. Vesper had also ventured into the mortal realm, but High King Romany banned him from his own court and cursed him to never return because of it. Her eyebrows lowered as she brought the rag back to the stone basin.

"Not all the courts had mortals around like you had in Bitter Thorn." She glanced up to confirm her suspicions.

Quintus nodded as he pressed his rag against a mud spot. "Exactly. The fae in Bitter Thorn and Mistmount were the first to accept mortals into their courts. Swiftsea eventually did the same, and Dustdune followed soon after. High Queen Alessandra's father eventually brought mortals to his court, though he mostly used them as servants. Ever since High Queen Alessandra murdered her father and took the Fairfrost crown, she has not brought many mortals into her court."

Elora's head snapped up even faster than before. "Queen Alessandra killed her own father and stole his crown?" She shook her head and turned back to the stone basin. "That doesn't matter right now."

When her interruption apparently stopped Quintus from telling more, she tried to prompt him with a question. "You are older than Brannick then?"

Quintus tipped an eyebrow upward. "The prince has more magic and more experience than most fae, which is how we measure age." He shrugged and dipped his rag in the bucket of water. "But I was grown before he was born."

"Fae do start as children then?" She gripped the edge of the stone basin as she leaned forward. "I assumed that at first, but then, I have never seen a fae child. I wondered if you just appeared as adults."

He chuckled. "Yes, fae begin as babies just as mortals do. Faerie itself keeps the number of fae nearly constant. So, a fae is only born when another fae dies. But since we are immortal, fae do not die very often. And, like in your case, sometimes mortals can become fae, which negates the necessity of a fae baby. The number is not always exactly the same, but it is always close to the same."

Elora bit her bottom lip, afraid to show too much eagerness but also being unable to stop it. "What was the prince like as a child? What was his childhood like?"

A hard swallow passed through Quintus's throat. He shifted and focused his eyes more intensely on the splotch of mud he was cleaning away from the stone basin. "Prince Brannick's father, Martin, lived in the castle until his death, but he was not allowed to raise the prince as a father usually does in Faerie. The fae of Bitter Thorn feared the prince would turn out too sympathetic to mortals if he did. Kaia and Soren mostly raised the prince, though he did get to visit with his father often."

A wistful look passed over Quintus's face as he scrubbed away more mud. "His father was audacious and creative. He taught me to craft like I never could have dreamed of on my own. The prince inherited his audacious side from his father, but he has not shown it much ever since…" Quintus swallowed and lowered his voice. "Ever since everything started to go wrong."

Clenching her rag tight, muddy water trickled down the side of the stone basin. Elora spoke through her teeth. "You mean ever since Queen Alessandra showed up and tricked the prince into falling in love with her?"

No answer came, but she didn't need one. He might have protested such an accusation if he could have, but since fae couldn't lie, he kept his mouth shut.

She released her grip slightly and dumped her rag in the bucket of water to clean it off. "But what about his mother?

Where was she when Brannick grew up? Why did Kaia and Soren raise him and not her?"

Again, he did not answer. Quintus dropped his rag into the bucket and marched out of the room. Apparently, the topic of High Queen Winola's death was the absolute touchiest subject in all of Bitter Thorn. She'd just have to force it out of Brannick sometime.

Without any distractions, she finished cleaning off the rest of the mud. A few bits still clung to the stone, but a bath would clear them away.

As she got to her feet, Chloe traipsed into the room and hooked an arm around her sister's. "Grace is making us stew. She says it's almost finished. Before we left the castle, Fifer gave her a bundle of herbs, which gave the soup the most delicious flavor."

A smile danced across Elora's face as they moved toward the door. Though they'd had an entire house to clean, it had gone much faster with so many of them. And it seemed Grace was already getting to learn how to cook just like she dreamed.

Chloe tucked a lock of blonde hair behind her ear as soon as they exited the room. Her eyes went glossy as she stared off. "Quintus said my dress was well crafted." Her lips pressed together in a playful smile. "That sounds like he wanted to compliment the way I looked in the dress, doesn't it? I think maybe he lost courage at the last moment, but he definitely thinks I'm pretty, don't you think?"

Her cheeks turned bright pink by the time she finished.

Stopping in the middle of the hallway, Elora took her sister by the shoulders. "No, Chloe. I told you, no falling in love with a fae."

She wriggled out of the grasp and pouted. "You fell in love with one."

Elora folded her arms over her chest. "*You* are still a child."

Chloe let out a *tsk* and flipped her hair over one shoulder. "I am fifteen, which is *nearly* an adult. But maybe Quintus isn't right for me after all. He is *very* dedicated to crafting. Maybe a little too dedicated."

Her blonde hair trailed behind her as she pranced away to the kitchen.

As she did, the front door swung open. Blaz entered first with his ears sharply pointed. Brannick came in next.

The prince slammed the door behind him and soon everyone in the house stared at him. He cleared his throat. "When day dawns, we will go to Swiftsea and beg for support from Queen Noelani."

CHAPTER 15

Cream palace walls of stucco towered over a sandy landscape. Copper tiles topped the turrets. Salt hung in the air, spreading sparkles across the landscape wherever the salt caught the light. Palm trees with sturdy trunks and bright green leaves waved in the light breeze.

Elora stood at Brannick's side, basking in the view of the palace before her. Lyren stood on Elora's other side. The dark-skinned fae shook her black curls back as she reached both hands out. Her eyes closed as she took in a long breath.

Behind them, Quintus used one hand to shield his eyes from the sun beating down on them. He nearly cowered at the lack of forest all around them.

Vesper watched Lyren enjoy the salty air with a note of longing in his eyes. Elora guessed it wasn't longing for Lyren,

133

but for Lyren's feeling of being back in her own court—Vesper seemed to want that for himself.

Elora's sisters had stayed back at Quintus's house where they would be surrounded by several enchantments. Both seemed glad for the protection.

Water trickled down from an aqueduct system that had been built into the palace walls. A group of fae, all carrying shimmery blue javelins, stepped down the staircase coming from the front palace entrance.

They offered short nods to Brannick and then beckoned his entire group to enter the palace.

Elora tried to catch the prince's eye to see what he thought of the invitation, but he was too busy patting his wolf on the head to notice her. When he followed after the group of Swiftsea fae, the others followed after him.

The Swiftsea fae took their group straight to a huge dining room with large fountains in each corner. Long open windows let in a salty breeze. It fluttered through the various seashell and reed wind chimes throughout the room.

Queen Noelani sat at the head of a table. Her silver and seashell crown sat atop her black hair that had been shaved close to her scalp. She wore a vivid blue dress with straight lines and a large print of white flowers. Her dark skin radiated even without direct sunlight shining down on her.

She gestured toward the chairs nearest to her. The wooden chairs were simple, but they had pearls of every color inlaid in their backs. Each one had a shimmery finish. Jars holding sea flowers and lily pads dotted the long table.

Once they were all seated, more fae entered the room carrying long metal trays. Plates were placed until everyone had something to eat. Elora's plate had yams spiced with cinnamon and a fillet of fish fried in oil with peppers, onions, and tomatoes on top. She was given a clear drink that had a hint of coconut throughout.

Brannick waited until everyone had been seated and had food, but then he finally turned toward Queen Noelani. "We need to discuss the high queen."

After popping a portion of fish into her mouth, Queen Noelani nodded. "We will get to that, but first, a story."

Vesper sat between Elora and Brannick, but she still managed to catch a glimpse of the twitch in the prince's eye at the sound of those words. He let out a sigh that was probably meant to be less audible than it turned out to be.

From across the table, Lyren shifted in her chair to glance at the others. "It is customary in Swiftsea to greet guests with a story."

Brannick offered a smile that looked more like a grimace.

A fae with short hair and tight curls came from the edge of the room to stand at Queen Noelani's side. The man brushed his loose-fitting blue shirt before he stood tall. "I received this story from the mermaid, Waverly of Swiftsea."

Elora's ears perked up at the mention of the name. After Ansel kidnapped her and brought her to his home, she and the mermaid had escaped together.

The male fae gave a solemn nod before he continued. "During one of Waverly's usual swims through the sea, pain and weakness overcame her body. Because of the decay, she was already weakened, and this she could not bear."

Reaching a hand across her stomach, Elora grimaced at the food on her plate. Apparently, this wouldn't be a happy story.

Across the table, Quintus pulled a notebook from his pocket and began sketching as the story continued.

The storyteller touched a hand to his forehead. "The weakness allowed Waverly to be captured. Soon, she found herself in Mistmount, in the home of the fae Ansel."

Next to Elora, Vesper flinched. Brannick glanced toward her for the briefest moment before jerking his head back to the storyteller.

With a frown that could have crumbled a lily pad, the storyteller closed his eyes. "Ansel tortured Waverly. He stole her blood. He constantly weakened her with iron. She did not know why until another fae arrived one day. High Queen Alessandra."

Brannick's chair gave a short skid across the floor as he sat up with a start. The scratching of Quintus's pencil stopped at the mention of the Fairfrost queen. Vesper gulped loud enough for everyone to hear.

Lyren had already told them that Queen Alessandra and Ansel were working together, but the mere mention of her still apparently filled everyone with fear.

Elora clutched her stomach tighter.

The storyteller opened his eyes again. His voice came out grave and weighted. "Waverly learned much that day. She learned enough that she fought to survive the torture so that she might eventually share the knowledge with her queen."

Slamming a fist against his palm, the storyteller stood taller. "When the chance to escape came, Waverly took it without hesitation. She aided the mortal, Elora, after the mortal also aided her. Waverly immediately shared all knowledge with her queen. The mermaid will forever be remembered for her great service to Swiftsea."

Brannick set one fist on the table as he turned to the Swiftsea queen. "What did you learn?"

With a wave of her hand, Queen Noelani dismissed the storyteller. Her eyes went alight as she turned back to her guests. "You know that Ansel draws power from blood?"

"Yes." Brannick's answer came quickly, eagerness lacing through it.

Vesper leaned closer to the queen. "We also know that Ansel cannot draw power from a fae's blood because the magic inside it will fight back."

A breeze rushed through the room, causing the wind chimes to move even faster. Queen Noelani raised an eyebrow. "What do you know of High Queen Alessandra's iron talismans?"

Brannick lips turned downward as he leaned back in his chair. He glanced toward Quintus and Vesper, but apparently neither of them knew anything.

Sitting up, Elora cleared her throat. "The iron in it makes it difficult for fae to remove or approach the talisman. It can also draw power from your court."

Queen Noelani raised a finger into the air as she shook her head. "Not power. The talisman draws *magic* from our court. With more magic, High Queen Alessandra can create more enchantments, which she uses to maintain control in her court."

A twinge of guilt raked over Elora's nerves as she remembered the enchantment that forced sprites to be captured in Fairfrost Palace. How many similar enchantments were there in Fairfrost?

Quintus scratched his pencil across his paper until it stopped with a start. His eyes widened as he spoke. "More magic means she can create more enchantments. But if she is conspiring with Ansel than she needs more than just magic. She needs power too."

137

Digging a hand into his curls, Vesper shook his head. "With more power, she could create an enchantment that covers a larger distance than it normally could."

Quintus's eyes widened even more. "She could create an enchantment that covered an entire court."

"Or all of Faerie." The weight in Queen Noelani's voice suggested she had been considering the consequences for too long.

The prince remained silent for a few more moments. At last, he placed a hand on top of his wolf's head and took a deep breath. "High Queen Alessandra cast an enchantment over my entire castle. It is still there now. The enchantment releases snowflakes that force any fae who touches them to feel the deepest anger. It led to great turmoil inside my castle almost immediately."

Touching a hand to the seashell necklace at her collarbone, Queen Noelani sighed. "Lyren informed me of the details already. If Ansel finds a way to give the high queen more power, there is no telling what havoc she could wreak."

Elora sat forward, leaning her elbows onto the table. "Why did Ansel kidnap Waverly then? They used an iron talisman against her, but if they didn't need magic from her, why capture her at all?"

Lyren shook her head as she stared down at her lap. "The iron talismans cannot draw magic directly from a fae, only from the land or the air."

The words might have settled the tension in Elora's gut if they hadn't been spoken through a grimace. She turned to the queen, hoping for a better explanation.

Queen Noelani took a breath. "The iron could not draw magic away from Waverly, but it still weakened her." She shook her head. "It weakened her magic."

Silence filled the air but for the gentle tinkle of the wind chimes. Suddenly, Brannick sucked in a sharp breath. His eyebrows flew upward as he jerked his head toward the queen.

She nodded, as if in answer to an unspoken question. "Ansel can draw power from a fae's blood, but he cannot use it because the magic fights back. But when the magic is weakened with iron, the magic can no longer fight back. Not very much at least."

Tucking black curls behind one ear, Lyren attempted a smile. "The iron weakens the power too. They have not found a way to get as much power as they desire from a single fae. Waverly said they plan to capture multiple fae and combine the power drawn from them, but—"

"One fae's magic will not combine with another like that," Brannick finished. "Even if weakened by iron, a fae must use careful magic to combine his magic with another."

Queen Noelani took her time chewing another bite of fish. Still, every eye was on her when she finally spoke. "Maybe it will not work. It *should* not work. But even if they fail, their experiments could be detrimental enough to cause irreversible damage to Faerie."

Lyren sat forward, as if she had been waiting the entire time for this one moment. "We need to find the high queen's talismans and steal them before they are used to destroy us."

Queen Noelani gave a respectful nod to Lyren before she turned to Brannick. "High Queen Alessandra has five talismans total. We have one and Ansel has one that he is allowed to use however he chooses. The other three are in the high queen's palace."

"Where?" The question leapt from Elora before she had a moment to consider how ridiculous it was. If Queen Noelani knew where they were, she probably would have stolen them already. Elora's head tilted to the side. But then again, they had needed Elora's wings and ability to touch iron to steal the first talisman. Perhaps they could not steal the others either.

"There are rumors the high queen's brother knows where the talismans are." Queen Noelani gave a significant glance toward Brannick.

He responded by lifting an eyebrow. "Severin? He would never defy his sister."

The queen's chin tilted upward. "There are rumors he has already done so." Her head lowered again. "Though no one knows where he is now."

Curling both hands into fists, Elora took a deep breath. "If we help you steal the last three talismans, will you help Prince Brannick with his plan?"

"Plan?" Queen Noelani shifted her gaze toward the prince.

He swallowed before answering. "That is the reason I came here today. I require your help if I am to succeed."

The slightest hint of deviousness passed through the queen's bright eyes. "Those words are like music to my ears." She stood from her chair with a start. "Come. We will discuss this plan as I take you to a place in Swiftsea that you must see to believe."

CHAPTER

16

Salty breezes drifted across Elora's face as she left Swiftsea Palace. Lyren walked at her side and Vesper and Quintus were near. Ahead of them, Brannick walked with his wolf on one side and Queen Noelani on the other. A small contingent of Swiftsea fae walked with them.

"Tell me more about this plan," Queen Noelani said as soon as they descended the staircase outside of the palace.

"I want to overthrow High Queen Alessandra." The answer came curt and definitive, but fear still lined the prince's words.

A fae from Swiftsea handed the queen a shimmery blue javelin. She held it fiercer than any of her subjects held theirs. Her eyes narrowed as she looked at the prince. "You will fight for your rightful place as High King?"

141

Brannick gave a short nod. Blaz nuzzled against the prince's leg. Brannick responded by patting the wolf's head. He cleared his throat. "There is only one way to overthrow High Queen Alessandra now."

One eyebrow twitched on Queen Noelani's face. "You intend to use the crown of Bitter Thorn?"

The prince gave another short nod, but his shoulders stiffened through the movement.

After a quick glance at those around them, the queen leaned forward. Her voice lowered, though not enough to hide it completely. "Do you know where it is?"

At the sound of those words, Brannick folded his arms over his chest. Blaz stood taller, his lips pulling back to show off his teeth.

The queen clicked her tongue and pulled back to a straighter stance. "There are rumors that you do not wear the crown because you cannot find it. I merely wish to know if your plan is viable before we begin."

Tension skittered for a moment, but then, Brannick let out a sigh. His wolf closed his lips over his fangs once again as he relaxed. Even still, the prince kept his arms folded. "The crown is meant for a king or queen only, and I am a prince. You should know why I do not wear it."

Waving a hand, Queen Noelani seemed eager to brush the whole thing aside. "I will give power to the crown of Bitter Thorn to help you overthrow High Queen Alessandra, but you must help me too."

The muscles in Brannick's arms squeezed as he raised a questioning eyebrow.

With a signal to the contingent behind her, a white boat with blue sails appeared in the sea behind them. The air shimmered around it, showing that a glamour had been hiding it only moments before.

Queen Noelani did not wait for any acknowledgement. She just beckoned the prince and marched toward the boat.

He followed her but dragged his feet as he eyed the blue sails. "Is there a reason we cannot open a door to wherever we are going?"

A flash of deviousness filled Queen Noelani's eyes before she answered. "I put an enchantment around the island we are going to visit. It prevents anyone from getting there except by boat."

The prince's steps slowed. "Why would you do that?"

Throwing her shoulders back, Queen Noelani stood taller. "To keep it safe from anyone who might try to go there and mess with things." Her lips turned up in a smirk. "Only a few fae have the skill to get past the sea monsters who inhabit our waters."

Her gaze turned toward Lyren, who gave a dutiful nod.

Elora stared at the sea. She had encountered the sea monsters in Swiftsea before. Even in a boat, she wasn't especially eager to be near them again.

Despite the tension that still rippled through his arms, Brannick followed the queen. He glanced toward the others to be certain they were coming too. Vesper and Quintus eyed each other carefully before they turned their gazes toward the prince.

He turned toward Lyren. She touched the white sea flower in her hair before answering. "It is about the decay." Lyren pressed her lips tight. Averting her eyes, she skipped past the prince to get closer to the white boat. As she passed, a quick rush of words left her lips. "You might need your magic against the sea monsters."

Tingles pricked at Elora's fingertips as she reached for her sword.

Magic.

Would *she* need magic? At least her sisters were safe back in Bitter Thorn. But how would she fare? Her feet almost bounced across the sandy shore. She tried to remind them how to step normally. Even once they made it to the dock that stretched out to the boat, her feet continued to stumble like an infant who had just learned to walk.

She had gone her entire life without magic. So why did she feel its absence so acutely now?

Her throat ached as she stepped onto the boat. She immediately lost her footing and grabbed onto the nearest arm to regain her balance.

Brannick glanced back at her, the light leaving his eyes when he did. Her throat only ached more at the sight of it.

But the arm she had grabbed onto began moving. She jerked toward it.

Vesper held her firmly, helping her regain her balance even more. His eyebrows knitted together under his brown curls. "I will use my magic to protect you if needed. I would not want to lose my sister so soon after finding her."

Some of the tension in her gut loosened at the sound of those words. She managed a slight smile, but it vanished once the boat began moving. It glided over the waves without a bit of resistance. Rather than becoming one with the waves, it seemed the waves were instead becoming one with the boat.

The bright blue sails rippled in the light breeze, but they did not seem to move in time with the boat's movement.

It took a moment to realize the fae who had once stood behind Queen Noelani now stood at the edge of the boat with their hands waving in gentle strokes.

Finally releasing her hand from Vesper's arm, she pointed her chin toward the fae. "Do they have water magic?"

Vesper's eyes went alight. "All fae have some ability to control water, but these fae are better at it than most. Still, their magic is even more specialized than that. That one there," he pointed to the nearest fae, "his greatest magic is in direction. He guides the boat while the others propel it."

It would have been nice to have a moment to be amazed by the words. It would have been nice to even nod at them. Instead, the entire boat lurched to the side. Her shoulder slammed into the deck as a crack resounded through the air.

"Lyren, the music." Queen Noelani shouted the words before dropping into a large chair upholstered with woven palm leaves.

Lyren touched a hand to her sea flower again before taking a deep breath. A mournful melody drifted from her lips. She released the sounds, not quite forming words but not evading them completely either. Each syllable danced on the air.

For a moment, the sea monster, who had beat against the boat only a moment earlier, dove deep into the water. Whether it was calmed by the singing or trying to avoid it, Elora didn't know. But at least it had gone.

Now the strange syllables in Lyren's song changed until they formed crisp words that pierced the waves around them.

Monster of the sea, let us be.
Let us be.
Writhe your tail and flail your jaw, but let us be.
Let us be.

145

Your strength is great, but magic is greater.
Choose to fight, and you will lose.
This command is given to protect you.
Let us be.
Let us be.

The boat moved faster with each new line of the song. The waves around them sparkled in the light of the sun. The water almost seemed to grow bluer. Brighter.

The light breeze churned into a whipping wind that rippled the sails of the boat.

Even if the sea monster ignored the words to the song, their speed would surely help them escape it anyway.

No sooner did that thought dance through Elora's mind than another crack resounded through the air.

Elora sucked in a gasp while the boat tipped so far to one side that water spilled over the edge. Her body tumbled toward one side of the boat. Every other fae remained in place.

Brannick caught her arm just before she slammed into the wall of the boat. She took in another sharp breath while trying to find her footing. Another sea monster slammed into the boat, this time toppling it in the other direction.

More water spilled over the edge until a puddle began forming on the deck. Brannick had to pull her close to keep her from falling in every direction. His own feet remained unmoved, as if stuck to the deck. After a closer glance, she realized gold shimmered around his feet.

Magic.

He had magic to keep his feet stuck to the deck. Glancing across the boat, it was easy to see that everyone else clearly had the same magic as well. Even Blaz.

She tried not to notice how her heart sank at the realization.

Even a wolf had more magic than her. Blaz also had a glamour that could make people look in any direction other than his. It didn't matter that he was only a wolf. As an animal, he wasn't technically fae, but Faerie itself had still gifted him with magic.

Vesper appeared at her side, waving his hands and pushing them toward her feet. His eyes closed while his mouth muttered silent words.

Soon, her own feet were magicked to the deck of the boat. It hadn't happened a moment too soon.

A wild screech punched the air around them. At the same time, ripples churned the waves on one side of the boat. A green sea monster leapt from the waves. Its snake-like body soared over their heads. It snapped its jaw over the largest mast at the center of the boat. The dragon-like head of the creature had shimmery scales that glinted as it clamped its teeth down harder on the splintering wood.

There must have been more than two creatures because something slammed into the boat on one side. It tipped and gathered more water into its belly, but the Swiftsea fae managed to use their magic to right the boat once again.

Lyren's voice continued strong, but the words stretched and pulled until they sounded more like mumbles. Now only the melody could be discerned.

Setting her jaw, Elora reached for the sword on her hip. Maybe the sea monster could destroy a mast in a single bite. Maybe it could tip the boat and use its snake-like body to crush it. And maybe she couldn't use magic, even though she had it.

But she still knew how to use her sword. She would die before refusing to fight.

The moment she began drawing her weapon, Brannick put a hand over hers.

"Do not." He gave her a sharp glance before jerking his head toward the sea monster.

Her jaw clenched and with it came the strong desire to completely disregard his words. But even Vesper shook his head. "The monster's scales are too strong. Your sword will not penetrate them, but your violent action will not be forgotten either. You will be marked by the sea monsters, never able to rest in Swiftsea because they will hunt you."

A grunt burst from her lips as she shoved the sword back into the belt braided with her mother's ribbons.

Why did she feel the lack of magic so keenly when she had only just acquired it? It wasn't fair.

Lyren continued to sing her song, her voice nearly a scream now. The sea monster's body writhed. Brannick and Queen Noelani both waved their arms about in some kind of magic Elora didn't understand.

Would she ever understand?

She had barely noticed that the boat continued to move forward. But it did, possibly even faster than before.

Queen Noelani let out a shout and hit the end of her javelin against the deck. A silvery stream of dust erupted from the javelin. The dust curled around the long writhing body of a monster. The moment it touched the scales, Lyren's song became intelligible once again.

Your strength is great, but magic is greater.

At the sound of those words, the sea monster let out a shriek while the silver magic seemed to envelop it. The scales turned dull. Its body jerked and twitched as it slithered back into the water.

Almost immediately after, the boat slowed and pushed onto a sandy shore.

Elora gripped Vesper's arm almost as hard as she clenched her jaw. Gesturing toward her feet, she said, "Release me."

With a wave of his hand, the magic holding her feet to the deck of the boat vanished. Her body shuddered as she popped the wings from her back. It may have only been a few steps across the deck and down a plank to get to the shore, but she couldn't wait to get off the boat.

The muscles in her back still strained when using her wings, but each time she used them, they got stronger. Her body floated toward the shore.

At least she got there before anyone else. What did she need magic for anyway?

It didn't take long for the others to join her.

No one said a word.

Queen Noelani gestured toward a cluster of trees that sat next to a clear, rippling stream. At the base of the trees, a thick black substance bubbled. It left sticky residue anywhere that a bubble popped.

Brannick glanced at it for only a moment before he turned to the queen. "You located the source of the decay."

Her grip on the blue javelin tightened as she scowled at the bubbling substance. "I will give power to your crown so that you may overthrow High Queen Alessandra, but you must help us too. We know the source, but we still do not know how to eliminate it. Once you overthrow her, you must help us with the decay."

"It is decided then." He gave a single nod. "Can I open a door that leads out of this island, as long as we are already here?" He didn't wait for an answer. With a wave of one hand, his swirling door of brown, green, and black gave off the scent of damp earth and crisp rain. Apparently, he *could* open a door once on the island.

Before he or anyone else could move toward it, the Swiftsea queen struck her javelin against the sand. "Prince Brannick."

He flinched before he turned back to face her.

Her hands settled on her hips as she raised an eyebrow. "I require a bargain if I am to give you what you seek."

Weighty resignation lined the sigh that left his lips. "Very well. Shall I propose it?"

She chuckled. Her shoulders rolled back. "I propose a bargain. I will give power to the crown of Bitter Thorn, as much as I am able to spare. Once you are High King of Faerie, you must rid my court of this decay for good."

His throat bulged against the beaded necklace at his throat before he responded. When he did, his voice came out tight. "I accept your bargain." His shoulders drooped as he said the words.

They all moved toward his door then, but a piece of him had been chipped away. When they entered the door, a piece of him was gone. Perhaps for good.

Only one bargain, but it had changed him.

And they still had two courts left. Two courts that might not be so eager to go along with Brannick's plan.

What bargains would they require?

CHAPTER

17

The moment Elora arrived back at Quintus's home in Bitter Thorn, her mind reeled. Now they had two goals. Two things to accomplish. They had to get the rulers of Mistmount and Dustdune to give magic to the crown of Bitter Thorn, and they had to steal Queen Alessandra's talismans before she could use them to create an enchantment that would cover all of Faerie.

Overthrowing Queen Alessandra hadn't lost any importance, but perhaps it would be better to prevent her from destroying the realm before they focused on overthrowing her.

Brannick must have agreed. He gestured toward Vesper, Lyren, and Quintus, and said, "Start thinking of ways we could infiltrate Fairfrost Palace and find those talismans. The iron in them might be strong enough to help us locate them inside the palace, but it would be good to have a backup plan in case that doesn't work."

It didn't escape Elora's notice that Brannick spoke to the others but not to her.

In the midst of his request, Chloe burst into the room. She held open a large book, pointing her finger at a certain passage.

"You were gone for ages. I thought you'd never return." Her eyes zeroed in on her oldest sister's. "I think I found something to help with…" Her voice trailed off as she glanced around. Once she saw Brannick standing nearby, her lips pressed tight together.

"With what?" Brannick narrowed his eyes at her. When she remained silent, he turned his questioning gaze toward Elora. Even Blaz leaned forward, as if eager to learn more.

Her stomach turned over on itself with the weight of his gaze. It had been too long since he looked at her properly. The colors in his eyes began to swirl almost at that same moment.

Once his eyes began to burst, he jerked away. "Never mind. It does not matter to me." His shoulders hunched forward as he stomped toward the exit.

Chloe skipped toward her sister, holding the heavy book out.

But Elora didn't look at it. Instead, she pressed a finger to her lips and glanced toward the others. Under her breath, she whispered, "Later. Tell me when night falls and we are alone in our room."

Snapping the book closed, Chloe gave a swift nod. Her eyes darted over the others before she let out a carefree laugh. "It's just about a recipe my youngest sister wants to try."

Perhaps it was because fae weren't used to being around someone who could lie, but Vesper, Quintus, and Lyren didn't seem suspicious of the words.

After a quick nod toward her sister, Elora slowly stepped out of the room.

Brannick had opened a door, though she couldn't have guessed where it led. He was just stepping into it with Blaz at his side. She could have called out to him or asked to come with him, but she doubted either of those actions would give the result she wanted.

Without thinking further, she stepped into the door behind him. Maybe it was impulsive, but she didn't care.

A moment later, she stepped onto a soft surface that sent stinging cold through her boots. Heavy snowflakes drifted down from above.

Her shoulders shivered while she took in the room. The snow at her feet made her think she had landed in Fairfrost. But then she noticed twelve trees growing out of the ground and a long wooden table in front of them.

Snow covered the Bitter Thorn council room. At least a foot's length of snow piled over the ground and over every surface. The wet snow weighed down the branches of the trees, smothering the leaves that grew there.

Brannick stood just in front of her. A small silver enchantment floated over his head. It blocked the falling snowflakes from reaching him, but he clearly hadn't expected the snow at his feet. The icy stuff covered his shoes and the bottoms of his pant legs. Considering the tight fists at his side, anger had already affected him.

He took in slow and heavy breaths. Perhaps he was trying to fight the effects of the anger-inducing snowflakes. Maybe, since he knew what to expect, it would be easier to overcome them.

Either way, Elora could help. Sometimes being impulsive *did* have its advantages. She crouched down and used her hands to scoop away the snow around his ankles. Blaz gave a happy yip at the sight of her. Then he used his snout to help clear the snow away from Brannick as well.

The prince grunted. She ignored it. The snow had almost been cleared anyway.

Brannick grunted a second time, but it started in the back of his throat like a growl. "*You*." He spoke through clenched teeth.

Using the side of her hand, she brushed away the last of the snow that had settled over his shoe. "It should be better now. Blaz, do you think you can snap him out of it?"

The wolf bounced his head just like a nod and nuzzled up to the prince's leg. Brannick sucked in a breath and blinked fast several times.

Pulling herself to her feet, she faced him with her arms folded over her chest.

He glowered in response. "What are you doing here? You were not supposed to come with me." He glanced to the side, narrowing his eyes at the spot where his door had been only moments earlier.

She tipped her chin upward. "You should be glad I followed you through your door. Without me, the snow could have taken over you."

With a huff and a grimace, he turned away. "I am still angry with you, regardless of the snow."

Her eyes rolled as she glanced around the room. "You are still mad that I saved you from your bargain with Queen Alessandra?"

"Yes." The word came out like a bite.

Rather than give weight to his uncalled-for feelings, she glanced around. "I wonder if there's a shield nearby. We could use it to clear a path in the snow for you to walk. Then the snow won't affect you."

He glared at her through the side of his eye. He then conjured a thin piece of metal that almost looked like a shield, except it had a rectangular shape and it curved slightly at the bottom edge. It would be perfect for scooping away snow to make a path.

Pushing it forward, he began to do just that. He also refused to look at her or acknowledge her presence. Maybe the snow that had touched him still affected him, but his anger seemed more genuine than she cared to admit.

It didn't take long before he cleared a path out of the council room and began heading down the hall.

"Brannick."

He bristled at the sound of her voice. When she moved to his side, she caught a glimpse of longing in his eyes. He forced his eyes shut and only opened them once his gaze had turned down toward the thin metal that scooped away the snow.

She took in a breath before speaking again. "*Do* you know where the crown of Bitter Thorn is?"

A scoff burst from his lips. "What kind of question is that?"

After a quick glance toward Blaz, she shrugged. "When Queen Noelani asked you if you knew where the crown was, you were evasive. You were evasive just now when I asked as well. Since you cannot lie, I thought maybe you were evasive because you did not want to admit you do not know where the crown is."

"Do not worry about the crown." He glanced toward her again, his eyes lingering a little too long on her hair and shoulders. His head shook before he tore his gaze away. "Do not read into every little thing."

155

It probably wasn't a good time to roll her eyes. "Have you checked in the throne room?"

"You need to learn how to use your magic." He said the words just as they turned the corner into a new hallway. A shriek filled the air, and a demorog shot toward them.

Before Brannick could do anything, Elora let out a shriek of her own. She threw her arms over her head and cowered in the presence of the thorn creature.

Even with her head covered, she could hear when the creature began beating its thorny wings in the opposite direction. After a quick peek, she saw it had gone away.

Showing cowardly fear went against her nature, but at least it was effective against a single demorog that wasn't too angry.

Brannick lifted an eyebrow at her as she stood from her position. "Where did you learn that showing fear works against demorogs?"

She rolled her shoulders back before moving forward once again. "Lyren taught me."

Again, his eyes lingered on her a little too long. It took another head shake before he started scooping a path in the snow once again. "I mean it. You *need* to learn how to use your magic. You are not a true fae without it."

Now *she* bristled. "I know."

The prince's voice lowered. "I allowed you to come with us to Swiftsea, but you cannot come with us when we steal the talismans from Fairfrost."

Her body jerked as she came to an immediate stop. "That's not fair."

"Fair?" Brannick chuckled as he pushed the thin metal even harder against the stone surface of the hallway. "Why do you think I care at all about being fair? I am trying to regain my

156

rightful place as High King of Faerie. That was all I focused on before you came along."

He glared at her, but it didn't stop her from noticing how his eyes shimmered and pulsed with color before they went colorless and then back again. At least his essence was doing better.

When his gaze lasted too long, he let out a huff and jerked his head away. "I do not like that my focus has wavered."

"I want you to be High King too." She clasped her hands behind her back and tilted her head until she caught his eye. "But can you not also care about other things besides regaining the crown?" Her head tilted down. Now she looked up at him through her eyelashes.

The words acted like magic. He leaned in toward her, as if he had forgotten that everything else in the hallway existed. The snow, the demorogs that might be lurking nearby, they were nothing.

But once his hand moved away from the thin metal to reach for her, he formed it into a fist instead. He turned away. "I must become High King. That *must* be my highest priority or all of Faerie could fall."

Before he could finish speaking, they both heard running footsteps coming from a nearby hallway. Elora gasped. Brannick gulped.

When they glanced at each other, Brannick set his jaw. "Perhaps it is Soren. He is still in the castle somewhere."

The footsteps moved fast. They were nearly upon them.

With one hand on the thin metal, Brannick let his other hand hover in the air, probably to do magic if needed.

It was smart of him to prepare because the face that greeted them around the corner was not Soren. Her gut writhed at the sight of the yellow eyes before her.

157

A wicked smirk curled on Ansel's lips as he stared far too intensely into her eyes. "You *are* alive. High Queen Alessandra will not be pleased." The growing smirk on his face suggested he felt the opposite.

Elora could feel his gaze trailing up and down her body. It scraped over her nerves, reminding her of every awful thing he'd done to her. He tricked her into killing someone. He kidnapped her. He tasted her blood.

Her entire body shuddered at the sight of him, but it didn't stop her from reaching for her sword. She had beaten him once in a sword fight, but one that had required she wouldn't kill him. Luckily, there were no rules against that now.

Ansel bent his knees and then lunged toward her. As he moved, he ripped a handful of thorns from a nearby briar and threw them at Elora.

Stinging pain erupted somewhere around her elbow, but she was too distracted to notice it. Even before her sword was drawn, Brannick threw the thin metal toward Ansel. With a wave of the prince's hand, the metal wrapped around Ansel's torso until his yellow eyes bulged.

Blaz bounded forward, clamping his fangs over one of Ansel's legs. The fae let out a series of shrieks as Blaz bit a chunk of flesh from his leg.

Brannick sent a blast of magic that forced Ansel off his feet. A vein in the prince's jaw pulsed. "You are not welcome in my castle."

He tightened his fist, which tightened the metal around Ansel's torso.

With his yellow eyes still bulging, Ansel tucked his chin against his collar. Once his chin met the blue gemstone on his collar, he seemed to gain greater strength. The blue gemstone vanished in a shower of sparks. He pushed his arms out, freeing himself from the metal.

By now, Elora had stomped forward, ready to sink her sword into any part of the fae's body that she could reach.

He didn't look eager to fight her a second time. With a wave of his hand, he opened a door and vanished through it.

She glared after the spot where the door disappeared, but finally shoved her sword back into her belt. When she turned to face the prince, his expression had evened.

He turned his eyes downward, probably noting how he could not step forward anymore without touching the snow. Now he glanced toward the thin metal that lay bent all the way across the hall.

Elora stepped toward it, but Brannick only shook his head. "Leave it. I will return later."

She didn't argue when he beckoned her. She wasn't surprised when he opened a door that led them back to Quintus's house. She *did* wonder why he had gone back to Bitter Thorn Castle in the first place. Was he looking for the crown? Or was it something else?

She had no time to consider the questions because her sisters jumped toward her with wide eyes as soon as they returned to Quintus's home. Apparently, they had noticed her absence. Even more important, they wanted answers.

CHAPTER
18

Pain stung into Elora's arm when she began walking forward. Only then did she notice the trickle of blood sliding down from her elbow to her wrist. Her sisters stood in Quintus's home with their mouths agape.

Grace pressed a hand over her lips. "Your arm is dripping with blood." As always, she spoke a little too abruptly with words too blunt, but at only twelve, she was still learning.

Shaking her hair back, Elora twisted her arm toward herself to assess the damage. The cluster of thorns Ansel had thrown must have hit her because two thorns stuck in her skin just below her elbow.

She plucked them out without ceremony. Though the wounds still stung, she could feel her fae nature beginning to heal them already. Was that not magic? How could her body heal a wound when she couldn't even access her magic?

At the nearby table, Lyren, Quintus, and Vesper pored over a large piece of parchment. Elora couldn't see what was on the parchment from her distance.

They offered looks of condolences at Elora's wounds.

Chloe rushed out of the room only to return a moment later with a clean cloth and a stone bowl filled with water. She dabbed the cloth over the wounds with her mouth in a pinch. After a moment, she shot a glare toward the prince. "Did you do this to her?"

Brannick stepped back, not managing to hide the look of horror on his face.

"No." Elora flinched at the cloth being pressed into her wounds. Before she spoke again, she turned toward those sitting at the table. "It was Ansel."

Even saying his name caused Elora to shudder. Her insides twisted, which probably turned her face into a scowl, but she couldn't help it. She closed her eyes while trying to forget the terror he managed to fill her with at the mere mention of his name.

Grace dropped a clay bowl she had just retrieved from the kitchen. The water splattered everywhere as the bowl split in two. When she dropped it, both of Chloe's hands flew up to her mouth as she gasped.

Lyren raised herself out of her chair, as if she couldn't decide whether to sit or stand. She looked at the two sisters. "What is it?"

Reaching for a lock of red hair, Grace spoke through a tremble. "If Elora is afraid..."

Chloe twisted the rag in her hands. "I've never seen my sister fear anything in my entire life. If she's afraid of this fae, Ansel..." Now Chloe's shoulders shuddered.

161

At least Elora's wounds had nearly healed now. "Forget that." She tried to wave off the fear she had shown only moments before. Now she glanced back toward the fae at the table. "Do you have any idea how to get the talismans?"

Vesper beckoned her forward. He gestured toward the parchment covering most of the table. Once Elora moved close enough, she could see that someone had drawn an outline of Fairfrost Palace with many of the rooms and hallways labeled. Many areas had also been left blank.

Quintus brushed a bit of dust away from the parchment before he picked up his pencil. He drew a quick sketch of a throne and then labeled the room *Throne Room*. Glancing toward the prince, he indicated the blank spots on the map. "We don't know about any other areas, but since you lived in the palace, we thought you could help with that."

The prince turned his gaze toward his wolf before he looked back at the parchment. Blaz took a stance beside the prince that looked strong and steady, perhaps to offer support.

Leaning back in his chair, Vesper shook the curls out of his eyes. "Getting inside the palace is the easy part. High Queen Alessandra has her citizens under strict control. We will enter the palace as easily," his gaze shifted to Elora, "as we did when we visited Fairfrost before."

Lyren raised an eyebrow at the pair of them. "You went to Fairfrost?"

When Elora nodded, her mind didn't settle on the two different times she had gone to Fairfrost with her fae brother. Instead, she thought back to the first time she had been there. Of course, since the memories were still hidden from her, she mostly thought about the fact that she had been there once before and couldn't remember it now.

Quintus pointed to the front entrance of the palace. "Once we enter, we will be escorted straight to the high queen. No one enters the palace without speaking to her."

"Are there no exceptions?" Elora rolled forward onto the balls of her feet, hoping for good news.

A twitch moved across Quintus's forehead that seemed more devious than anything. "A mortal *might* be able to enter. We believe High Queen Alessandra has enchantments in place to detect magic, which is how the guards know whenever someone enters the palace. But a mortal with no magic *could* get in undetected."

The cause of his devious twitch wasn't clear until he finished his explanation by giving a pointed glance toward Chloe. Now that Elora was fae, Chloe was the oldest mortal there.

"No." Both Elora and Vesper spoke at the same time, recognizing Quintus's intention immediately.

Though she wasn't right next to it, Chloe stepped even farther away from the table. With a gulp, she plucked a book from off a nearby chair. "I want to help, but I couldn't do that." She pressed the book against herself and folded her arms over it. She continued backing away, closer to the room where she and her siblings slept at night. "I'm not like Elora. I can do research and clean a wound and recite poems like you've never heard before." She gulped again, almost ready to step into the bedroom completely. "But I can't help with anything dangerous. I don't do well when I'm frightened."

Elora turned to her sister wearing the most reassuring expression she could muster. "You are not going to Fairfrost, Chloe. And neither is Grace."

Her youngest sister let out a heavy sigh of relief as Elora turned to the other fae, daring them to defy her.

163

Quintus opened his mouth, but Vesper leaned forward and shot his own glare toward the fae. Finally, Quintus shrugged. "Fine."

Both of Elora's sisters glanced toward each other then. Grace crept closer to the door while Chloe waited. Once there, they both disappeared into the nearby bedroom. Apparently, even talk of dangerous plans was too much for them—though they did leave the door open, so maybe they still wanted to hear.

A thought tickled at the back of Elora's mind. She pinched the belt braided with the remains of her mother's skirt. "What about me? You all insist I'm not really fae because I cannot use magic. Could I get in undetected?"

"No." For the first time since approaching the table, Brannick spoke. His eyes remained studiously on the parchment though. "Your magic may be dormant, but it is still detectable."

The small well of hope in her chest crushed to nothing at the sound of those words. She huffed, but everyone ignored her.

Using one hand to pet his wolf, Brannick used the other to point to an empty space on the drawing. "This is a library. These are guest quarters. Many of her personal guards live there, though some of them live in the quarters for the royal family." His finger shifted to another part of the map. "Those are here."

Quintus's pencil scurried over the parchment while he drew and labeled to fill the spaces the prince had indicated. When finished, he jabbed the end of his pencil at another empty space. "What about this room? I thought its strategic position could be good for an armory."

Tilting his head to the side, Brannick closed both of his eyes. They snapped open a moment later. "No, those are all sitting rooms. The armory is here." He pointed and then moved to another area of the map. "And these are the dungeons. There are more cells than there are living quarters inside the palace."

A soft hum escaped Lyren's mouth while her face looked deep in thought. When the others turned to her, she looked at the prince. "Do you know where she would hide the talismans?"

Brannick pinched the bridge of his nose before answering. "She would likely keep them separate from each other, so they are more difficult to steal, which makes our job harder. I would guess she has one hidden in the library, one in the armory, and one in a box that she keeps in her pocket."

The soft scratch of Quintus's pencil stopped as his mouth dropped. "Her *pocket?* We could not recover that without incapacitating her first."

A wild grin danced over Vesper's face, turning his blue and gray eyes bright. "Or maybe we could trick her into removing it from her pocket. If one of us incites her wrath, she might try to use the talisman against us as a form of torture."

Lyren kneaded her temples as she tried to hide her smile. "Your desire for adventure is quite deadly sometimes. You know that, right?"

Chuckling, Vesper shook his curls to one side. "Yes, but at least this time it is useful too."

Lyren snorted as she shook her head.

Quintus tapped his pencil on the table. "How do we take the talismans when they are made of iron?"

A more serious expression adorned Lyren's face when she sat forward. "Queen Noelani gave me three boxes we can put

165

the talismans in. It will be painful getting close to the talismans, but hopefully we can recover quickly once the talismans are inside the boxes."

Sucking in a sharp breath, Quintus's eyebrows flew up to his forehead. "You think we can all recover if we *touch* the iron? Maybe we would recover eventually, but I doubt we could do it fast enough to escape Fairfrost Palace."

"I can conjure gloves that should help." Brannick rubbed the back of his neck before throwing the tiniest glance toward Elora. "I believe my essence is healed enough for it."

Though the glance lasted only a moment, it spread warmth all through Elora's chest. A smile pricked at her lips as she leaned over the parchment. She stuffed one hand into her pocket to touch the crystal holding his essence. With her other hand, she trailed a finger over the throne room and then over the hallway leading to it. She stopped it over a room that hadn't been labeled yet.

Her heart skipped, beckoning the words from her throat. "This room here is where the sprites are held captive. If someone glamours me to be invisible, I could save them while the rest of you get the talismans."

"You are not coming with us." Brannick didn't even look her way when he spoke.

Pulling the hand from her pocket, she curled it into a fist and pressed it against the tabletop. "*Yes*, I am."

Though he often made expressions that kept his face entirely still, the one he wore now spoke of resolve. Great resolve. His voice sounded the same. "This is not up for debate."

Huffing loudly, she narrowed her eyes. "You cannot stop me." She pointed her nose in the air and turned away from him.

"I'll just follow you the way I did when you went back to your castle." She glanced over her shoulder at him then.

A crack in his expression formed, beginning with one eyebrow. It twitched and that made his nose wrinkle, which then made his jaw clench. He raised himself higher until he towered over her. "You are not coming!"

His mouth opened as if to shout more. Instead, he turned away from the table and stomped toward the room where Chloe and Grace had gone. Gesturing toward the door, he lowered his voice. "What about your sisters? You want to leave them here alone?"

Once he had moved close enough, he glanced into the room. His eyes widened at something he had seen inside, but he quickly tried to hide it.

With her eyes still narrowed, Elora trailed closer to him. Had he really seen something that surprised him? "They will be fine. They were fine when we went to Swiftsea." Her retort came out more distracted than she meant it.

Brannick looked over his shoulder into the bedroom. His eyes widened a second time. Again, he smothered the expression. "And what if…"

His voice trailed off as he stepped fully inside the room. He looked at something without wavering.

Unable to resist her curiosity, Elora stepped into the room after him.

Before she could even glance toward the direction Brannick had been staring, the prince leapt outside the room once again. She jerked her head toward him, but it was too late.

Shimmery gold erupted from his fingertips and soon surrounded the entire room. While it spread, the door flew of its own accord to slam shut.

Letting out a scream, Elora pounded against the closed door. "Let me out!" The enchantment Brannick had just placed stopped her fists a hair before they could even touch the wood.

From the other side of the closed door, she heard Brannick's smug voice. "This enchantment will vanish as soon as we have traveled to Fairfrost. Until then, perhaps you should enjoy your sisters' company."

Her fists slammed into the golden enchantment over and over again, even though she knew it was hopeless. Her two sisters tried to pull her away, but she just screamed.

Finally, Chloe caught both of Elora's fists and tipped her head toward the door. Her blonde hair seemed as bright as the gleam in her eye. "Listen," she whispered. "Even with the door closed, we can still hear them. But you have to stop screaming first."

The fight went out of Elora immediately. Clamping her mouth shut, she leaned toward the door. Just as her sister claimed, she could hear the fae's voices clearly. Her lips pulled up into a grin. If she knew their plans, then maybe she could find a way out of this mess.

CHAPTER
19

Sleep tickled at the back of Elora's eyelids. Her head was tucked against the door with her legs curled to the side. She cursed herself for falling asleep while the others were still planning their mission to Fairfrost.

The last thing she remembered was their plan for once they got into the palace. They would go straight to Queen Alessandra and pretend they had come for peaceful negotiations. When those didn't go as planned, they would pretend to leave.

They hoped the enchantments inside the palace would simply detect their magic once they entered. Then, instead of leaving, they would glamour themselves to be invisible. They hoped the queen wouldn't detect their presence any longer after that, or at the very least, that she'd be too distracted to notice they had never left. Then, they would be free to roam the palace in search of the three talismans.

The conversation came back to her, hitting her like a rush of running water. She stood up with a start and pressed her ear against the door. The soft rays of light streaming in from the window indicated day had dawned. Had they left already?

After attempting to leave the room, the enchantment provided the answer. She was still locked inside the room, which meant they hadn't left yet. Her ear strained as she tried to listen for any sounds outside the door.

"Elora."

She jumped at the sound of her name. Placing a hand on the door, she answered. "Vesper, let me out of here."

He cleared his throat before speaking. "We will not be gone long if everything goes according to plan. Please do not do anything stupid while we are gone."

"Vesper." She said his name louder this time but was met with silence. "I know you can still hear me."

Again, no response came.

A whooshing sound indicated that a Faerie door had been opened.

"Wait!" Pleading filled her tone. "Do not go without me."

She slammed her fists against the door. It did no good. She knew the exact moment they left because the enchantment around the room let off a shimmery burst before vanishing into the air.

While a hard lump settled in her throat, she yanked the door open. No one sat at the table. No one lingered near the edge of the room. She pushed open the door to the other bedroom, but of course it stood empty as well.

Grace left their room while pulling her red hair into a bun with one of the ribbons from Elora's old skirt. "Would you like porridge for breakfast? Vesper was kind enough to find us some. We could also have beans and muffins, but those will take longer to prepare."

"I say we have porridge." Chloe rubbed the sleep from her eyes as she plopped into the nearest chair.

Hissing, Elora turned toward her sisters. "I do not want to eat. I want—"

"Oh, just let the others take care of the talismans." Chloe waved a hand toward her older sister, as if to shush her. Then she turned to her youngest sister. "Shall I ready the table and drinks while you make the food?"

Grace nodded as she lifted the lid off a woven basket in the corner of the kitchen. "Yes, please."

Elora stomped over to them, her mouth twisting into a knot. "I need to get to Fairfrost. Maybe I can do it. I just have to open a door. That should be easy enough."

Her eyelids dropped as she tried to visualize the area just outside Fairfrost Palace as best she could. Maybe she should have paid more attention when Vesper brought her there. Still, she remembered a few things. There was snow as far as she could see and nearby, a forest of trees that were covered with ice and frost. The ice had been iridescent and magical-looking.

With that thought in her mind, she waved her hand in a circle just like the other fae did when they opened a door.

Peeking through one eye, she checked to see if a door had appeared.

It hadn't.

She kicked the nearest wall, which sent an ache through her toes.

"This is cooking up nicely." Grace tucked an errant strand of red hair behind one ear as she bent over the cast iron pot that hung over a fire. She stirred the contents with a wooden spoon.

Chloe continued to rub the sleep out of her eyes in between setting clay bowls on the table. Each had green and brown geometric designs painted around the outside rims. Without warning, her head snapped up. "I found some honey yesterday."

She scurried over to the edge of the kitchen and dug through the large clay pots and woven baskets sitting there. Soon, she drew out a small clay pot with a wooden stick poking out of it. "Here it is. Should we put some in?"

Red hair bounced as Grace nodded. They both grinned while Chloe poured in a few dollops of honey.

Tension writhed in Elora's gut before she let out a scream. The second time she kicked the wall, she kicked even harder. Now her eyes turned upward at the floating sprites above. "Can you help me? You know I want to free the sprites while I am in Fairfrost. Can't you open a door for me to get there?"

Nothing about the sprites' floating or glowing changed at all. Elora kept staring at them, but that did nothing. She even lifted one hand, hoping a sprite might come and land on her palm. None did.

"It's ready." For once, Grace sounded as young as she really was.

While her youngest sister spooned the porridge into the bowls, Elora began pacing across the room.

Chloe dropped into a chair while a big yawn escaped her. "Come sit down." The plea came out annoyed.

"I cannot," Elora snapped. "How could I possibly sit at a time like this?"

Her two sisters glanced at each other. She saw the concern in Grace's eyes as she bit her bottom lip. And then she saw the frustration in Chloe's eye roll.

With a dramatic flourish, the middle sister pushed out of her chair. Once standing, she grabbed Elora's bowl and spoon and shoved them into her oldest sister's hands. Chloe shook her blonde hair before she moved back toward the table. "Eat while you walk then."

Maybe it was because she was too full of emotion to fight back, or maybe it was because she was hungrier than she realized, but Elora began shoveling porridge into her mouth.

Her sisters sat at the table looking perfectly content with eating porridge and living in a small house in the middle of a Faerie court they knew almost nothing about.

Grace took a delicate bite of porridge and then turned to her middle sister. "What books will you study today?"

By now, Chloe had fought off the last of her exhaustion. She sat up with a back so straight it would have made their mother proud. "Oh, probably that one I..." She trailed off and suddenly her spoon clattered into her bowl. "That reminds me." She jumped up from her chair. "I never told you what I found."

She disappeared into their room for only a moment. When she returned, she held the large book she had tried to show Elora yesterday.

The book stopped Elora's pacing. She told herself it would only be for a moment, but once the book was open, she had already forgotten the pacing entirely.

Chloe pointed an ink-stained finger at a passage in the middle of the page. "A memory elixir is difficult to make. It has an intense creation process requiring exact magic. It also requires ingredients that are nearly impossible to come by."

173

Reaching for a ribbon braided into her belt, Elora leaned closer to the book. "That does not sound like good news."

A chuckle rippled in Chloe's throat before she answered. "If we were trying to make a memory elixir it wouldn't be, but we want a memory *restoration* elixir."

Elora lifted an eyebrow. "And that's easier to make?"

Chloe's lips twitched with a grin as her finger pointed to another passage. "Technically, there are two ways to restore memories. The first way involves essence and some very complicated magic, but I don't think it would work for you."

The urge to pout came over Elora. "Why not? I'm fae."

With a shrug, Chloe turned back to the book. "Yes, but you were mortal when you lost the memories. I think that makes a difference, and anyway, the second method is much easier. You just have to make a restoration elixir. The ingredients are much more common."

"That's all?" Elora narrowed both eyes. If it were so easy, then why would Kaia say it might be impossible? Why did Queen Alessandra fly a dragon to steal a piece of Bitter Thorn Castle in order to get her own memories back?

Chloe turned a page. "I don't think the knowledge is common in Faerie. This was one of the dustiest books in the Bitter Thorn library. There *is* a little more to it than just the restoration elixir. There are important rules to follow or else the memories will be lost permanently. The person who gave you the memory elixir also has to give you the restoration elixir. And it has to be administered under the same conditions as when it was given. I think that means it has to be the same time of day, but if you had any injuries, you might need similar injuries when you receive the restoration elixir."

Elora snorted. She tried to say something about how delightful it was that she might have to injure herself in order to get her memories back, but since it wasn't actually delightful, she was unable to speak the lie.

She had never realized how often she lied before becoming fae.

Chloe's ink-stained fingers brushed a bit of dust off the page. "Since Kaia gave you the elixir, and since she'll probably know the conditions and everything, it shouldn't be too hard to get your memories back."

The thought of excitement sprouted inside Elora, but it never quite blossomed. If her mind hadn't turned to the others in Fairfrost Palace, she might have been able to appreciate the moment more.

"I am impressed you found that information, Chloe. I will have to visit Kaia and explain everything to her." Elora glanced toward the green lights floating just under the ceiling. "Or perhaps I should send her a message."

"Oh, Elora." Chloe shuffled across the floor to a corner of the kitchen. "Prince Brannick left you flowers."

After traipsing across the room again, Chloe gave Elora the bundle of purple wildflowers. They had been tied together with a forest green ribbon.

"How do you know they're from Prince Brannick?" Elora ran her finger over the ribbon as she asked.

With a smirk, Chloe dropped a note into her oldest sister's hand.

I did it for your safety. -B

Now Elora found herself tracing over the words. She spoke again, almost in a hush. "How do you know the flowers were meant for me?"

From her place at the table, Grace snickered. Her eyes were bright as she glanced up. "He only makes the purple ones when they're for you."

175

Chloe snickered too. "Exactly." She took the empty bowl of porridge from her oldest sister while Elora was left to read over the prince's words again. Maybe she would have reacted more to them, except a knock suddenly sounded on the door.

Elora blinked. Had it come from somewhere inside the house? She had already checked all the rooms, but maybe Brannick or Vesper had opened a door to return. Her heart sank. They couldn't be back already, could they? Maybe she had been wrong to want to go with them if they stole the talismans so quickly.

When the knock came a second time, the questions in her mind transformed into a terror that seized her gut.

Grace whispered from her spot at the table. "Someone is at the front door."

Without thinking, Elora stepped toward the door.

A whimper shuddered from Grace's mouth. "What if it's that scary fae?"

Chloe stood from her chair, pulling Grace closer to their bedroom. "Yes, what if it's Ansel?" She spoke his name even lower than the rest of her words.

Terror continued to twist in Elora's gut, but that only brought more conviction to her footsteps. If there was danger ahead, it was almost always better to face it head on. Maybe she needed magic to be a true fae, but she didn't need it to be her true self. She took a deep breath and moved closer to the door. Even without magic, she would not sit back and do nothing. "Ansel does not know we are here."

She waved her sisters toward the bedroom. Once they were inside with the door shut, she spoke again. This time, the words were just for her. "And if it is Ansel," she reached for her sword, "he will regret coming here."

CHAPTER 20

Elora cracked open the door, peering outside it while flutters whipped under her skin. Two figures stood just outside Quintus's home, a male and a female. After determining that much, it seemed silly that she hadn't swung the door open all the way. She had already betrayed her presence by simply opening the door.

It swung on its hinges as she pushed it open fully. Setting her feet in the middle of the doorway, she tried to take up as much space in it as possible. A little intimidation never hurt. For good measure, she gripped her sword and wore the darkest glare she could manage.

Despite her theatrics, the two fae in front of her didn't react in any way. She had never seen either of them before. They both had fair skin, which meant they most likely came from Mistmount, Noble Rose, or Fairfrost. The male fae had blue eyes with silvery threads. The female fae had white-blonde hair and a friendly smile.

But Elora had been in Faerie long enough to know that friendly smiles could be deceiving. Nothing about their clothes gave any hints as to which court they belonged. They wore simple tunics and trousers in a nondescript tan color. The fabric even seemed rougher than any she had ever seen in Faerie. It almost looked like it had come from the mortal realm.

After her moment of observation, Elora finally glanced behind them. The lush forest of Bitter Thorn had moss and black briars growing everywhere as usual. As dense as the trees were, they didn't quite cover a large creature with purple and white scales and veiny wings.

A dragon.

Clutching her sword tighter, Elora took a step back. "You are Fairfrost fae." Fairfrost was the only court with dragons, at least as far as she knew. Sliding the sword from her braided belt, she narrowed her eyes at the pair of them.

The fae with the blonde hair and the friendly smile stepped forward. She held both hands out with her palms up. "We are not here to hurt you. We are here to help you."

It seemed like an appropriate time to scoff in disbelief right up until the moment Elora remembered fae couldn't lie. The fae had spoken with simple, blunt sentences. Was there a way she could have deceived with them? It didn't seem likely.

The blonde fae gestured toward herself and then to her companion. "My name is Tindra, and this is Severin."

White teeth flashed behind the male fae's smile. Severin. Elora had heard the name recently, though it took her a few precious moments to place it. The two fae continue to grin at

178

her while she thought, as though they could win her over with nothing more than their smiles.

After a sharp intake of breath, Elora ripped her sword from her belt and shoved the tip of it just under Severin's jaw. In her other hand, she still held the cluster of purple wildflowers. "You are Queen Alessandra's brother."

He snorted. It wasn't from fear either. Actual delight filled his eyes at the sound of her accusation.

Her eyes narrowed again. "What is it?"

A playful chuckle tumbled from his throat. "She is *High Queen* Alessandra now. And yes, I am her brother, but that is not my fault." He cleared his throat and stood taller, completely disregarding the sword that still pointed at his neck. "I heard you need a way to get inside Fairfrost Palace."

Elora blinked. Despite herself, the sword lowered slightly. "Where did you hear that?"

His mouth quirked into a grin. "From a friend." He held his palm out and a green light from above zoomed down until a sprite landed on it.

"Thisbe?" Elora recognized the yellow-haired sprite at once as the one who had visited her while she was still in Bitter Thorn Castle.

The tiny creature glowed bright green before he nodded. "Severin is a friend to the sprites the same way you are. He will help you get into the palace, but you must promise to rescue my brothers and sisters while you are there."

Her sword fell away completely from Severin. It almost seemed to move of its own accord, but deep down, Elora knew she had nothing to fear anymore. She tucked the weapon back into her belt. "Of course I will rescue the sprites in Fairfrost. I made a vow to rescue them."

A knot in her chest twisted at those words. Though she had been able to ignore the subtle feeling, it reminded her that something physically changed inside her when she made that vow. She knew the twist in her chest would not release until she had fulfilled her promise.

And of course, the sprite who had helped her defeat King Huron and who had taught her how to fly would be the most important rescue of all. Even as the knot twisted, her chest still felt lighter. Soon, Tansy would be free.

Reaching into his pocket, Severin pulled out a long necklace with opal beads and a bright gemstone pendant. He held it out to her. "You will need this."

Her eyebrow lifted. "A ward necklace?"

"Sort of." Tindra pressed her lips over to one side, as if trying to decide how to explain. "Technically, it is a ward, but it only protects against one particular enchantment. It will prevent High Queen Alessandra from detecting your magic inside her palace."

A sheepish grin took over Severin's face as he nudged Tindra with his shoulder. "Only my Tindra could create such a ward. She is the most brilliant fae in all of Faerie."

Tindra's cheeks flushed with pink as she nudged Severin with her own shoulder. "Careful. Even if you believe it, saying something like that is dangerously close to a lie."

His only answer was a wider grin.

Elora took the necklace while they were busy gazing into each other's eyes. As she lifted it over her head, she snapped her head up. "Do you have more of these?" In her mind, she counted Brannick, Lyren, Vesper, and Quintus. "Four more?"

The pink in Tindra's cheeks vanished at once. "No. I only have one more, but we might need it. This is the only one we can spare."

"That is fine." Elora's head still hung down as she voiced the reassurance. Hopefully the others had evaded Queen Alessandra's detection after meeting with her like they had planned.

Severin nodded toward the sprite who still stood on his palm. "I will glamour you to be invisible so that no one will see you while you are in Fairfrost Palace. Go straight to the room with the sprites. Do you know which one it is?"

Elora ran her finger over the green ribbon around her wildflowers as she nodded. "Near the throne room."

"Good." Severin glanced over his shoulder before turning back toward her again. "To free the sprites, you must give them a message to deliver. It does not matter what the message is. Their magical obligation to deliver a message is the only thing strong enough to defeat the enchantment that forces them into that room. Send every message to me specifically. I will go to a place in Faerie where the sudden appearance of many sprites will not look suspicious."

Now Tindra leaned forward, her eyes wide with worry. "You will need an offering for every message you send. Do you think you can find enough offerings?"

The question dropped like a weight onto Elora's shoulders. It wasn't until her thumb brushed the ribbon around her bouquet once more that her lips finally turned upward. She lifted the bouquet and counted a dozen wildflowers, and there were still at least a dozen more that she hadn't counted yet. She could give one petal each as an offering, and if she ran out of those, she could give leaves and stems.

Her head bounced as she lifted the flowers. "These will work. Can you glamour me to be invisible now?"

Tindra nodded as her eyes narrowed. A glamour shimmered over Elora until her entire body disappeared from view.

Even with her invisible now, Severin still managed to look her way. His features turned serious. "You should avoid the throne room. If something happens to the glamour, do not worry too much. No one else in the palace will recognize you, and if they do, they will not say anything to my sister. They do not like her at all."

Memories spilled into Elora's mind. Queen Alessandra had tricked Brannick into falling so in love with her that he willingly entered a bargain to follow every order she ever gave him. Soon after making that bargain, he learned that her love for him was false. She had merely used him to gain another guard for her palace. If her other guards had been obtained in the same way, it made sense that they didn't like her either.

"Are you ready?" Thisbe's yellow-green eyes sparkled. He lifted off Severin's palm only to hover in front of Elora's invisible face.

"Yes." She gripped her sword as she spoke.

With a solemn nod, Severin whirled his hand around. A tunnel of spinning white whirls and iridescent icicles appeared before them. A chilly breeze fluttered through it, making the hairs on Elora's arms stand on end.

Severin gestured toward the door. "This will take you directly into my bedroom inside the palace. To get to the sprites, you will need to go left down the hallway and then right down the next hallway. After going down a short staircase, you will be in the correct hallway. The room with the sprites is at the very end and on the left. It is right across from the throne room, so move quietly enough that my sister does not hear you."

Tindra let out a dry chuckle. "Her hearing is impeccable, even for a fae."

Stepping forward, Elora let the white swirls and the chilly air engulf her. She would save the sprites. Every fiber of her being committed to it. Her heart skipped as she took another step forward.

But she would find the others first.

CHAPTER

21

Plush carpeting met Elora's feet as the room in Fairfrost Palace came into view. The room was even larger than Brannick's inside Bitter Thorn Castle, but this room had none of the same charm. For one thing, it was almost completely dark.

No glowing green lights floated up above to offer any light source. It also had blankets, clothes, and books scattered over every surface. The floor was especially littered, which made it difficult to trek across it in the dark.

When Elora tripped over a shoe for the second time, she hissed. The moment the sound left her lips, she clapped a hand over her mouth.

At least she was still inside Severin's bedroom. Making a sound like that in the hallway would have dire consequences.

Only then did she notice how her feet shuffled across the floor in a far from silent manner.

Her stomach dropped. This would be harder than she anticipated. Taking a deep—but silent—breath, she stepped into the hallway. She went to the left.

When she reached the end of the hallway, she turned right, just as Severin had told her to do. Nearby voices froze her feet in their tracks. Her heart thumped in her chest as she forced herself to hold her breath.

Turning as slowly as she dared, she began tiptoeing down the hallway. Now she moved opposite of Severin's directions. She could go off the path he explained, just as long as she remembered which hallways she had taken. That would help her find her way again.

But right now, she couldn't ignore the voices she had heard.

Peeking her head around a corner, the owners of the voices came into view. Two guards wearing white brocade uniforms marched down the hallway. They held chains of shimmery gold that look more magical than physical. Behind them, Prince Brannick, Lyren, and Quintus all walked with their chins dropped to their chests.

The magical chains wrapped tight around their wrists and ankles. Perhaps something about the chains also suppressed their magic because none of them tried to escape. Or maybe they *had* already tried. Tried and failed.

Seeing their condition sent a weight to the pit of Elora's stomach, but then it dropped again. Where was Vesper? It took all her focus to keep from gasping on the spot. Had Queen Alessandra done something to him?

One of the guards glanced back at the prince before shaking his head. "You should not have returned to Fairfrost

185

Palace. High Queen Alessandra is still angry that you escaped." The guard rubbed his shoulder, which Elora now noticed had a bit of blood seeping from it.

Brannick huffed as he spoke under his breath. "She can control others' emotions so well, you would think she could control her own anger."

The second guard spoke in a gruff voice. "You should have known she would never let you leave once you entered the palace. She has been trying to think of a way to lure you here to recapture you ever since you escaped."

For the briefest moment, Brannick glanced up. "Did Severin really defy her?

A smile flitted across the face of the guard with the injured shoulder. "He recently escaped. He is now the second to do so." His smile suddenly pulled down to a frown. "I suppose his escape is less impressive now that you have been captured again. Perhaps he will return again someday just like you have."

Brannick flinched at the sound of those words. His face fell.

Elora continued to tiptoe after them. With so much conversation, she didn't have to worry as much about being silent. The urge to fight came fast and strong through her gut, but in this case, it would probably be better to spend a few more moments to assess the situation.

Raising his chained wrists, Quintus ran a finger through his black hair. "We should have realized this would happen. She did not even listen to a single word we said. She just sent us straight to the dungeons."

The guard with the gruff voice turned back with a smile that looked oddly comforting. "But at least you put up a fight before you got captured. Not all fae are brave enough to do that."

Tension curled Elora's toes as she forced herself to move closer to the group.

Lyren increased her speed, just enough to catch up to the fae with the gruff voice. "Is there no way you can help us? You do not want High Queen Alessandra to succeed, do you?"

The first guard rubbed his shoulder once more before turning to face her. "We would help you if we could."

With a near growl at the back of his throat, the second guard nodded. "No one loathes the high queen more than her guards."

Rolling his shoulder, the first guard spoke again. "But we are bound by a bargain. We must take you to the dungeons and lock you inside."

Lyren's feet faltered as she fell back into step beside Brannick and Quintus. But then her curls bounced as her head perked up again. "Can you take us to the dungeons, lock us inside, and then let us free after that?"

A gruff sigh escaped from the second guard. "Alas, we are ordered to keep every prisoner locked up until she orders otherwise."

Elora had one hand on her sword hilt, but the thought of using it became less appealing by the moment. These guards may have carried out Queen Alessandra's orders, but they were not on her side. She didn't want to injure them if she didn't have to.

Quintus smoothed his hair until it lay flat against his head again. "What if we knock you out? You could not fulfill your orders if you were unconscious, correct?"

The first guard's shoulders slumped as if someone had dropped cast iron pots on top of them. "You can try, but we are ordered to fight back and call for help if anyone attempts to prevent us from completing an order."

187

Elora's hand continued to grip her hilt, but this time it merely aided her thinking. Maybe she wouldn't try to kill the guards, but knocking them out might be an option. Her feet stepped carefully over the red and gold rug at her feet while she eyed the walls.

Tall decorative candlesticks hung against the wallpaper. The flickering candlelight provided the only light source in the hallway, since there were no sprites anywhere nearby. More importantly, the ornate candlesticks were long and heavy. They could be used as a weapon.

Brannick had decent sword training now, and Lyren knew how to wield a javelin. If Elora pulled the candlesticks from the wall, those two could use them as weapons.

She glanced around at her surroundings once more just to make sure she hadn't missed anything. When she took a deep breath, her arms were ready for action.

Stepping to the edge of the hallway, her body bent at the waist. She ripped the plush rug with as much strength as her arms had. The unexpected movement caused the guards to tumble to the ground.

Brannick, Lyren, and Quintus tumbled to the ground as well, their magical chains clanking the whole way down.

Her feet moved lightning fast as she bounded to the guards' sides. The moment she got there, they both let out loud cries of help.

She jabbed the guard with the gruff voice with her elbow and then slammed her foot against the injured shoulder of the first guard. Both actions caused the guards to gasp in surprise. Their shouts cut off almost as soon as they began.

But their cut-off shouts just led to fists flying. The two guards punched toward her, despite the fact that the glamour making her invisible was still in place. Without thinking, her wings popped from her back. They flapped hard, somehow even quieter than usual too. Both guards continued to swing fists toward the air she had just filled, but since she had moved up instead of back, their fists met only air.

By now, Brannick had gotten to his feet. He charged toward the guards with a determined look in his eye.

Elora sucked in a breath as she flitted even higher. Her feet dangled just above Lyren and Quintus's heads, but they didn't seem to hear anything unusual. Flying closer to the wall, Elora began pulling a candlestick off it. When gentle movements did nothing, she dug in deep and yanked it off. It clattered to the ground.

Lyren didn't seem to notice a candlestick floating away from the wall on its own, but she did notice it when she nearly tripped over it. She snatched it up right away and slammed it into the neck of the second guard.

His eyes fluttered closed as he dropped to the ground unconscious. The first guard put up more of a fight, despite his injured shoulder. Brannick had clamped his hand over the guard's mouth to keep him from shouting, but the guard still kicked and hit in every direction he could.

One particular jab caused Quintus to fly across the hallway and slam into the wall. Quintus shook his head before whisper-shouting toward the prince. "Can you break the chains?"

Brannick nodded and tilted his head toward the guard. "You two hold him down, and someone keep his mouth covered."

Still flying, Elora pulled the sword from her belt. She glanced at the pommel. If she hit the guard in the neck just right, she could knock him out the way Lyren did with the other guard. Even acknowledging that in her mind did nothing to spur Elora into action. Her sword training had taught her more about how to kill than to render unconscious. She didn't want to make a grave mistake she might regret.

Luckily, Lyren and Quintus managed to tackle the guard to the ground. Quintus stuffed crumpled papers into the guard's mouth until his every sound was nothing more than a muffled growl. Lyren used a fist to knock him out.

Brannick held the ends of all their chains in one hand while his other hand hovered above it in waving motions. It took a few moments, but the magical chains soon vanished into the air.

Elora fluttered to the ground, waiting for one of them to ask how the rug had moved out from their feet. Instead, Blaz appeared at Brannick's side, growling at the unconscious guards. The prince dug his fingers through the black fur while eyeing the rest of the hallway. "Well done, Blaz."

The wolf must have been using his glamour to hide as well. Did they think Blaz had pulled the rug out from under them?

Quintus swiped his forehead with the back of his hand. He leaned against the wall at his side. "That was close."

Letting out a sigh, Lyren touched a hand to her chest. "I thought we would actually get locked in the dungeons."

"So did I." Dark weight tightened around each of Brannick's words.

After another quick sigh, Lyren stood tall and whipped a portion of curls over her shoulder. "Should we split up then? Quintus and I will get the talisman in the library while you get the one in the armory?"

Brannick nodded, scratching his wolf behind the ear. "Do you still have the gloves I made to protect you from the iron?"

Pushing himself off the wall, Quintus tapped his pocket. "Yes. Once we retrieve our talisman, we will meet you just outside the throne room as planned."

Another set of nods rippled through the group before they started down opposite halls.

Elora stared after them, still wondering if she should make her presence known. It seemed strange to hide, but then again, Brannick *had* locked her in a room to keep her from getting to Fairfrost Palace. If he found out she was there, he might try to force her back to Bitter Thorn. Perhaps it was best if they didn't know she was there.

Turning on her heel, she moved down the hallway to get back to the area that would lead her to the sprites. This way, she could rescue the sprites in peace. And if the others were going to meet up at the throne room anyway, she would be close by to know when they got there. She'd meet up with them then.

First, she'd rescue the sprites.

CHAPTER 22

Being invisible made Elora hyperaware of her noises. Even in the empty hallways, she could hear each time her boots met the plush carpet. Since her wings were still out after using them against those Fairfrost guards, she tried flying down the hallways instead.

It went faster, and it was quieter too. Maybe it was because they were magical, but her wings did a much better job at being silent than her own feet did.

Eventually, she reached the hallway with the sprites. A guard stomped down it. Toward her. With her wings spread out, she filled much of the hallway. The guard would run into her. If she trusted her flying ability a little more, she would have just flown closer to the ceiling.

For something like this, she couldn't take any chances. Instead, she sucked in a silent breath and lowered herself to the ground. Her heart thumped in her chest as she edged herself up against the wall.

Now her wings fluttered against the wallpaper, but they managed to do it without making a sound. She held her breath.

The guard continued to stomp down the hall, completely unaware of her presence. Soon, he turned the corner and stomped even farther away.

It took skill to suppress the sigh of relief that wanted to escape her mouth. The hallway lay empty before her, but it didn't stop the skittering of her heart. She curled her hands into fists, hoping it might distract her from the fear growling in her belly.

Lifting off the ground, she flew down the hallway at her slowest pace yet. Though she feared another guard would appear at any moment, none did. Once she reached the door with the sprites, she glanced every which way.

Still no guards appeared. Fear told her it must be a trap, but intuition told her everything was going according to plan. If she expected to free all the sprites before Brannick and the others returned to the throne room, she needed to hurry.

Throwing one final glance over her shoulder, she ducked into the room.

Green light glowed so bright she had to use one arm to shield her eyes. A swarm of sprites floated inside a shimmery white bubble. Ice trickled down her spine as she remembered what the enchantment did. It took the essence from a sprite. If they were sent to deliver a message, the offering they received from the message-giver would be the only essence they would have left.

A short table with an opalescent top sat against one wall. A white and gold vase stood upon it with an empty candlestick at its side. Other than that, the room was empty. No windows. No food. Not even a guard stood inside.

Elora's eyebrow cocked up. Considering the enchantments Queen Alessandra had in place throughout her court, maybe the room didn't need one. Maybe the consequences for entering that room were so dire that no one dared to try. Or perhaps she had an enchantment to detect the presence of magic inside the room, but because of the pendant from Tindra and Severin, Elora was safe. Whatever the reason, she had made it safely. It was time.

Taking a deep breath, Elora whispered toward the creatures. "I have a message to send."

Every sprite inside the white bubble jerked to a stop. They all glanced toward her, but none of them moved.

Clearing her voice, she tried again. "I know I am glamoured to be invisible, but I am still here. I need one of you to send a message for me."

Throughout her speech, one of the sprites at the top of the bubble began pushing her way through the others. It wasn't until she got closer that Elora saw the sparkle of pink in her green glow.

"Elora?"

Even though the sprite couldn't see it, Elora still smiled wide. She couldn't help it. "Tansy."

The sprite's pink dress hung down to her ankles. She was shorter than before, but her dress was still the same length. Her arms looked thinner and frailer than ever. Even her green and pink eyes were gaunt and empty. It didn't matter. All that would change once she could escape Fairfrost.

Pulling the wildflowers from her pocket, Elora cleared her throat. "I have enough offerings for all of you. I will send as many messages as it takes until you are all free."

Plucking a petal from one of the wildflowers, she turned back to the sprite still hovering in front of her. While Elora held the petal in her hand, it stayed invisible like the rest of her. So she placed it onto the table with the vase and the candlestick. "I am saving you first, Tansy. There is your offering."

The slightest gleam appeared in Tansy's eyes before she floated down toward the table. Her soft pink shoes padded onto the opalescent surface without a sound. She bent at the waist, but just before she could pluck the petal up, her hands froze. Soon, her wings were carrying her backward, closer to Elora again.

Tansy's velvety hair bounced as she lowered her head. "Do not save me first. There are others who are much weaker than me. They should be the first to go." Her mouth quirked up as she stared not quite at the spot where Elora stood. "I will stay with you until you are done. I will deliver the final message."

Elora nodded before she realized Tansy couldn't see it. Elora said, "I like that plan. Will one of the weaker sprites please come forward to deliver my message?"

After some shuffling, a little sprite with a red cap and pointy shoes flew forward. He was half the height of Elora's thumbnail. The glow his body gave off was almost more gray than green. He landed with a thud on the table's surface.

While the sprite examined her flower petal, Elora cleared her throat. "I am Elora of Bitter Thorn. I have a message for Severin of Fairfrost. Tell him, the rescue has begun."

The little sprite nearly toppled over as he tried to shove the flower petal into his pocket. Once he managed it, he floated away, disappearing through the wall like it didn't exist. Maybe it was her imagination, but his glow looked a little greener just before he disappeared.

She dropped another flower petal onto the table. "Who is next?"

Another tiny sprite flew forward, her wings twitching as she moved. This time, Elora's message said the sprites were very weak. The next message said there were many of them to save.

It turned out, coming up with messages was the hardest part of the rescue. Soon, her messages contained single words like *hello* and *greetings*.

Nearly all the flower petals had been given now, but several sprites still remained. She'd have to start using leaves and stems as offerings soon. If she ran out of those, she'd just start plucking hairs from her head to give to them.

Footsteps sounded outside the door. Brannick and the others were coming. With a gulp, she began sending messages even faster than ever. The sprites had formed a line leading to her, which thankfully sped up the process even more.

Soon, voices accompanied the footsteps outside the door. Brannick and Quintus spoke quietly to each other, but another set of footsteps suggested Lyren would be there soon as well. Elora would have to join them if she didn't want to get left behind in Fairfrost.

Dropping a wilted leaf onto the table, Elora freed one more sprite. Over a dozen sprites still remained, but if she didn't hurry, she'd be stuck in Fairfrost with no way back to Bitter Thorn. She took a step toward the door. She froze. Her throat burned when she tried to swallow.

She had vowed she would save the sprites. All of them.

Even knowing how fast she had to move, she still turned back and quickly freed three more sprites.

The voices in the hallway moved farther away from the room. Brannick and the others were leaving. Elora's eyes darted from the remaining sprites to the table and then to the closed door. There were still ten of them left, including Tansy.

With her pink dress sparkling, Tansy flew toward the door and jerked her chin toward the voices outside it. "Are those your friends?"

"Yes." Hopefully they all heard the hesitation in Elora's voice. Biting her bottom lip, she freed two more sprites and then jumped toward the door. "I will come back for the rest of you in just a moment. I only need to tell the others to wait for me."

Trust settled in Tansy's eyes as she nodded. The look tugged at Elora's insides, twisting that knot in her chest just a little bit tighter. She had made a *vow*.

With a gulp, Elora dropped the rest of her bouquet onto the table. It was nothing more than a few empty stems now. "I need to send more messages to Severin of Fairfrost. Tell him, it is done. All of you should send that same message."

With the softest tug, she pulled the door open. She had never asked more than one sprite to send a message at one time. Hopefully it would allow all of them to leave. She glanced back to see the sprites flying toward her offerings. They examined the stems, so it must have worked. Her wings popped out automatically as she hovered above the floor.

Though she had just heard them, Brannick and the others were nowhere to be seen. Holding her breath, she flew down a hallway with her eyes searching wildly. A voice stopped her in a single breath.

Brannick. He was in the throne room.

CHAPTER

23

Circling back toward the throne room, Elora's heart twisted. Her flying turned jerky because her shoulders shuddered so much, but she couldn't help it. What was Brannick doing *in* the throne room? Weren't they supposed to meet outside it? She gulped. Would he get captured again?

She floated into the throne room without a single guard or other fae even glancing in her direction. She reminded herself that she was only invisible, not silent. If her heart could stop pounding so hard, she would be a lot safer.

Queen Alessandra sat atop a shimmery ice-blue throne with frost on the steps leading up to it. She gripped an axe with an opalescent handle in one hand while gripping an arm of her throne with the other. Her fingers curled tight enough over the throne's arm that her knuckles had turned white.

She sneered at the back of the room.

Taking in a slow breath, Elora forced herself to look in the same direction.

Brannick leaned against the back wall with a smirk. His long hair was messy, like he had just run his fingers through it. Lyren and Quintus stood on either side of him, showcasing identical expressions of arrogance. Blaz was nowhere to be seen, but he was surely nearby wearing his glamour.

There were no chains. They looked to be free. But if that were the case, then *why* did they risk returning to the throne room? And why was Vesper still missing?

The questions slammed to a halt when Queen Alessandra sent icy words across the room. "How did you escape my guards?"

Smirking wider, Brannick pulled heavy, leather-like gloves onto his hands. Once they were on, he pulled items from his pocket. With his hands closed over the items, no one could see exactly what they were. He lifted one eyebrow. "We have your talismans."

Queen Alessandra flashed her teeth before sitting back in her throne. "Not all of them."

She tried to maintain an air of arrogance as effortlessly as Brannick, but her performance lost all heart when he peeled his fingers open.

In one hand, he held one talisman. In the other, he held two. "Are you sure?" he asked, flashing a devious smile.

With his hand open, the iron of the talismans began drifting into the air. It hit Elora like a pommel to the gut. It took everything in her not to audibly gasp at the sudden pain. Something seemed to flicker around her. Or perhaps it was *her* that flickered. Was her glamour failing with the iron nearby?

199

Brannick immediately closed his hands over the talismans once again. The stinging pain took another moment to subside, but at least her glamour appeared to be steadily in place.

Elora had a single moment to grin. They had gotten all three talismans, even the one in Queen Alessandra's pocket. Although, considering her surprise at their appearance, maybe the third talisman had been hiding in another room and not in Queen Alessandra's pocket after all.

It felt like ages in her mind, but the entire conversation had happened in two blinks of an eye. On the third blink, Queen Alessandra threw her opalescent axe straight at Brannick's heart. He jumped out of the way just in time. By then, she had ordered her guards to capture him once again.

Before any of them could approach, Brannick waved a hand and stepped into the door he had just opened. Lyren and Quintus immediately stepped in after him.

"Use your magic to keep that door open!" Queen Alessandra screamed more than shouted the words. Two guards sent some kind of magic into the door. They tried to step into it, but it shrank to half the size before they got there. Their arms waved as they sent magic toward the door. It opened a little wider for only a moment. Tension split across their faces as they waved their arms harder.

With a pop, the door vanished completely.

Brannick and the others had escaped.

A breath of relief might have left Elora, except she immediately realized she was now stuck in Fairfrost. Her wings jerked as she shuddered, but soon she was flying normally again. It didn't matter. She'd find a way out.

Queen Alessandra muttered under her breath as she yanked her axe from the wall it had embedded in. Her mutters turned angrier as she stomped back to her throne.

"It was only a trick," she said as she fell onto her throne. Shaking her head, she shoved both hands through her hair. The perfect curls that had been cascading down her back a moment earlier now had several flyaway strands that stuck out at odd angles.

She huffed as she ran a finger over the opalescent handle of her axe. "A trick." She shook her head again. An exasperated sigh tumbled from her mouth. She slammed her axe onto the arm of her throne and then she reached into her pocket.

With a manner approaching reverence, she pulled out a marble box Elora recognized. The same box had held her father's sword not so long ago. Queen Alessandra leaned forward until her nose nearly touched the box. She held her breath.

Even lifting the lid slowly, the sting of iron in the air still sliced through Elora. Red splotches appeared on the queen's face, probably from the iron. Still, she smiled.

The sight of it caused Elora's gut to curl into a knot. They hadn't succeeded after all. One more talisman still clearly remained in Queen Alessandra's possession. Brannick must have glamoured a third talisman to make it seem like he had all three of them.

The queen sighed in relief while another set of red splotches broke out across her neck.

When she tried to close the lid of the box, something stopped it. Her eyes narrowed as she tried to close the lid again.

She must have seen something Elora didn't because the queen immediately stood and swiped the air in front of her. "No!" She swiped again, and this time, she caught onto something. Whatever she held must have been glamoured because Elora still couldn't see anything.

Queen Alessandra screamed as she waved her hand. Something was pulling her forward as she worked. She continued to wave her hand and shout.

The glamour fell away.

Vesper stood in the middle of the throne room. He wore the same type of gloves Brannick had been wearing. He held one hand in a fist. Since the stinging pain of iron had gone out of the air, Elora guessed he now had the third talisman in his hand. The real one.

Queen Alessandra had a handful of his vest in her fist. She swiped at his face, cutting three lines across his cheek with her fingernails. He yanked and did everything he could to get away.

Beating her wings faster, Elora flew across the room and grabbed the back of the queen's brocade dress. It only took a single yank to make her lose grip on Vesper.

A door appeared at the back of the throne room. Brannick's door.

They had planned this all along.

In one glorious moment, Vesper sprinted toward the door. It looked like he would actually get away, but Queen Alessandra had ordered her guards forward once again. One of them grabbed Vesper by the arm and one grabbed his pant leg.

Vesper faltered, but he continued to run toward the door. He was nearly there.

The queen let out an icy laugh that froze in the air. "My guards can hold your door open indefinitely."

Elora grabbed the back of the coat belonging to the guard who held Vesper's arm. She yanked with all her might to pull him away.

Without knowing an attack came from behind, the guard lost his footing immediately.

Glancing over his shoulder, Vesper smirked. "Your guards can hold my door open, maybe, but we both know they cannot hold Prince Brannick's door open for long."

He shook his leg as he ran, trying to kick off the guard who held it.

Maybe helping this much would reveal her position, but Elora didn't care anymore. She yanked the guard's coat as hard as she could. When that didn't work, she flew closer and dug her nails into his arm.

The guard's grip faltered just as Vesper was stepping through the door. The two guards had gotten back to their feet and struggled to keep the door open as they had before. Just as before, they only held it open for a moment before the prince's magic forced it shut with a pop.

Letting out a breath, Elora glanced around her. Neither of the guards seemed to have noticed her presence, despite her yanking. She took in controlled breaths as she flew backward. Only a little farther, and she could leave the throne room without anyone knowing she had ever been there.

She eyed the doorway. Her heart thundered, but at least she had found a way to breathe silently. Just a little farther.

An icy hand clamped down on her arm, yanking her closer to the ground. Elora gasped as her feet met the floor in a crash. For some reason, hiding her wings seemed like the most important thing to do.

Just as they curled into her back, the glamour keeping her invisible vanished.

Queen Alessandra stood above her, still with a firm grip on her arm. She ripped the ward necklace from Severin and Tindra off Elora's neck. With a sneer that could have killed, the queen spoke only one word.

"*You.*"

CHAPTER

24

Shimmery golden chains appeared around Elora, wrapping over her wrists, but also holding her arms against her body. When Queen Alessandra clenched her fist, the chain pulled tight, stealing the breath from Elora's chest.

It took a few coughs before Elora could breathe again.

A guard approached from a corner of the room. His face pointed downward. "Should we take her to the dungeon?"

"No." Flecks of spittle flew from the queen's lips. She dug her fingernails into Elora's arms as she yanked her to her feet. "This one is not leaving my sight."

The queen's grip tightened as she dragged Elora out into the hallway. Her icy blue eyes seemed to crystalize with wildness. They focused on the door to the room that once contained the sprites.

"I need to send a message." Frosty air drifted from Queen Alessandra's mouth as she spoke. Her nails dug deeper into Elora's skin. Her jaw clenched as she continued to stomp forward. "I need a sprite *now*."

Elora's gut had already twisted into the tightest possible knot from the moment the queen caught her and removed her glamour. Now it dropped down. When the queen glared at the door, Elora's stomach dropped even more.

The sprites were gone. Maybe she hadn't given individual messages for all of the last ones specifically, but she figured it was close enough. How would the queen react when she discovered her sprites were gone?

Just as they reached the door, a glow of green popped through the door. The light zoomed down to the queen's palm with a sparkle of pink inside it.

Tansy. Had Tansy stayed for Elora?

"Finally." Queen Alessandra kept one hand holding Elora while she dug into her pocket with the other.

Tansy's eyes widened at the sight of Elora in chains. An audible gulp sounded from her tiny throat, but the queen was too busy to hear it.

Queen Alessandra pulled her hand from her pocket and dropped a white bead into Tansy's little palms. Without even waiting for the sprite to examine the offering, Queen Alessandra gave her message. "Tell Ansel of Mistmount that High Queen Alessandra of Fairfrost has a message for him. The message is this: I have the girl."

Stuffing the bead into her pocket, Tansy began flying away from the queen.

Elora took a step toward the sprite. "And tell Prince Brannick I have been captured."

Tansy's pink dress swirled as she gave the subtlest nod.

For a moment, Elora feared the queen would notice. That fear turned out to be unfounded because the queen was too busy shoving Elora to the ground. "You know nothing of Faerie. Sprites only give messages for those who provide offerings."

It definitely wasn't a good time for Elora to admit she had already given Tansy an offering. And even if that didn't technically count, Tansy would certainly deliver the message anyway. Elora was a friend to the sprites, after all. When the sprite flew away, the twisted knot inside Elora's chest released. The sprites were free. Her vow had been fulfilled.

Nails dug into Elora's skin as the queen dragged her back toward the throne room. Elora allowed it for two steps. On the third, she acted.

She jerked herself out the queen's grip and lifted one foot for a kick. With chains pinning her arms down against her sides, she would have to forgo using her sword. But that didn't mean she was useless.

The moment her foot swung toward the queen, a clattering shock sliced all throughout Elora's body. Pain erupted inside her. She gasped hard as she fell to her hands and knees. It took effort just to force air in and out of her body.

Queen Alessandra grabbed her by the collar and forced her to a standing position once again. The queen's icy eyes looked more like daggers now. "Do *not* try that again."

Despite the warning, Elora did try to yank herself away from the queen's grasp. The attempt was met with an even stronger shock of pain slicing through her. She was still trying to catch her breath as the queen dragged her into the throne room.

Under the queen's direction, guards used Elora's chains to secure her up against the wall. More chains appeared around her ankles and legs. Those fastened to the wall as well.

While the guards looked on, Queen Alessandra stared at her captive. She stared too hard. It wasn't the look in her eye that grated against Elora's nerves. It was more the unwavering intensity.

Even after the guards were standing back in their previous positions, the queen continued to stare. And stare.

Was it simply meant to intimidate?

Elora never did respond well to intimidation. Showing as much defiance as she dared, she closed her eyes. The queen could continue to stare as much as she liked, but Elora refused to watch it.

That plan didn't work out at all because Elora could still feel the stare under her skin. Even with her eyes closed. Her nose twitched as she opened her eyes again. "What?"

Ice and anger filled every line and every curve of Queen Alessandra's face. It turned her stunning features into a painful sight. But something lingered deep in her eyes, something she was probably trying to hide. The tiniest speck of vulnerability glimmered like candlelight deep in the queen's irises. When she opened her mouth to speak, the tiny light grew.

"Why does he love you and not me?"

"What?" The word flitted from Elora's mouth too fast for her to stop it. She narrowed one eye. "You mean Brannick?"

Queen Alessandra flinched and the vulnerability flickered across her every feature for the shortest moment. "*Prince* Brannick."

A huff of laughter spilled from Elora's throat. "Are you serious?"

Instead of responding, the queen merely continued to stare.

That spark of vulnerability was nothing now. Elora's jaw clenched as she formed her words. "You tricked him into a bargain that forced him to do your bidding. You deceived him. What did you think would happen?"

The queen pointed her nose toward the ceiling, but the aloof body language fooled nobody. "What have you ever done for him?"

Each new moment seemed like a more appropriate time to laugh. This conversation was turning more unbelievable by the second. Elora shook her head as she spoke. "I helped him win the testing. I helped him *survive* when you tried to injure him with your orders."

Anger fell away from the queen's face while pain engulfed it. "But I earned his love once. How can he turn away from me now?"

Elora leaned forward as much as she could while being chained to the wall. "Love is not something you earn once and never fight for again. Love requires constant nurturing. In return, it often gives more than deserved." She lifted an eyebrow. "But you must give more than deserved too."

The mask of anger returned to Queen Alessandra's face as she sneered.

Before either of them could say a word, someone charged through the throne room door. Elora hardly needed to see the figure to know who had arrived.

Ansel's yellow eyes seemed to glow when he locked eyes with her. His mouth twisted into a sick grin as he stepped toward her. "The once mortal is now in chains." His grin turned even more twisted than before. "I have never seen such a glorious sight."

It didn't matter that magical chains bound her. It didn't matter that Queen Alessandra had magic that could create shocks of pain.

Elora tried to get away anyway. She shoved against the shimmery gold chains, fighting with all the strength she had.

This only delighted Ansel even more. He moved across the floor until he stood directly in front of her. Too close. She could smell sour milk on his breath.

He eyed her neck with too much fascination. His lips parted and then his teeth opened too. He leaned toward her, still staring at her neck.

Was he going to bite her?

Queen Alessandra scoffed and shoved something against his chest. "Use a knife, will you? We do not need a bigger mess."

His yellow eyes glowed. He continued forward without any change in his movement.

When the queen shoved him again, he shook his head. "Fine." He took the knife she had shoved against his chest and brought it to Elora's neck.

It scared her how much less disturbing a knife was to the alternative. She was so relieved he wasn't touching her that she barely even felt when the blade sliced open her skin.

Ansel wiped up a drop of her blood with one finger and brought it straight to his mouth. He sucked off every bit of it with a little too much pleasure. He glanced toward the queen while delight danced in his eyes. "It is as we suspected. Her blood has the power of a fae, but her magic is still dormant and cannot fight against me when I steal the power from it."

The queen tapped a foot impatiently. "It will work then? I do not need the talismans anymore?"

209

Elora shuddered when Ansel brought his finger to her neck once more.

This time, he closed his eyes as he licked the blood off his finger. When he opened them, they crackled with a yellowish glow. "The talismans are nothing to her blood. It will be more powerful than you can imagine."

Queen Alessandra turned away from them to march back to her ice-blue throne. "Prepare the gemstones quickly then. I want to kill her as soon as possible."

Ansel had his hand stretching toward Elora's neck again, but it stopped midair. He spun around. "You cannot kill her."

"Why not?" The queen glared as she lowered herself onto her throne. "Will the gemstones not work if she is dead?"

Even with him facing the other direction, Elora could see a vein in Ansel's neck bulge. He curled his hands into fists. "Of course it will still work. But you cannot kill her. You must give her to me once we are finished."

He turned around to get more blood from Elora's dripping wound. After licking only a portion of it off, he stroked her cheek, leaving a thin trail of blood behind. "I must have her for my collection. Breaking the strong ones is so much more fulfilling than breaking the weak ones."

Ice and shudders and every disgusting thing writhed under Elora's skin. She considered trying to bite off Ansel's finger, but he would probably just enjoy it. She did the next best thing she could think of, which was to go limp against her chains. No reaction showed on her face. Her arms didn't move. They didn't twitch. If he wanted to break her, she wouldn't give him the satisfaction of knowing how much he disturbed her. She would give him nothing.

Oddly, Queen Alessandra seemed intent on giving him the same thing. She laid both arms on her throne and sat forward.

"I will not give you a fae who can give you enough power to defeat me."

Ansel whirled around to face the queen again. "Then I will make a bargain that I will never use her power against you."

Her eyebrow lifted. "The answer is still *no*."

"Then I will not help you."

She maintained her regal position, refusing to speak. But he refused to speak as well. They stared at each other, which gave Elora enough time to try and think of a way out of her predicament. At the moment, she had no ideas.

Reaching for the collar of his shirt, Ansel began twisting the yellow gemstone pinned to it. "Come now, you know I have only helped you thus far because of how it benefits me." He shrugged. "If you do not give her to me, then I will not make the gemstones you need."

They continued to stare at each other while Elora continued to try and think herself out of the situation.

Magic.

That was the only way she'd get out, and she knew it. Maybe she couldn't access her own magic, but she had accessed her sword's magic once before. It only worked when her life had been in danger. But her life was more in danger now. And if she understood what Ansel and the queen were saying, all of Faerie was in danger too. Apparently, her blood had exactly what Queen Alessandra needed to take over Faerie completely. Never had she needed magic more than in this moment.

With the chains binding her, Elora couldn't reach for her sword. Instead, she tried to imagine using it. She imagined its magic cutting away the chains until she could grab it. And then she imagined plunging the sword straight through Ansel's chest.

Her imaginings came to a halt when the queen finally spoke. "I propose a bargain. If you make me gemstones full of her power…" She trailed off as her head tilted to the side. "If you make me *four* gemstones full of her power…"

Ansel flinched at the number, but he didn't refuse.

The queen continued. "Then I will release," she turned her nose up as she gestured to Elora, "this vile creature into your possession." She looked into Ansel's eyes. "Though you must never use her power against me."

A sick delight filled Ansel's voice. "You must say her name for the bargain to be binding."

Pressing her lips together, the queen folded her arms over her chest.

Ansel let out a chuckle. "You know what her name is."

Queen Alessandra flinched. She glared at the ground and folded her hands into her lap. "I will release *Elora*," she flinched again, "into your possession, though you must never use her power against me."

"I accept your bargain." Wicked delight danced in his eyes as he turned to face Elora. He pulled four clear gemstones from his pocket and brought the knife close to her neck once again. His eyebrow raised. "Shall we begin?"

CHAPTER

25

D ays must have passed. Elora couldn't be sure because the Fairfrost throne room had no windows. Queen Alessandra and Ansel had both taken several meals since Elora had been captured. They both slept at least two or three times. Memories had turned fuzzy in Elora's mind. Or maybe it was the lack of food that weakened her.

They had given her liquids. She got one cupful of water for every three meals Ansel and the queen ate. They did not give her any food.

Drips of warm blood trailed down her neck. Ansel had made several cuts. Too many to count. All of them stung and pricked. Maybe it was in her head, but the wounds didn't seem to be healing as quickly as they should have been. Maybe it was just because she had nothing left.

She had failed.

She tried. Over and over she tried. Again and again.

She hadn't accessed a single spark of magic. Her sword dangled against her leg offering nothing more than a weight to tire her out more. Chains held her arms against her body. They held her ankles and legs together too, but she couldn't rest at all because the chains still held her against the wall.

Every time her eyes would droop and allow sleep to overtake her, the position would jerk her awake just as fast. Why wouldn't they just let her rest?

Tears cut down her cheeks, but she barely even noticed them. Too many tears had fallen in the past few days to notice any of them now.

Making the gemstones had taken energy from Ansel. He had to rest after each one, often for what felt like an entire day.

He took her blood and used magic to trap it inside a clear gemstone. It took concentration. Effort. He often had to sit down in the middle of the process because it took so much out of him. Little by little, her blood turned the clear gemstones into a bright and clear purple.

Purple. Just like the wildflowers Brannick had conjured for her. Would she ever see him again?

Ansel and the queen were arguing about killing her again. They had repeated the same argument many times over the past few days, but never more than now that all four gemstones were finished.

It really didn't matter. Queen Alessandra was bound by the bargain. Though she hated it, Ansel would take Elora away soon enough.

The queen paced across her throne room, her white brocade dress giving off iridescent glints in the candlelight. "Technically, I could do anything to the girl once I release her into your possession. That still allows me to keep my side of the bargain."

Ansel shoved a fist to his side. He probably glared at the queen, but he stood too far away for Elora to tell for sure. He knocked his fist against his side again. All four gemstones sat in that fist. The movement offered a not-so-subtle threat. "I know how to keep my possessions safe. Release her now, or I will crush these gemstones at once."

A cold laugh broke from Queen Alessandra's mouth. "I thought you said it would kill a fae to use more than one gemstone at a time. And is there not a rejuvenation period after using a gemstone? Did you not tell me that I should wait to use another gemstone until the rejuvenation period had passed?"

Ansel's foot tapped against the throne room floor at a tense speed. "You proposed the bargain yourself. Release her into my possession."

Weak breaths moved through Elora's nose. She was broken. All that bravery, and it had only gotten her here. How much more would Ansel break her? Could she bear it? Would death be kinder?

The skin wrapped around her limbs felt like saggy, threadbare wool. Her once strong determination had turned to mush in that throne room. Her heart had been chipped away until there was nothing left. It didn't matter that she could still feel a steady thump in her chest. Whatever beat inside her now wasn't a heart. It was an empty weight, one that she couldn't possibly bear.

Brannick had not come for her.

Maybe Tansy never delivered Elora's message to him, but she doubted it. He must have been angrier with her than she realized. She must have made one mistake too many for his love to bear.

215

"Fine." Queen Alessandra scowled. "Take her. I release her into your possession." Her head whipped around to stare Ansel right in the eyes. "But if I ever see her again, I will kill her the first chance I get."

Ansel probably made some sickening expression that could turn any fae's stomach. Elora had learned by now not to look him in the eye. His fist curled tight as he approached the back of the room.

She could feel her muscles twitch the closer he got.

Even his voice sent a shudder down her spine. "Once she is in my possession, I will place her gemstones on the floor for you."

Her gemstones.

Elora's blood would give the queen everything she needed to gain complete control of Faerie. Only Elora's blood had the power of a fae with none of the magic to fight back.

Brannick was right. She should have stayed in Bitter Thorn. The sprites were free now, but at what cost?

Most fae probably went their entire immortal lives without threatening all of Faerie, but Elora had already done it twice. First, when she conspired with King Huron, and now, when Queen Alessandra would use her blood.

A scratchy finger trailed down her cheek, then down her neck, and then down her arm all the way to her hand. Ansel breathed in her face. He liked how it made her shudder.

She didn't have to suppress the urge to shudder anyway. The lack of sustenance in her body made her too weak for it. Even if her chains were removed, she probably wouldn't have the strength to fight against him anyway. Nothing broke her more than that knowledge.

With a tight squeeze on her fingers, Ansel bent to his knees and began unlocking the chains that held her against the wall.

Of course, he did nothing for the chains that wrapped around her ankles, legs, and arms. No, he'd probably keep those on until he brought her to his home. Maybe he'd even keep them on long after they arrived.

Even that didn't make her shudder. She was too tired for it still.

As the last of the chains holding her against the wall fell away, her body gave out. He welcomed it, yanking her straight into his stiff arms. The urge to fight finally came. The scent of sour milk on his breath curdled in her gut. Could she muster any strength? Any at all?

Just as Ansel set the four gemstones onto the ground, a loud crack sounded through the room. It reverberated off the walls with a screech. Ansel clenched her tighter.

"What is that?" He whipped his head toward the four purple gemstones on the floor and then toward the queen. "Did you plan this? Taking her away from me right now is against our bargain."

The queen might have offered a snide retort, except she wasn't even listening to Ansel. Her jaw hung slack as she stared toward the ground at her feet. A small crack had broken through the marble floor. Another crack sounded, a little quieter this time, but the crack in the floor stretched longer.

Queen Alessandra stepped away from it, her eyes growing wider.

A third crack sounded, this one loudest of all. With it, the entire marble floor completely split apart. Half of the throne room fell to one side. The guards on that side of the throne room tumbled off their feet. They shouted as they tried to stand upright again.

By the time the broken half of the room stopped moving, the edge of the floor that had cracked pointed toward the sky and the side wall lay against the ground. No guards could get back to the throne room now. At least not soon.

Sucking in a breath, Queen Alessandra jerked her head toward the guards on the other side of the room. "Get in the hallway. That is where the magic came from."

Before she even finished speaking, another crack jabbed the air. This one worked faster than the others. Another piece of the throne room split away and fell on its side just like the first. Those guards could do nothing for the queen now.

Only a thin strip of marble floor remained. It trailed from the throne in the middle of the room all the way down to where Elora had been chained to the wall. Only the queen, Ansel, and Elora stood on the portion that remained. Somehow, the four purple gemstones had survived as well.

Ansel's grip turned sharp as he yanked Elora closer to him. "You will not get away this time."

Despite the absence of any energy at all, Elora still wanted to stab her sword through his chest. Unfortunately, chains still held her arms against her body.

Queen Alessandra continued to ignore the two of them as she lifted her axe. She raised her other hand and an opalescent enchantment shot from her fingertips toward the hallway that had once bordered the throne room wall.

The enchantment didn't hit anything particular. It seemed like odd aiming until movement in a nearby part of the hallway caught Elora's attention.

For the first time in days, she found the strength to turn her head.

Brannick. Her Brannick.

He was there.

He leapt from the hallway onto the narrow strip of the throne room that still remained. Never had his agility been so

218

impressive. He leapt across the chasm as if it were nothing more than a small stone in his path. Blaz leapt at the same time, landing next to the prince just as his feet touched down on the marble floor.

No glamour hid Blaz now. He snarled and spat from his bared fangs. Even without wolf teeth, Brannick wore an identical expression.

Another blast of opalescence left the queen's fingertips, but Brannick simply leapt into the air to avoid it.

Only when Ansel's grip changed slightly did Elora realize he had opened a door. It was a rocky gray and smelled like open air.

With a deep breath, she jolted her body to one side. The attempt would have seemed pathetic days ago, but given the circumstances, she was proud of it now. Her body jerked again, which weakened her more than she cared to admit. She settled for wriggling as much as possible after that.

It wasn't enough. She glanced toward the prince, but he was too busy avoiding Queen Alessandra's enchantments to do anything for Elora.

Knots twisted in Elora's gut. If Brannick got captured while trying to rescue her, she'd never forgive herself. Not that she could do much about it in her current position.

She continued to wriggle and writhe, but it was useless. With the chains, she didn't even have her limbs to help in the fight. Ansel's door swirled only one step away. Her breath caught in her throat. Was she holding it?

If she went through that door, she'd never come back. But who could stop him from taking her?

Ansel let out a blood-curdling shriek and nearly dropped Elora from his arms. A snarl immediately answered who had come to her rescue.

Blaz.

He took another bite out of Ansel's leg, tearing off a chunk almost as big as a fist. If he bit again, he'd probably crack a bone.

"Stupid wolf." In his crazed state, Ansel tried to send an enchantment toward the wolf, but Blaz easily evaded it. Ansel stepped to the side, forgetting to avoid the leg Blaz had just taken several bites out of.

Elora hit the ground with a thud. It took all her energy just to find her feet again. Ansel dragged his injured leg across the ground while aiming his hands toward Blaz again. This blast would not miss.

No thought passed through Elora's mind as she lunged toward Ansel. Her heart was the one that acted. That thick lump of nothing hadn't been so empty after all. She wouldn't let Blaz get hurt after he had come to her rescue. She couldn't.

The move worked perfectly to protect the wolf, but now Ansel had a grip on her again. He slung her over one shoulder and limped toward his still-open door.

With her heart properly feeling again, it wasn't difficult to find more strength. She wriggled and twisted against Ansel's hold. He clenched tighter on her, but she still slithered out of his grip.

Falling from a greater height, she hit the marble ground with an even harder thud than before. Her head slammed into the cool stone, causing blood to drip into her hair.

From behind, she could hear Blaz snapping his jaw. Ansel shrieked again. Her throat ached anyway. She was dangerously close to Ansel's door. If she didn't get away, he would take her for sure.

Blaz let out a growl that shook through the air.

When someone reached for her waist again, she automatically began to writhe against the grip. It wasn't until a comforting voice brushed across her ear that she stilled.

"I have you." Brannick lifted her into his arms with more strength and more gentleness than Ansel ever had. She melted into him, her body relaxing for the first time in days.

Considering the wrath he showed, she almost expected the prince to give some grand speech or admonition. Something to put the queen in her place. He said nothing.

When the queen threw her axe at him, he ducked. At the same time, he opened a door.

Apparently Brannick only cared about one thing, and it had nothing to do with putting Queen Alessandra in her place.

He stepped into his swirling door with Blaz at his side, leaving the chaos of the Fairfrost throne room behind him.

Crisp rain and mossy trees had never smelled so good.

CHAPTER 26

Elora's head bounced against Brannick's chest each time he took a step. His arms enveloped her in a grip that made her feel safe. Sand seemed to line the inside of her eyelids, begging her to keep her eyes closed. The exhaustion plaguing every corner of her body begged for the same. The shimmery gold chains around her withered away. Watching them made her eyes close for just a moment.

She didn't know she had fallen asleep until her head bounced up with a start.

"Not yet." Brannick's voice had never been so soothing. "You will sleep soon but wait just a little longer."

Even though it wasn't a command, she forced her head up, eager to do as he asked. He had earned that much at least.

The swirling tunnel of brown, green, and black faded around her until the kitchen of Quintus's home came into view.

The prince's feet landed gently on the ground, but it still caused her head to bounce. She leaned into his chest, taking one last sniff before forcing herself to glance around.

Chloe and Grace rushed forward. They must have had rags and ointments ready because they were already wiping away blood and patting her gently.

"Set her in this chair here. I need to examine her for wounds." Chloe brushed her sister's hair out of her face and let out a little gasp. She had probably just discovered the blood caused from falling onto the marble floor.

It made sense that Elora's injuries needed to be tended to, but she was suddenly loath to leave the comfort of Brannick's arms.

Perhaps he read her mind, or maybe he just felt the same way, but the prince didn't set her down at all. He just sat in the chair with her on his lap. He faced her outward so that her sisters might reach her better.

Grace blushed at the sight.

Dropping a hand onto her hip, Chloe shot the prince with a glare. "I said to set her on the chair."

He responded in a near growl. "You can reach her fine from where she is."

More crimson burned across Grace's cheeks.

The tension broke when Lyren stepped forward. Her curls hung limp as she wrung her hands. "How... how is she?" The fae glanced toward Elora. "Can you speak?"

"Yes." Elora forced the word out her mouth, but it certainly didn't help that it came out as scratchy and dark as the black briars that filled Bitter Thorn.

A slight tremble moved across Lyren's chin before she clapped a hand over her mouth.

From Elora's side, a movement caught her eye. Vesper stood close enough to lay a hand on her arm. "You are safe now." Pain flickered in his eyes.

"Get me that pot. The one with the spiky herbs." Chloe's voice sounded more determined than it had in all her time in Faerie. Quintus moved toward the pot she indicated and quickly handed it to her.

Was it a good sign that Elora could barely feel her sisters work as they tended her wounds? At least it didn't hurt too badly, but the lack of pain probably indicated a deeper problem.

Shifting slightly, Brannick reached for her shoulder. He must have leaned closer because she could feel his breath on her neck. Even coming from him, it gave her the urge to shudder. "Ansel gave you these wounds."

It was more a statement than a question, but Elora nodded anyway.

Several fingers began touching her neck then. Even though she knew they came from her sisters, she still flinched. Grace's eyebrows pinched together, but she didn't stop cleaning blood away.

Chloe followed behind her, smearing something cool and soothing over the cuts that sliced across the neck. "Kaia made this ointment herself. Your wounds will heal in no time."

Elora's body still cringed at their touch, but her eyes were so heavy she could barely…

Her head snapped up as she awoke suddenly.

Brannick brushed featherlight fingers across her skin as he moved her collar back slightly. Every muscle in him stiffened. "How many times did he cut you?"

She had to gulp before she could answer. "I do not know." She gulped again. "I lost count."

The arm he had around her waist curled in closer as he clenched his jaw. "I will kill him."

Though her sisters continued working, the other fae in the room seemed to freeze. Quintus cleared his throat. "I know you technically killed King Huron, but that was different. He tried to kill you first, *and* he intended to kill half the fae in Faerie. But Ansel?"

Brannick's jaw clenched tighter as he looked up with a sneer. "I will *kill* him for this."

"My blood." Elora cleared her throat, trying to ignore the tears welling in her eyes. "Queen Alessandra..." The words stuck to her throat. She couldn't get them out.

The tension in the prince's muscles relaxed as he set his face closer to hers. "Your blood has the power of a fae without the magic to fight back."

Her eyelids dropped, still begging her to sleep. They snapped open when she turned toward him. "You knew this would happen?" Her stomach twisted. "Is that why you locked me in the bedroom before you went to Fairfrost?"

"Do not think of it anymore." His voice was so gentle compared to the growling earlier. "We still have a plan to overthrow the high queen. You have no need to worry."

An uncontrollable shiver shook through her entire body. "You do not understand." Tears poured down her cheeks. "She has four gemstones. Each one is filled with my power."

"You need to rest." He glanced toward Chloe.

Her blonde hair shifted as she gave a short nod.

Afterward, Brannick stood from the chair, lifting Elora close to his chest as he did. As he carried her toward her bedroom, he whispered gently. "Vesper, Quintus, Lyren, and I are traveling to Dustdune soon. The newly coronated Queen

Nerissa is inexperienced, and we already have Swiftsea on our side. We believe she will help us without much persuasion needed."

Soft blankets enveloped Elora as the prince set her onto a plush sleeping mat. Her eyes dropped from exhaustion, but she still noticed how his eyes swirled and burst with mesmerizing colors.

He leaned just close enough to squeeze her hand. "Sleep now. Everything will be fine."

She was asleep before he had even finished the final word.

When consciousness tickled into her mind again, it felt like several more days had passed. Nothing indicated that except she actually felt well rested. Her aches and pains didn't even throb. It took a few blinks to nudge the sleep out of her eyes.

She tried to sit up, and two heads jerked toward her immediately. On her left, Blaz was snuggled up to her side. His ears perked as he looked toward her.

Brannick sat against the wall on her right side. He had a piece of parchment with a list of rooms in Bitter Thorn Castle on it. A few of the rooms had been crossed off. He dropped the parchment to help her sit up properly. He pierced her with an unwavering gaze. "How do you feel?"

Her muscles creaked as she tried to stretch out her shoulders. "Better. How long did I sleep?"

A smile pricked at his lips.

"What?" Her question came out like an accusation, but a smile pricked at her lips too.

His grin curled upward as he brushed a few strands of hair out of her face. "There is no time in Faerie."

He got a glower in response. "I *meant*, have you gone to Dustdune already?"

"We can talk about that later." There was an edge to his response, though it wasn't directed at her.

Blaz repositioned himself until his head rested in her lap. She ran her fingers through his soft black fur, but then she reached for her hair.

"There is something I need to tell you." Brannick stared at his hands, which now sat in his lap. He gulped and glanced toward Blaz. The wolf dipped his head like a nod, and Brannick took a deep breath. "My mother saved my life."

Elora had been using her fingers to comb through a knot in her hair, but she stopped immediately. "While she was still High Queen?"

He continued speaking as if she hadn't spoken, but maybe it was just too painful to answer her question directly. "You already know the other courts overthrew my mother by giving power to High King Romany's crown. They stripped her of her title as High Queen, making her only a princess. But the crown of Bitter Thorn did not recognize their actions. The crown never reverted to the crown of a princess. Even worse, she could still wear the crown, which gave her enormous power. Faerie itself continued to recognize her as the high queen."

Raising an eyebrow, Elora went back to combing through the knot in her hair. "I imagine that did not go over well with the other rulers."

He snorted. "No, it did not. She and my father grew closer during that time. It is rare for fae to have children because a

227

baby is usually only conceived when another fae dies. Since fae are immortal, that does not happen very often."

With the knot loosened, she began stroking Blaz's fur once again. "So, no one expected it when you came along?"

"Exactly." Brannick shoved a hand through his shoulder-length hair. "They knew she would be weaker while pregnant, so that is when they chose to act."

Elora's nose wrinkled at the thought.

A sigh fell from Brannick's lips as he rubbed his forehead. "They poisoned me. They ensured that I would grow while in my mother's belly, but I would die immediately after my first few breaths."

Trembling filled Elora's fingers as she stroked Blaz's fur. They poisoned a baby? An *unborn* baby? Her heart clenched at the thought. She whispered her next words, almost unable to speak them. "But you are alive."

He nodded. "Only a life sacrifice could save me."

Elora swallowed hard as she met the prince's eyes. A life sacrifice, just like the sacrifice Elora had given when she used the balance shard. Something told her, Brannick's mother hadn't had the same outcome as her. "She *died* to save you?"

He dug both hands into his hair, but it didn't hide how his face twisted. "Yes. She made a choice and suffered for it. She lived long enough to take the crystal from her crown and fill it with my essence. Kaia said she tried to kiss my head, but she died before she could."

If his hands hadn't been in his hair, she would have reached for one of them. Instead, she placed a hand over his elbow. "Brannick."

"I never understood why I should be grateful for her choice." His hands dropped to his lap, leaving his hair poking in all directions. "I have lived all my life without her. She suffered in that one moment, but I have had to suffer always."

His chin dropped to his chest. "I have had to live all my life knowing I would never be as noble or as good as her."

Guilt rankled through Elora's limbs, but no matter how she tried, she still didn't regret plunging that shard into her chest. She knew Brannick was angry at her for doing it. She knew it hurt him because his mother had done the same thing for him. It didn't matter. If given the choice, she would have done it again. She gulped. "I wish I had known. I—"

He cut her off without ceremony. "When Tansy delivered your message..." His eyes closed as he took a breath. "When I finally realized what you had done..."

Lifting his head from her lap, Blaz gave her one last nuzzle. Then, he left the room without making a sound.

Brannick moved in closer, tucking a hair behind her ear. Every color in his eyes twisted and sparkled like they never had before. He took her hand and held it close to his chest. "I would have done anything to save you. My own life was nothing at all."

When he met her eyes, she could feel the look deep inside her. It curled around her. It set a fire within that would never extinguish.

He brushed a thumb along her jaw, pulling her closer. "I have been slow to learn, but I think I finally understand her choice." He leaned in until his nose nearly touched hers. His gaze captivated her like it never had before. "And yours."

Her heart had already bloomed even before his lips met hers, but when they did meet?

She could barely breathe.

There was so much more behind his kiss than just the feel of his lips. She could feel his muscles shift, his arms pull her closer, his heart beat in time with hers. The sensations trickled through her, leaving nothing untouched.

For a fae who supposedly knew nothing of emotions, he gave everything of himself and more. He had pulled her nearly onto his lap. Her head rested in the crook of his arm.

Whatever happened, she knew one thing for sure. His essence would never suffer again.

CHAPTER 27

No one noticed Elora as she emerged from her room the next morning. She snuck into the kitchen while everyone busied themselves with their own tasks. Apparently, breakfast was already over. She had explained everything about the gemstones the night before. Everyone looked properly horrified by it, but they all seemed to think the crown of Bitter Thorn would still overthrow Queen Alessandra like they planned.

Not wanting to deal with a barrage of sympathetic glances, Elora moved into the kitchen as quietly as she could. Her youngest sister stood over an empty pot. Maybe something of breakfast still remained.

Wisps of red hair danced across Grace's forehead. She tried to wipe them away, but it left a smudge of flour across her forehead. At the sight of her sister, she gave a small gasp but quickly followed it with a smile. She lifted a cloth and revealed a wooden tray carrying two biscuits and a pot of berry jam.

Elora gave a nod of gratitude as she took it.

Brannick sat at the table with Lyren, both of them arguing over words of some sort. They were trying to decide what to say to King Jackory when they went to Mistmount.

Turning into her youngest sister, Elora whispered, "Did they go to Dustdune already?"

Grace nodded as she used the cloth to wipe the remaining flour off her fingers. "Yes." Her lips tilted downward. "Queen Nerissa refused to help."

The words cut into Elora's heart. She sank onto the ground, nearly squeezing the air out of her biscuit. "The queen said *no?*"

Grace's little nose tucked down. "They thought it would be easy to convince Queen Nerissa. She was only just coronated." Her shoulders shivered. "They think she fears High Queen Alessandra more than she trusts Prince Brannick. And now they fear she will tell the high queen of their plans."

Scowling, Elora plopped a dollop of jam onto her crushed biscuit and tore a bite out of it. "Queen Nerissa will regret refusing." Her heart thumped. "Or maybe we will."

"We must not be so aggressive when we go to Mistmount." Lyren tapped the table. Both of her eyebrows were raised, giving off a look that showed she wouldn't back down. "You know he is not the type to align himself with anyone. He prefers neutrality."

Prince Brannick rubbed a hand down the side of his face as Blaz stood taller at his side. The prince shook his head. "But we have to be aggressive if we want him to help us. Obviously, our aggression wasn't enough with Queen Nerissa."

Lyren rolled her eyes before she responded. "It is easy for King Jackory to hide in his mountains and open spaces. The mountains provide a natural barrier between his court and the rest of Faerie. He does not have to get involved if he does not want to. We need a stronger argument."

The words sent an ache into Elora's heart. Lyren had a point.

The more they talked about Mistmount, the more Elora's gut roiled. Ansel lived in Mistmount. Anything about Mistmount reminded her of him, mostly how those chains had wrapped around her wrists and arms and how blood had dripped down her skin for days. And she'd been unable to do anything to stop it.

When another bite of biscuit crawled down her throat, she could barely even feel it.

In another corner of the room, Quintus and Chloe argued with each other. Quintus was crafting a harp meant for Grace. It was smaller than any harp they had ever used before, but since they lived in such a small house now, that was probably best anyway.

Either way, Quintus did not appreciate how Chloe watched over his shoulder. She suggested that he make the smallest string even smaller, which only made him shake his head. "I know what to do. I made the harp you all used in the castle you know."

Chloe put both hands on her hips tilting her head just so. "Why do you think I'm giving so many suggestions?"

Quintus's nose twitched before he answered. "Are you implying I made a mistake with that harp?"

Lifting one eyebrow, Chloe stood taller. "I'm not implying anything. I'm saying it outright. Now make the pillar bigger and start with a smaller string."

His black hair rustled as he shook his head. The strands of his hair were usually neat, but ever since living in the same house as Chloe, his hair grew more disheveled by the day.

Vesper stood staring out a window. He gazed over the landscape, as if it could provide an escape. "We've been sitting in this house too long."

No one stood near him, so it was unclear who he spoke to exactly, but maybe he only spoke to himself anyway.

Adjusting the ribbon on her wrist, Chloe turned toward him with a smirk. "What are you going to do out there? Fight with the demorogs?"

He shrugged. When he spoke again, it was loud enough to address the entire room. "Do you think the demorogs have nests?"

His question stopped Brannick and Lyren immediately. The prince tilted his head to the side. "Why?"

When Vesper turned away from the window, his eye sparked with a wild gleam. "I wonder if we could attack a nest and destroy a dozen of them at once."

Chuckling, Lyren touched the white sea flower in her hair. "Your need for adventure is going to kill you."

Turning back to the window, Vesper muttered under his breath. "That would be better than being cooped up all day."

Grace lifted a burlap sack, frowning at how it sagged. "We need more flour." She didn't speak as loud as Vesper, but it was still loud enough for everyone in the room to hear.

Elora stood up, brushing the crumbs off her skirt. "I'll get more flour for you."

The moment Elora spoke, everyone jerked their heads toward her. She had forgotten how she had snuck into the room. None of them had realized she was there.

Lyren pressed her painted blue fingernails to her lips. It didn't quite hide the smile that hid underneath them. "Do you even know where to get flour?"

The hairs on Elora's arms stood on end. She attempted to smile away her unease. "In a village somewhere? Or can we conjure more?"

A snicker escaped Vesper, but he tried to cover it up with a cough. "Only sprites can conjure food items."

Carving into the pillar of the small harp in his hands, Quintus shook his head. "How will *you* travel to a village when you cannot even open a door?

It took too much effort to keep her chin from trembling, so Elora turned away from them. She pretended to arrange the kitchen items in front of her. She still could not do magic. The truth of that hurt almost as much as the memories of those chains. But with all the talk of Mistmount, she had to get away.

Glancing over her shoulder, she shrugged. "Vesper will take me."

Vesper folded his arms over his chest. He threw his head back until his curls moved off his forehead. "You volunteer me without even asking? Just because I am your brother does not mean—"

"Would you rather stay here doing nothing?" Elora raised an eyebrow as she asked.

The hesitation painting his features dropped away while a light sparkled in his blue and gray eyes. "Yes. I will take Elora to the village."

"No." Brannick stood up from the table. Shadows curled around his cheek bones and jaw, making his features more striking than ever.

Lyren blinked twice.

Curling a fist, Elora glared at him. "No?"

The prince gave no hint of expression as he placed his hand on top of his wolf's head. "*I will take you to the village.*"

Now Lyren stood from the table, her black curls shaking. "We are in the middle of preparing for our visit to King Jackory."

"We will finish later." The prince waved her words off with his hand.

With a longing gaze toward the window, Vesper turned back with a sure expression. "I am still coming with you. If I stay in this house any longer, I will lose my mind."

Quintus announced that he would come too. Elora had a sneaking suspicion that Chloe's numerous suggestions had something to do with his desire to get away, but he claimed he merely needed more supplies.

The thought of more companions only eased the tension in Elora's chest. She wanted to get away, but she definitely didn't want to be alone. Hopefully, getting flour would the simplest adventure. Or better yet, no adventure at all.

CHAPTER

28

At Elora's side, Brannick opened a door. The smell of crisp rain and moss fluttered around her, but it felt heavier than usual too. Her feet moved slower, holding her back for some unknown reason.

They were just going to a village. Yes, Queen Alessandra had the gemstones with Elora's blood, but surely she hadn't used any of them yet. They would know. Then again, Brannick had all kinds of enchantments around Quintus's house, so maybe they wouldn't know.

Memories of chains and dripping blood twisted in Elora's mind. She wrapped her hand around the crook of Brannick's arm. Hopefully, he assumed she just wanted to be close to him. She *did* want to be close to him. But she also had fear slithering through her gut. Was it wrong to seek comfort?

The village looked more like a forest than she expected. Dwellings had been built not just next to the trees but *with* the trees. Trunks and branches curled to provide shelter. Where the trees didn't cover, moss and clay filled the gaps. Tables of wicker and branches stood in front of fae. All of them glanced around with their eyes shifting.

The fae did not barter with money. When Elora had first come to Bitter Thorn Castle, her brownie, Fifer, had explained no one used money in Faerie. Instead, they traded their skills and their magic.

Some fae were good at conjuring clothing while others excelled at conjuring pots and containers. Others still were skilled at making weapons.

Maybe it was just the recent memories of Ansel and Queen Alessandra that plagued Elora, but the fae seemed more suspicious than usual.

Brannick placed his hand over hers that still sat in the crook of his elbow. His long hair tickled her ear as he leaned toward her. "Something is not right."

She could feel it too, but she couldn't explain it any more than he had already. Thickness filled the air but with what she didn't know.

Quintus and Vesper walked ahead of them, each searching the wares on the tables.

With every step forward, the memory of chains tightened in on Elora. She struggled to keep her breathing even.

A small rock in the path caused Vesper to trip. He let out a hard gasp. Stumbling backward, he clutched his chest. When a villager spoke beside him, he clutched his chest even harder and stepped back again.

It was such a little thing to be startled by. He seemed to realize that, and yet, it still took a moment for him to breathe normally again. Quintus ignored him and moved toward a nearby table. He plucked a small tool from off the table, examining it closely. Next, he picked up a chisel.

The moment his fingers touched the sharp chisel, a nearby fae jumped toward him. "What are you doing with that? Do you intend to use it as a weapon?"

The angry villager produced a long spear from inside his magical pocket. He rapped the spear against Quintus's knuckles hard enough to send a smack through the air around them.

Quintus's eyebrows drew together so tightly, they were nearly touching. His teeth ground as he shoved the villager out of the way. "Are you trying to destroy my hands?" Even as he spoke, red welts appeared across Quintus's knuckles. Why had the villager assumed Quintus meant harm with chisel? He had only lifted the tool to examine it.

A shudder worked through Quintus's shoulders as he lifted his fists. "I am a craftsman. Without my hands, I am nothing."

Vesper curled his own fist and gestured toward the villagers nearby. "Look at how they are gathering." His jaw clenched. "They want to attack us."

Even just the word *attack* would never be the same as it had been before. Elora could feel chains around her body, even though they weren't there anymore. Her memories of being trapped inside Fairfrost Palace were too vivid. Her neck prickled as memories of Ansel's blade filled her mind. Her stomach turned in on itself because now she could feel his fingers on her neck and the smell of his sour breath in her face.

Pulling away from Brannick, she shoved her palms over her eyes. It did nothing to eradicate the memories that refused to leave.

"Elora." Brannick placed his hand at the small of her back. She didn't ignore it exactly, but she couldn't focus on it either.

Blaz nudged his head against her leg. Even that took effort to recognize.

No chains bound her, but she still felt trapped.

Brannick leaned closer. "Do you have the crystal? The one with my essence?"

He whispered low enough that no one else could hear. With the flood of memories inside her, it was difficult to comprehend his question. She forced one eye open, hoping to catch sight of him. Instead, she was met with the sight of a dozen angry villagers glaring straight at *her*.

Her eyes slammed shut again. Brannick slid his hand over her waist and tugged her a little closer to his chest. Blaz nuzzled into her leg again. For a moment, she could breathe.

"Yes, I have it." She always had it. Did he need her to hold it and think of his true self the way she had during his fight with Queen Alessandra during the testing?

Her eyes opened as she reached into her pocket. Perhaps opening them had been a mistake.

A wild voice pierced the air. "This is her fault." A fae wearing a gauzy green dress jabbed a finger toward Elora. "Chain her up, and we will bring her to High Queen Alessandra."

Whatever calm Elora had found a moment ago vanished like an extinguished candle flame. The villager with the spear whacked it against Quintus again, but this time it hit his shoulder. Quintus and Vesper shoved the fae away, but more emerged from the shadows of the forest. Their pointed ears looked sharp as they rushed toward Elora.

One managed to grab onto her shoulder. With a scream, she wrenched herself out of the fae's grip. Her heart was beating too fast. She ducked behind a wicker table. Her knees shook as she pressed them into the mossy ground.

Another fae leapt toward her. Flashing his teeth, Brannick jumped between her and the fae. He shoved the fae away and then sent a blast of silvery magic toward him.

Glancing over his shoulder, Brannick gave her a look that made the colors in his eyes shimmer. "Get the crystal."

Her hands trembled, but she reached into her pocket. He needed it. She knew he needed it. Why couldn't she make her hands stop shaking?

A fae came forward with a raised spear. How could the fae of Bitter Thorn attack their own prince? Perhaps they didn't know it was him. That seemed unlikely. After glancing up, she realized they had no intention of attacking the prince. They only wanted to attack *her*.

Brannick produced his own spear from inside his magical pocket. He shoved the nearest fae away. He waved his hand in a circle, which sent a blast of forest green wind to knock a group of fae off their feet.

Blaz growled at a fae who moved toward Elora. The wolf bared his fangs, but it didn't stop the fae from charging forward. She eyed Elora while her fists curled. Blaz growled hard this time, aggression dripping off his features.

Elora clutched the wicker table beside her, as if it might offer protection. Why were there tears welling in her eyes? She was not the type to be afraid. She was supposed to be the brave one. But her fingers shook so hard she could barely reach into her pocket. When she finally found her pocket, her thoughts twisted.

The palace.

Ansel.

Her heart beat too fast again. She could barely breathe.

The crystal sat at the bottom of her pocket. She squeezed it as soon as she touched it, hoping that was all she had to do.

It would have been easier if her shoulders didn't shake so much.

Brannick shoved fae with his spear. He sent enchantments out from his fingertips. It probably didn't even matter that she held the crystal now. He was too busy fighting.

Why wasn't *she* fighting?

Tears slipped from her eyes as she shook her head. This wasn't working. Maybe Brannick just needed to hold the crystal himself. She clearly couldn't help him in a state like this.

When she drew it out of her pocket, a fae leapt down from the tree nearest to her. He tackled her to the ground.

Her breath hitched as the crystal slipped from her fingers. Her heart leapt into her throat.

The crystal.

When she gasped, the fae attacking her followed her gaze. Wicked delight curled his lips upward as he reached for the light green stone.

Her fingers clenched into tight fists. Pushing herself off the ground, she reached for the weapon that was always at her hip. She swung her sword, finally able to ignore the fear that twisted through her.

The fae stepped back but still stared at the crystal. She swung again. With a gasp, the fae clutched his chest and took several steps back.

Elora's heart still beat too fast, but at least for one small moment, the fear of losing the crystal had been worse than the fear of being chained and imprisoned once again. She snatched the crystal off the ground. With it tight in her palm, she thought of Brannick, of his essence, of who he truly was.

Fear closed in on her once again, swift and unforgiving. Her hands trembled as more fae crept around in the shadows nearby. Blaz howled at the sight of them.

Brannick used his magic to tear a root from the ground. It whipped across the nearest fae, shoving them off their feet. He jumped in front of Elora, using one hand to push her behind his back.

The fae surrounding them hardly looked deterred.

But then, a golden enchantment erupted from Brannick's fingertips. It did not come out like a blast or even a canopy like he'd used to block the snowflakes in his castle. Instead, the enchantment filled the space around them like a thick fog.

Elora could only see through the enchantment if she looked closely. The scene ahead was not pleasant.

Tables had been overturned. Tools and weapons were strewn across the mossy ground. Still, something had changed the moment Brannick's enchantment released.

Fear continued to slither inside Elora, but not with the same tightness it had moments ago.

Vesper shook his head, staring at the fae at his feet. Vesper had punched the fae only moments earlier. Now, his curls seemed to go limp. "High Queen Alessandra manipulated our emotions again."

The villager who lay on the ground and had just been punched, stood up as if nothing had happened. The copper in the villager's light brown skin looked even more vivid under the light of the golden fog around him. "No, it cannot be that. We heard about the attack on Bitter Thorn Castle. We did not have any snowfall."

Brannick slipped an arm around Elora. He lifted his other hand into the air, as if touching it. He took in a long breath. When he spoke, it was not to the villager or Vesper or even Elora. He spoke to everyone. "High Queen Alessandra sent snow to the castle because she wanted us to know that attack came from her." He rubbed his thumb across one finger. "This

243

time, she did not want anyone to know they were being manipulated. She did not use snowflakes this time, but the fear around us still came from her."

The explanation was obvious once he said it. Fear had crippled Elora. Fear so strong she could barely move her hands and grab a crystal. Considering how Vesper had been so startled by that rock and how Quintus had been so quick to assume the fae wanted to destroy his hands, everyone appeared to have been affected.

Queen Alessandra had indeed attacked again. But how far had her fear seeped this time? Had she used one of the gemstones containing Elora's blood? Had the high queen sent fear through all of Faerie? Perhaps it was because they all knew it was likely that no one spoke a word.

Brannick stood even taller. He tugged Elora closer before speaking to everyone once again. "My enchantment will fade away soon. If you have protective enchantments around your homes already, they might protect you from this manipulation. Stay inside as much as possible. When you must leave, remember, your fear is being heightened by magic. The knowledge that you are being manipulated will not be enough to overrule the fear completely, but it will help."

Without another word, he strode forward and plucked a burlap bag off the mossy ground. A small dusting of flour poofed out around it. Then, he turned and opened a door. Quintus and Vesper moved toward it, leaving their destruction behind without a word.

Elora took Brannick's arm again as they stepped into his door. She lowered her voice to a whisper. "Why did the queen's magic affect me? I was the only one safe last time." Her chin trembled. "Why was I afraid too?"

He squeezed her hand. "Your memories are too fresh. Do not think of it too much." By now they were back in Quintus's home. Lyren raised an eyebrow at the moss stains on Vesper's knees.

Brannick clenched his jaw. "We must go to Mistmount as soon as possible. The longer we wait to overthrow High Queen Alessandra, the more control she will have over Faerie."

Perhaps Elora should have been motivated to help in some way, but she wasn't. All she could think about was how the queen's magic tore her apart just like it had every other fae.

If she couldn't even control her own emotions, what good was Elora to anyone? She had no magic, no control, and while afraid, even her sword skill had been mostly useless. For the first time, she worried Queen Alessandra might be too powerful to overthrow.

CHAPTER 29

Mountain air chilled Elora's bare arms. She wore a sage green dress with a tight bodice and several layers of skirts. Her sword bounced against the gauzy fabric while her hair rustled in the breeze. Gravel crunched under her feet.

The openness around her might have brought her comfort back when she craved freedom more than anything. Now it suffocated her as effectively as a pillow over her face.

She could barely breathe.

Brannick had formed a bubble of enchantment around their little group before they ever entered Mistmount. It protected them from the fear Queen Alessandra had put in the air all around Faerie. They knew with certainty now that the queen of Fairfrost had used her first gemstone.

Brannick's enchantment didn't protect Elora from everything, though.

They were still in Ansel's court.

Elora didn't need any of Queen Alessandra's magic to make her fingers tremble. Fear swirled inside her just because they were in Mistmount.

A small bird flew overhead, which caused her to jump back. She clutched her heart. Was she to fear even small birds now? Controlling her breath took too much effort.

When she dropped her hand to her side, Brannick took it in his. He glanced toward her, offering the smallest smile before he turned forward again.

Maybe it would have been better if she hadn't come. She had asked the prince if she could stay at Quintus's house with her sisters while the rest of them went to Mistmount. But all he had to do was look at her with his mesmerizing eyes that held every color in the realm. When he said that he did not wish to be parted from her, she agreed without even thinking.

She probably should have refused and stayed at Quintus's house anyway. But deep down, she knew she would do anything the prince asked.

A fae with leather shoes and a wide-brimmed hat stuck his head out of a cave. "This way," the fae whispered. He glanced at the open space around them before ducking deep into the cave.

Lyren tossed a few curls over her shoulder. "You are not alone anymore, Prince Brannick. Even the fae of Mistmount have had to abandon their castle. They must live in these caves because it is easier to block High Queen Alessandra's magic in a smaller area than inside an entire castle."

Pulling out a sketchpad, Quintus nodded absently. "They must miss their castle very much."

Vesper replied to that comment with a snort. "Nonsense. The fae of Mistmount love hiding away and avoiding others.

Caves are their favorite dwellings. They might never return to the castle even after we defeat High Queen Alessandra."

Defeat. The word was too big to comprehend at the moment. Elora gripped the hilt of her sword, but it didn't bring comfort the way it had so many times in the past. Would she ever feel safe again?

They passed through a smokey gray enchantment upon entering the cave. Brannick immediately took down his golden bubble of enchantment around them. The fae with the hat beckoned them forward.

Gemstones and slivers of gold twinkled out from the rocky walls of the cave. They passed a metal bucket holding a milky substance, but the stool next to it was empty. Or maybe the fae sitting on it had simply been glamoured to appear invisible.

The cave path twisted and opened up into a large area. King Jackory sat on a plaid sofa across from a female fae with striking violet eyes. A gray ceramic plate between them held various cheeses, crackers, and small slices of bread. There were even a few clusters of grapes and a pile of dried apricots.

King Jackory's braided crown glinted in the light of the sprites above. His eyebrow twitched at the sight of Brannick and the others. "We do not get many visitors in Mistmount."

It did not sound like an invitation to visit more often. In fact, it almost sounded like a reprimand.

Brannick didn't move, but he seemed taller. More regal. Maybe it was just the intense look in his eye. He raised an eyebrow. "As you well know, Faerie itself is at stake. This meeting is necessary."

Sighing, King Jackory took one last wedge of cheese from the plate. He then gestured that the fae across from him should take it away. While she moved, Brannick nudged Elora with his elbow and tilted his head inconspicuously toward the fae. "See if you can find out any information from the king's consort. I have heard that one is his favorite."

Though Elora nodded, she doubted she would learn anything. Brannick probably only gave her a task to help her feel more useful. Knowing that was likely the reason only made her feel less useful.

She should have stayed in Bitter Thorn.

Letting out her own sigh, Elora stepped toward the king's consort. The fae's violet eyes sparkled like gems. She wore a full maroon skirt and a loose white blouse. Her light hair was in two braids that were wrapped around her head like a crown. She gave Elora a wary look as she set the ceramic plate onto a small wooden cabinet with a glass door.

"I am Elora." Elora gave an expectant look at the fae in front of her, hoping to get a name in return.

Instead, the fae only raised both eyebrows. "Everyone knows who you are." But something in her face changed as she stared a moment longer. "You can call me Briella."

"I hope you did not have too much trouble when Queen Alessandra's magic fed fear into your court." A smile probably would have helped sell Elora's words, but she couldn't bring herself to do it.

The fae's violet eyes glistened as she lowered herself to the ground. "We live in a court of giants and cliffs. We know how to manage our fears."

Elora dropped to the ground, crossing her legs under the gauzy layers of her skirts. "Did the magic not come here, then?"

Lowering her eyes, Briella frowned. "Yes, it came here. It is everywhere in Faerie."

"Even in Fairfrost?"

A snort escaped Briella. "The fae in Fairfrost do not need any magic to make them fear. High Queen Alessandra does that well enough on her own."

Ice curled around Elora's spine, sending a shiver down it. Queen Alessandra did have a way of making people fear her. Elora knew that a little too well.

"You wish for me to give power to your crown?" King Jackory's voice carried across the room as he spoke in a voice loud enough for all to hear.

Brannick sat on the sofa across from the king. He spoke with no hesitation. "Yes."

King Jackory narrowed his eyes as he leaned forward. "Do you still have it?"

Glancing toward his wolf, they both gave each other a look that clearly communicated something. Brannick rolled his eyes. "Why does everyone ask me this? Do you think I have lost my own crown?"

The king responded with a shrug. "If it still looks the same as it did when your mother wore it, then perhaps it is not *your* crown at all."

Shifting his features into a glare, Brannick sat forward. "Will you help us or not?"

Elora turned back to the fae with violet eyes. "The sooner your king helps us, the sooner we can get rid of Queen Alessandra."

Briella stared back intensely. "There are some who say the high queen's magic will remain even after her death."

Sitting forward, Elora's eyes widened. "Even after her death? But surely her magic cannot last forever."

Now a devious smile flickered across Briella's face. "There are other ways to defeat her magic." The expression on her face closed as she waved a hand. "Maybe those ways will not be necessary though. We have heard rumors about fae in Noble Rose who can overcome the fear that floats around us. They carry roses that protect them, but they will not explain where the roses came from or how they work. We only know that it takes no magic or effort from the fae of Noble Rose to overcome the fear, as long as they carry those roses."

Across the room, Brannick stood from the sofa. The movement drew every eye in the room. "You expect me to enter a bargain where I must grant an unknown request *before* you give magic to my crown?"

King Jackory looked extremely relaxed as he sat back in the sofa. "I will tell you my request just before I give power to your crown. If you wish to refuse, you may."

The prince narrowed one eye. "But if I refuse, you will not give power to my crown?"

"Exactly." King Jackory's smirked as he relaxed even more.

Both the prince and his wolf let out a huff before Brannick flopped onto the sofa again. "Then why not tell me your request now? Why wait until just before you give power to my crown?"

King Jackory glanced across the room. His eyes locked onto Briella's for only a small moment before he turned back to the prince. "I have my reasons."

Brannick folded his arms. "I do not like agreeing to the unknown."

The king offered a shrug that very clearly said he knew the prince had no choice. "I propose a bargain…"

He continued to speak, but Elora's attention turned when fingers pushed the hair away from her ear. Elora sucked in a breath and jumped away from the touch.

Moving hair didn't bother her, but the fingers that moved it came close enough to Elora's neck that she could feel them.

The sensation was followed by the memory of knife slits and dripping blood.

Briella seemed completely unaware of how her action had affected her companion. Her eyes were only on Elora's ear. "It is true then. You have changed."

Thumping heart beats filled Elora's chest as she tried to control her breathing once again. Would these memories ever fade? She gulped. "I still cannot access my magic."

One of Briella's eyebrows raised. "You should not share that information. There are fae who would use it against you."

Elora nearly laughed out loud. Little did the fae know, that information already *had* been used against Elora... in the worst possible way.

Brannick huffed loud enough to draw Elora's attention again. His mouth twisted into a knot. "Very well. I agree to your bargain." He had never sounded so resigned. He stood from the sofa again, but his shoulders slumped forward. He gestured toward Vesper, Lyren, and Quintus, who stood on the other side of the room.

By the time he turned toward Elora, she was already moving toward him.

No matter how beautiful the sparkling caves were, and no matter how fresh the mountain air smelled, she wanted to leave Mistmount. Though maybe the prince had been wise after all for asking her to speak to Briella.

It intrigued her that fae from Noble Rose had a way to overcome High Queen Alessandra's magic. If Queen Nerissa had refused to help them before, she might be more willing if they could present her with the special roses that could overcome Queen Alessandra's magic.

They just had to find the roses first.

CHAPTER

30

Elora had only been to Noble Rose three times, but more than anything, she remembered the overwhelming scent of roses that filled High King Romany's throne room. Even during the tournament when she had been outside among the rolling hills, the smell of roses still lingered in the air.

That missing scent offered the first clue that things in Noble Rose had changed. When she stepped out of Brannick's door and onto a grassy hill, it wasn't the chill in the air or the frosted greenery that stole her attention first. It was the smell of nothing.

A light dusting of snow covered every surface of the once bright and warm landscape. Ice crystals formed over wooden trellises. Flowers wilted under the weight of frost and ice.

It smelled like snow and snow smelled like nothing. Coming from the rich scents of crisp rain and wet bark, the absence of smell would have been disconcerting on its own. But after expecting a strong scent of roses, the lack of smell hit that much harder.

Glancing to the side, she saw that she wasn't the only one surprised. Brannick scowled at the landscape before them. Blaz growled at the snow beneath his paws, as if that might help in some way.

"What happened here?" Elora shivered as she ran a hand over her bare arm. They had returned to Quintus's home just long enough to drop off the others. Brannick had then taken her to Noble Rose as soon as she mentioned the roses that could defeat Queen Alessandra's fear.

The scowl on the prince's face grew. "After High King Romany died without a successor, it fell to the next High Ruler to choose one. As you already know, High Queen Alessandra chose herself. She is now Queen of Noble Rose, and the land is changing to reflect that."

When Elora shivered again, Brannick conjured them both leather coats. The soft leather molded around her body, offering comfort and warmth.

At least one part of Noble Rose hadn't been touched yet. Glowing green lights floated overhead. The sprites seemed to fly slower than usual, but their lights still shined bright. Had they been affected by the fear in the land? Maybe that was the reason she hadn't seen Tansy since being in Fairfrost Palace.

A bubble of golden enchantment floated around Elora and Brannick to keep them protected from the fear. He gestured forward. "There is a village just ahead. We should be able to see if any of the fae have the roses Briella told you about."

At least Elora had worn her boots. The dusting of snow was light, but it still would have been unpleasant in softer shoes. She had considered asking to stay in Bitter Thorn but decided not to. Somehow, she knew the prince would just ask her to come, and she couldn't refuse that. She glanced toward him. "Are you going to take me along with you everywhere you go from now on?"

"Yes." He kept his eyes on the path ahead, but when silence met his response, he flicked his eyes toward her. "How else will I know that you are safe?"

Her fingers wrapped around her sword hilt as she scowled at the frosted ground. "I used to be able to protect myself, but the smallest things frighten me now." She huffed. "I cannot even use the magic I was given, and all of Faerie is suffering for it."

Not even Blaz glanced her way after that. The prince and his wolf marched forward in silence, leaving her to dwell on her own insignificance. What could she do except sigh?

She waved her hand in front of her, trying for the tenth time that day to open a door. It seemed like the easiest place to start, but nothing she had done so far had been successful. Her lips pulled downward. "How do you know where to open a door? Does it have to be somewhere you have been before? Can you open a door to a person instead of a place?"

"It must be a place, but it does not have to be somewhere you have been before." Tension curled around the prince's words. Or maybe he was just cold. The air *did* seem even chillier than before.

They had reached the outskirts of the village now. Quaint brick homes with white picket fences lined a cobblestone street. Fae carrying vases of wilting flowers or pouches darted across the streets. None of them held roses. The fear must have been affecting them because none of them stayed out in the open for long. Red and gold enchantments shimmered over each doorway.

"Perhaps we should try a different village," Elora suggested.

Brannick sighed. "We might have to, but I would like to speak to some of the fae first. They might be able to answer some questions."

Even the cobblestone street had a thin layer of ice covering it. Elora had to step carefully to keep herself from slipping. "King Huron opened a door inside my room in Bitter Thorn Castle. That is how I got to Dustdune to speak with him. How did he do that if he wasn't opening a door to me?"

With eyebrows knitted together, Brannick glanced toward her. He stood for a moment while he stared off in the distance. "He must have sent the door to your room in Bitter Thorn Castle. He probably assumed you would be in your room."

"But he could not have known which room was mine. Doors always seem to open in exactly the right place."

The prince shrugged. "That is how magic works. Faerie itself can sense your intention. The magic does what you want it to do. King Huron did not need to know exactly which room you were in. He just had to send the door to your room. Faerie did the rest."

They neared a small cottage with wilting lilacs that framed the doorway. Brannick opened the little gate in the picket fence before they moved up the path to the door.

Elora bit her bottom lip. "Is there ever a way to open a door to a person instead of a place?"

Brannick had lifted his fist to knock on the door, but he held it still instead. His head tilted to one side while he narrowed one eye. "I wonder…"

Before he could finish his thought, the door in front of them swung open. Two fae stood in the doorway, each holding a weapon high. The fae nearest to them gripped a long wooden handle with a mace on the end of it. She glared and jabbed the weapon toward Elora.

With a gasp, Elora jumped backward. The fae swung her mace again. The wings at Elora's back released with a pop. They lifted her high enough to avoid the weapon, but now she had also escaped the bubble of Brannick's enchantment.

Fear carved into her from all sides. Her wings beat harder. She flew higher into the sky, ragged breaths shaking through her. The prince was yelling at the fae. They'd dropped their weapons to the ground. Their heads bowed.

She clutched her chest. Her heart felt like it was being squeezed by an enormous hand. The door to the cottage slammed closed. Now the fae were nowhere to be seen.

It should have brought comfort.

But Elora still couldn't breathe.

Not enough.

She gasped, trying to gulp in air. Her wings continued to pull her higher into the air. She had never flown so high on her own, but perhaps it was no surprise that fear had given her the ability.

Finally, Brannick shot his bubble of enchantment upward until it enveloped her once again. Her heart still clenched, but at least her mind cleared. She took in a deep breath. Tears stung down her cheeks, freezing against her skin.

She continued to take deep breaths as she forced herself to the ground once again. Brannick pulled her into his arms the moment her boots hit the cobblestone path. More tears came, but those fell onto his shoulder. He held her tight, but it wasn't tight enough to keep her body from shuddering. Shivers shook through every part of her.

"How do I use my magic? How do I find it?" The words came out more in gasps than anything.

Brannick brought her close enough that he could whisper in her ear. "I cannot explain. You must discover it on your own."

A wracking sob shook through her. "I do not want to be helpless anymore. I have never felt…" She sucked in a breath. "I have never been afraid like this before. I want to go back to who I was before." Her head buried deeper in his chest. "Before he cut me open and stole my blood."

It took several moments before Brannick responded. He spoke carefully. Slowly. "If I close the portal to the mortal realm, you will not feel fear anymore."

Her head shot upward as she took a step backward. "The portal? If you close the portal, we will be cut off from *all* emotion. I would not just lose fear. I would feel nothing instead."

His eyes shimmered as stared at her. "Yes. Nothing." Again, he spoke the words slowly. Deliberately. He gazed into her eyes, trying to say more but without words. He reached for his heart, which was unnecessary. She understood.

With the portal closed, they would both lose the love they had found for each other.

She shook her head as she wiped away the remaining tears on her cheeks. "Do not close the portal." She shook her head again. "If I cannot forget what happened in Fairfrost Palace, how do I move past it?"

A breath of air escaped him that almost sounded like a chuckle. "I do not know. You are much more adept at handling emotions than I am."

He continued to gaze into her eyes. The look killed her. Pressing her lips together she turned away. Her arms folded over her stomach. "How can you still want me? I am not even the same person you fell in love with anymore."

The air went still around them. Using one hand, he lifted her chin upward. His eyes continued to shimmer with the same brilliance they always had. No, not the same. They were *more* brilliant. More mesmerizing than ever. The lightest smile played at his lips. "You have helped me through my worst. Did you think I would not do the same for you?"

He followed the words by placing a gentle kiss on her lips. The touch warmed her insides and expanded her heart. With his thumb, he stroked her chin. "Yes, you are different now, but different is not always bad."

Despite herself, she smiled at the words. How could he make her feel so full when she had been so broken?

The smile on his own face grew. "When change comes, you must embrace it. When magic calls, you must answer."

Her heart thumped at the sound of those words. It was almost like a puzzle piece finally clicked into place. More things might have fallen into place, but a glowing green light flew toward them. Her mind changed focus immediately.

Soon, Tansy hovered right in front of Elora's face. The sprite's body had grown tall enough that her pink dress fell to her knees again, but her face still looked gaunt. She glanced over her shoulder with a shudder before turning to the pair of them again. "You must hide at once."

CHAPTER 31

Clapping a hand to her mouth, Elora gasped. "Tansy." The word came out hushed. "I thought maybe something had happened to you. I haven't seen you in so long, and—"

"Hush." Tansy's pink dress sparkled as she glanced over her shoulder again. When she turned back, her pink and green eyes looked duller than before.

Brannick took a step closer to Elora. His eyebrow lifted at the sprite. "Why are you here?"

Ignoring him, Tansy closed her eyes and waved both arms in wide circles. After three rotations, she pushed her palms outward toward the two of them. No enchantment appeared from her fingertips, but Elora, Brannick, and even Blaz's bodies turned invisible. Even Brannick's golden enchantment turned invisible.

Elora opened her mouth with several questions hanging on her tongue.

Tansy's velvety hair shook as the sprite pressed a finger to her lips. "Do not make a sound."

Even before she finished speaking, a door opened just ahead of them on the cobblestone path. The glittery white swirls and icy breeze coming from the door showed exactly who had opened it.

Moments later, Queen Alessandra stepped out onto the cobblestone with her head high and her sharp crown even higher.

Another gasp ignited at the back of Elora's throat, but she forced herself to swallow it down. Brannick grabbed her hand and tugged her backward. They stepped into a frosty garden. Even invisible, it seemed like a good idea to get as far away as they could.

Queen Alessandra tipped her nose upward. "I command all fae of Noble Rose who can hear my voice to come hither."

Silence hung in the air. Elora moved onto her tiptoes to reach the prince's ear. She whispered in her softest voice possible. "Do they *have* to do it if she commands it?"

Brannick tugged her deeper into the frosty garden, but they were still within eyesight of the cobblestone path. "They do not, but she is High Queen now. She can punish them if they do not listen."

The fae seemed to realize that truth at the same moment Brannick whispered it into Elora's ear. Several doors creaked open. Most of the fae who stepped onto the cobblestone had trembling shoulders or hands.

Some held fists up, but they all jumped at even the slightest noises.

Queen Alessandra tapped her toe on the cobblestone, which made everyone gather around her a little faster. She looked down at them, as if they were nothing more than filth. "Who among you can conjure roses?"

Every fae on the street flinched at the sound of her voice. Most of them still shivered, but a few of them cocked their heads in disbelief.

The queen narrowed her eyes, which wasn't exactly a threat, but they all treated it as such. Several hands shot into the air.

She gestured toward the fae nearest to her who had risen a hand. "You. Conjure me enough roses for everyone in this crowd." She pushed back her cuticles while she waited, giving off an air of impatience.

Once the fae finished conjuring the roses, Queen Alessandra plucked one from the bunch. Her hand waved over it while she muttered under her breath.

The red in the petals melted away until a pure white rose was left behind. An iridescent glow surrounded it. The queen smirked.

She jabbed a thumb toward the next nearest fae. "You. Come here."

The fae's hands trembled more with each step he took toward the queen. He stumbled over his feet. But once he was an arm's length away, the tension in his shoulders vanished. He let out a breath that calmed his trembling hands right away. By the time he stood directly in front of the queen, his entire demeanor had relaxed.

She plastered a saccharine smile onto her face as she held the rose out to him. "Here. Feel my love. It will free you from the fear that plagues you."

The fae's eyes grew wide as he took the rose. His demeanor continued to shift. Once he held the rose in his hand, a smile of relief overtook him. "My queen." His voice came out breathless. "Thank you."

He swallowed and took a step backward as soon as the words escaped his lips. Fae rarely expressed gratitude. If they did, they were required to offer a gift in return for saying such a thing. It was clear the fae had not intended to speak the words, but he didn't seem to regret it either. He tapped his chin. "I will give you—"

Queen Alessandra held up a hand to stop him. Her voice came out lilting. "There is only one thing I ask of you. I ask that you will defend and protect me, especially from anyone who tries to hurt me or my reign."

The fae held the white rose close to his chest. "Of course, my queen. It would be my honor. I vow to defend and protect you, especially from anyone who tries to hurt you or your reign."

A wicked smile danced across the queen's face as she waved him away. Now she gestured toward the next nearest fae. "You. Come here."

Elora swallowed, but it did nothing to ease the lump in her throat. She watched helplessly as one by one the queen gave roses to the fae before her. Fear no longer plagued them, but they were far from free. They simply had a new emotion manipulating them now.

At some point, Elora had found Brannick's hand. She only noticed it when she squeezed it so tight that her fingers ached. But even after the queen finished and left through a door, Elora still could not bring herself to release her grip.

Each fae on the cobblestone street had a white rose, which they held close to their chests. They moved across the stone wistfully, almost unaware of anything around them.

"Is this not wonderful?" one fae said before bumping into a picket fence. The fae giggled at the sight of the fence, completely unbothered about accidentally running into it. "I can no longer feel any fear at all."

"We are free," another fae said.

But of course, they were anything but.

Tiny wings fluttered next to Elora's ear. "Back away slowly." Tansy's high voice came out tighter than usual.

Brannick continued to hold Elora's hand tight as they both backed away as quickly as they could without making too much noise. They moved until they had reached the bottom of the hill. Now they were out of sight of the fae with the roses.

Tansy waved a hand toward them, and suddenly, they were visible again. The sprite's face had fallen. "She is traveling all throughout the court to deliver those roses."

"The roses are full of her love." Elora didn't say it as a question exactly, but both Tansy and Brannick nodded anyway.

The prince shook his head. "During the testing, she vowed to High King Romany that all fae in his court would feel loved by her." At his side, his wolf let out a whimper. "Now they do, but she intends to use it as a weapon against anyone who tries to oppose her."

A brighter glow emanated from Tansy's wings. "Whatever plan you have must be enacted soon. She is growing too powerful to stop."

It didn't matter that Brannick's enchantment blocking fear was still in place. Elora's gut twisted all the same. The air around them thickened with horrifying possibilities.

Tension continued to mount when Tansy flew directly in front of Elora. "You will always be a friend to the sprites for how you rescued us from Fairfrost. We are still recovering, but I will visit you again as soon as I can."

The little sprite flew away with a sparkle of pink inside her green glow.

Elora's stomach dropped as she turned to her side. "What will you tell the others?"

Brannick's eyes still looked magical, but they weren't as shimmery as they had been before High Queen Alessandra's appearance. He gave a hard swallow that pressed against his necklace. "We must get Dustdune on our side. We do not have a chance to win otherwise. King Jackory has agreed to help us now. Surely, Queen Nerissa will not refuse again."

"We should leave as soon as we can." Elora crouched down and ran her fingers through Blaz's fur. "Now, even."

Brannick nodded, his face growing even more serious. "Yes. And when night falls tomorrow, we will gather the other rulers, including High Queen Alessandra. Once my crown has enough power, we can overthrow her for good."

Elora's heart clenched. "Even Queen Alessandra? Does she *have* to be there when you overthrow her?"

Before opening a door, Brannick's face fell. "Yes. The magic will not work unless she is nearby."

Pressing her face into Blaz's black fur, Elora shuddered. Fear continued to writhe inside her with no care for how little she could stand it.

But it didn't matter. Fear was a part of her now, and she would embrace the change.

CHAPTER
32

Dry heat clung to Elora's mouth, and sand tickled her nose. The warmth of Dustdune accosted her, mostly due to the leather coat she still wore. After shrugging it off, her bare arms and gauzy dress could appreciate the heat much more.

Brannick took her coat and the extra one he had conjured for himself and tucked them both into his magical pocket. She still had no idea how Faerie pockets could hold so many things and yet take up no space at all. Once she learned to use her magic, the first thing she would do was find her own magical pocket and stuff it with whatever useless items she could find.

They traipsed across orange sand dunes until they reached the gilded doors of Dustdune Castle. Once inside, Elora brushed away the layer of sand that had clung to her dress. "Maybe we should have gone back to get the others. Lyren is much better with words than either of us. What if we need her?"

Brushing sand off his shirt, Brannick shrugged. "We will be more approachable with just the two of us."

She lifted one eyebrow. "Maybe that is true, but I know you simply did not want to wait for the others."

A swift but genuine smile fell across his lips. "You are beginning to detect deception as well as a fae." He ran a hand through his glossy hair, shaking out a few grains of sand. "Your magic is brewing."

His words had a way of lifting her spirits even when things felt dire. She shook out her own hair and tried to pretend his words hadn't warmed her down to her toes. The golden bubble of enchantment continued to glow around them. They did not meet any servants or fae on their way to the throne room, though.

Once they entered the grand room, they saw how a silvery enchantment partitioned off a corner of the room. Queen Nerissa's dark knee-length hair swept over one shoulder. She knelt on the ground, working with different fibers to weave a rug of some sort. Two guards stood near, but they didn't speak to her. A light sheen of sweat glistened along her hairline. The silver enchantment around her made the golden ornaments in her hair sparkle.

Once Elora and Brannick stepped through the enchantment, Queen Nerissa began to speak. She didn't lift her eyes from the rug on her lap. "Prince Brannick. I did not know if you would return." Her eyes flicked upward. At the sight of Blaz, her nose twitched. When she spoke again, her voice had an edge to it. "And with your wolf again I see."

"He will not hurt you." Brannick set his hand on top of Blaz's head.

Elora had a neutral opinion of Queen Nerissa up until that point, but once she looked at Blaz with disdain, that quickly turned downward. She didn't like this queen, Elora decided.

The queen mirrored that sentiment when she noticed Elora. Queen Nerissa's nose twitched again. "Ah, and you have brought the infamous mortal."

Elora's hand itched to curl into a fist. She grabbed her sword hilt instead. "I am fae now."

Queen Nerissa spared only a small glance before she looked back at her rug again. "So I have heard."

Brannick cleared his throat. "I ask again for your support. Will you give power to the crown of Bitter Thorn so that we may overthrow High Queen Alessandra?"

"You killed my father." Her eyes never left the rug, but she still managed to send her words out like jabs.

A muscle twitched in Brannick's shoulder as he folded his arms over his chest. "He tried to kill half the fae in Faerie."

Her fingers pulled a piece of the rug back before attempting to weave it into a small opening. "That does not change what you did."

When Elora scoffed, every eye turned toward her. She raised both eyebrows at the queen. "Did you even care for your father?"

Queen Nerissa blinked twice before she plucked one of the golden ornaments from her hair. "No." She turned the piece on its side and then used it to force a piece of the rug through the small opening. "He sent me away while I was young. He never liked me, and I suppose I always felt the same about him."

Elora spoke again but threw softness into her tone. "How has your court fared since the attack of Queen Alessandra's fear?"

The queen's fingers froze as she glanced up at Elora. She stared with a different expression than before. Perhaps she was realizing Elora was not who she had expected. The thought sent guilt crawling down Elora's spine. Perhaps she had been too quick to judge the queen as well.

A touch of vulnerability snuck into Queen Nerissa's features when she turned back to the rug. "Not well," she said, almost under her breath.

Brannick took a step forward. "Then you must wish to rid Faerie of her manipulation as much as we do."

Both the rug and the hair ornament dropped from Queen Nerissa's hands as she jumped to her feet. "I do not understand why you need my help. Can you not just steal her crown and take it for yourself? Then *you* would be High Ruler of Faerie."

"That is not…" Brannick blinked and shook his head. Whatever he was about to say, he swallowed it down. He was probably just trying to find a more diplomatic way to phrase his words. "A crown only accepts one ruler at a time. Once a ruler places a crown on their head, it is bonded to them. No one can ever wear that crown and access the power within it until that ruler dies."

The queen gestured toward one of the nearby guards. "My advisors tell me a ruler may also give up their claim to the crown. By doing so, the rule is transferred to another, but the first does not have to be dead."

Again, Brannick swallowed, looking very much like he was carefully measuring each of his words. "That is true." He raised an eyebrow. "But High Queen Alessandra would never give up her claim to the crown. The only way to overthrow her is with a more powerful crown. No one will be able to defeat her or even kill her until she is no longer High Queen."

Queen Nerissa narrowed both of her eyes to tiny slits. "Someone killed High King Romany."

269

Brannick pinched the bridge of his nose before he answered. "Prince Fabian gave his father the poison unknowingly. He thought it was a strength elixir. If he had intentionally tried to kill High King Romany, the crown would have helped the high king sense it. I am certain High Queen Alessandra would see through such trickery anyway. The only way to overthrow her is with a more powerful crown."

Scowling, Queen Nerissa glanced to the side. "Do you have the crown? I have heard—"

"Would I bother asking for your support if I did not even have the crown?" Brannick's fingers curled into fists as he leaned forward.

The Dustdune queen stared back with an even expression. "I require a bargain if I am to help you."

Elora reached for a lock of her hair, hating how Brannick's face fell.

The colors in his eyes dimmed as he let out a heavy sigh. "Very well."

Queen Nerissa plucked the golden ornament off the ground and fastened it back into her dark hair. "You must grant me a request before I give power to your crown."

Brannick lifted an eyebrow. "What request?"

She continued fiddling with her hair ornament. "I will reveal it just before I give power to your crown."

Elora placed a hand on her hip while she gripped her sword hilt with her other hand. "That sounds familiar."

"Does it?" Nothing about Queen Nerissa's voice sounded innocent.

Elora's eyes narrowed. "King Jackory said the same thing."

The queen nodded. "Indeed. He suggested the request I plan to make."

A tiny huff escaped Brannick's nose. "And you will not tell me the request now?"

"No."

He huffed louder this time. "Fine."

She proposed the bargain, which he agreed to immediately, but his shoulders drooped as he did. The colors in his eyes dulled again, and even his muscles looked weaker than usual.

After agreeing to the bargain, he said nothing. He just turned and walked away. He only slowed long enough for Elora to catch up to him. Once she did, he opened a door.

Quintus's home looked exactly like it had when they had left, but nothing felt the same anymore.

Brannick flopped onto the nearest chair and began explaining about the roses from Queen Alessandra.

Vesper stood at the window. He tore his gaze away once the prince explained how the fae each said *thank you* when they received a rose and then proceeded to vow that they would protect the high queen.

Vesper's mouth dropped. "She is using love to build an army."

Brannick shoved two hands through his hair, disheveling the long strands. "It will be a strong army too. We must enact our plan when night falls tomorrow. We cannot wait any longer."

Lyren strummed her painted blue fingernails on the table. "What about Dustdune? I do not think your crown will be strong enough without Queen Nerissa's power."

Elora cringed as she dropped into the nearest empty chair. "We already got Queen Nerissa's support."

Lifting an eyebrow, Lyren glanced between Elora and Brannick. "Then why do both of you look displeased?"

Maybe a groan would ease the tension in Elora's chest. It didn't. She scowled instead. "She forced Brannick into a bargain where he must grant an unknown request just before she will give power to his crown."

271

The scratching of Quintus's pencil across his sketchpad stopped. His eyes flicked upward. "That sounds like the bargain you made with King Jackory."

Brannick buried his face in his hands. "I do not want to discuss that."

Elora frowned. "She admitted that she spoke to King Jackory about it, which seems ominous, but what can we do?" With a turn, she surveyed the room. "Where are my sisters?"

Lyren pressed her lips together to hide a smile, but Vesper did nothing to hide his chuckle. Quintus glared at his sketchpad. His mouth twisted before he finally answered. "Chloe got mad at me for trying to enchant her voice to be quieter. Even though it did not work, she still yelled at me like I had really done it. Then she took Grace into their room and insisted they would not come out until I learned to treat them with more respect."

The urge to chuckle bubbled at the back of Elora's throat. She tried to suppress it because Quintus looked so upset, but that only made it more difficult.

Without warning, Brannick stood from the table. "We need to finalize our plans, but first, I must return to Bitter Thorn Castle for..." He forced out a very unnatural cough and looked at Blaz. "Something."

"I will come with you." Elora practically jumped out of her chair to get to his side before he could open a door.

For the first time since her return from Fairfrost Palace, he did not look eager to bring her along. It didn't matter. If he tried to argue, she would simply insist. He didn't know it yet, but he needed her. Because she realized she knew exactly what he needed to find.

CHAPTER

33

Thorns twisted through cracks in the walls of Bitter Thorn Castle. On the ground, piles of thorns sat as high as Elora's knees. A thick layer of wet snow weighed the thorns down. Her boots crunched over them, but a few points still found her legs. The scent of decay overpowered any hint of moss or rain that usually filled the castle walls. The ever-falling and melting snow probably only made it worse.

When a swarm of demorogs hurtled toward them, Brannick sent a blast of silvery enchantment from his fingertips. The demorogs gave off a high-pitched whistling sound as they tried to break through the magical wall he had just created. This time, he had been careful to create an enchantment around them that would protect them from the fear in the air *and* the snowflakes all around.

A squeal sounded from around a corner behind them. Thumping footsteps followed the sound, and soon, a figure came into view. The brownie held a short spear pointed upward.

Fifer had traded his normal bare feet for thick swaths of leather wrapped tightly around his feet and legs. The brownie's suede shirt and pants had slices cut through them and several worn spots that faded into holes. His bulbous chin and spindly fingers looked the same as ever, but his floppy ears hung limp down to his shoulders.

At the sight of them, Fifer's big eyes grew even wider. "My prince." He swallowed. "I hope nothing is wrong."

Brannick rested a hand on his wolf's head before he answered. "You stayed? You did not have to stay."

Fifer let out a laugh and lowered his spear. "Nonsense. Who else would stop the demorogs from tearing our castle apart?"

He stepped into the bubble of enchantment that protected them from Queen Alessandra's magic. A long sigh escaped his mouth when he did. "I can create my own enchantments, but I usually lower them while fighting the demorogs. It is simply too difficult to keep them in place while fighting."

Both Brannick and Blaz lifted their heads in unison. They seemed to have the same remarkable idea at the same moment. The prince glanced down at the brownie. "Could you create an enchantment that will protect both you and Elora while I go to another part of the castle?"

Elora whipped around to face him. "Where are you going?"

"To my mother's room." His tone was a little *too* innocent. "The thorns are much worse in there. I would not want you to have to fight through them."

Before she could protest, he turned back to Fifer with an expectant look.

The brownie created his own enchantment, which was more green than gold. Brannick immediately turned and left them in the hallway while he opened the door to the room next to his own.

Both of Fifer's eyes narrowed. "He left you quite eagerly."

She waved away the words with one hand, turning down an adjoining hallway. "It does not matter. I know what he is looking for, and it is not in his mother's room. Apparently, he does not want anyone, even me, to know he cannot find it."

Hiking up her skirt, she began to trudge through the piles of snowy thorns. Two large doors stood at the center of the hallway. Bundles of thorns twisted around the gold handles of the throne room. Using her sword, she sliced them away.

A confused expression fell across Fifer's face, but he did not say anything when she pushed open the doors to the throne room.

If possible, the smell of decay was even worse. She pressed her face into her elbow, using it to block some of the smell. Soon, she knelt down in front of the throne, and pushed away the thorns that curled at the side of it.

When she grabbed the object, it was still invisible. Once she brought it closer to her face, the glamour around it vanished.

A crown of branches and obsidian sat in her hand.

It looked exactly as she remembered it. The tines stretched toward the ceiling looking regal, but they looked as wild as something formed by nature as well. An empty setting in the center of the crown sat waiting for the crystal it had once held. As before, she knew instinctively that the crystal in her pocket containing Brannick's essence was the one that used to fill that setting.

No dust lingered on the obsidian. Even the branches looked like they had only just been cut from a tree to form the crown. The other crowns in Faerie had their own beauty, but nothing compared to this breathtaking display of nature before her.

She moved the crown even closer to her face, hoping to examine the small purple gems she hadn't noticed the first time. As she moved it closer, the gems let out a burst of sparkles.

Fifer clapped a hand over his mouth and took several steps backward.

The entire crown began popping with energy. Sparkles burst out around it, showering Elora's hand.

"The crown..." Fifer grabbed onto one of his limp ears. "It has chosen you."

Such words might have caused a crisis within her, except a swarm of demorogs shrieked in the hallway. They broke down the doors, each trying to be the first to enter the throne room.

Without thinking, Elora drew her sword. She continued to grip the crown tight in her other hand, somehow ignoring the sparkles that still burst from it.

Her chest tightened at the sight of the demorogs. Her hands shook. Maybe fear would always be a part of her now, but she would not cower anymore. Instead, she embraced the change.

She swung her sword, cutting away the first demorog's wing. Her sword glowed when it met the thorny creature. The glow grew brighter as she sliced and jabbed at the remaining demorogs.

Magic.

The thought pierced her as surely as her blade pierced the demorogs. They withered to the ground, turning to dust at her feet. As she swung her sword, magic even began to trail off her hand in waves. It encased her sword, lending even more power to her blows.

Only a few breaths had passed through her before all the demorogs lay at her feet in piles of ash. She stared down at the sword in her hand, which still gave off a purple glow. "I have never accessed my magic like that before."

Fifer waded through the snowy thorns on the throne room floor to stand at her side. He gestured toward the crown in her hand, which still gave off bursts of sparkles. "That is the power of the crown. For now, it will only give you power while you touch it, but if you place it on your head, that power will stay forever."

Maybe her mind should have twisted at the thought. Instead, it glowed. The feeling enveloped her too completely to ignore. She swallowed and glanced down at the brownie. "Would you tell Kaia I need to speak with her?"

He gave a pointed glance at the crown. When he turned his gaze upward, his ears perked up. "The crown has chosen you as one who is worthy. It would not be wrong for you to wear it." He did not speak again before leaving.

His enchantment shimmered around him as he disappeared through the throne room doors. With only a wave of her hand, she created an enchantment of her own to protect herself from the fear in the air.

Magic danced on her fingertips. It filled her with a strength she had never known.

She thought her decision might be easier with the brownie gone, but that proved to be untrue. The crown had *chosen* her. If she put it on, *she* could be Queen of Bitter Thorn. She would finally have access to the magic that belonged to her now that she was fae.

She deserved the magic, didn't she? Faerie itself had given it to her. And she had endured the trauma of reliving all her emotions in order to get it. She would never be helpless again. She would be as powerful as when Brannick first met her. Even *more* powerful.

He would have a true reason to love her again.

Memories of knife slits and chains and dripping blood accosted her mind, but they didn't hurt so much this time. If she had the power of the crown, Ansel could never touch her again.

And they could still enact all the rest of their plan. The other rulers only ever promised to give power to the crown of Bitter Thorn. They never said the crown would have to go to Brannick. She and the prince could be together, but she would be ruler instead of him.

That wasn't so different from the life she already imagined.

Her fingers seemed to move of their own accord as she lifted the crown higher. Soon, it hovered just over her head. Only a tiny drop and the crown would be bonded to her. Still, it hovered instead of dropping. Questions filled her mind, though she tried to ignore them.

Would Brannick forgive her if she took his crown? Would their love survive such betrayal?

Her fingers raised the crown a little farther from her head.

Could *she* live with herself after such betrayal?

The memories of Fairfrost Palace hit her again, even stronger than before. Her stomach churned as if someone had jabbed an elbow into it. Fear slithered inside her like it never had before. The enchantment blocking out the fear withered away.

If she ever saw Ansel again, she would fight. But she had fought inside Fairfrost Palace. She had fought and lost. Her own skills had not been enough to save herself.

She brought the crown closer to her head.

If the crown had chosen her, didn't she deserve it anyway? How could she refuse such protection? Such power?

A new memory flitted through her. Brannick had worn a light smile as he stroked her cheek. He had spoken plainly, so his meaning would be clear. *You have been there for me through my worst. Did you think I would not do the same for you?*

Another memory flowed in immediately after. This time, Elora's own words filled her mind. Words she had spoken to Queen Alessandra. *Love is not something you earn once and never fight for again.*

Sucking in a deep breath, she transferred the crown to one hand and pulled it down to her side. All her life she had dreamed of adventure and freedom. Love was always an afterthought.

But it turned out, love meant more to her than anything else. It even meant more than the ability to never know fear.

Yes, she was different now. Fear had settled inside her in a way that might never be undone. But she *didn't* want to go back to way she had been before. She had gained too much to risk losing it.

Holding the crown behind her back, she left the throne room to find Brannick.

Just outside the door, a swirling tunnel met her. Kaia stepped through it. An enchantment surrounded her that quickly enveloped Elora as well. The dryad's dark skin looked fresh. Her emerald hair looked even longer than it had ever been. Her brown and green eyes turned bright as she offered a smile. "I may be able to help you find your magic. It could make up for how I led to your parents' deaths."

Elora nearly chuckled as she tightened her grip on the crown. She already had a way to access her magic, but she was still willing to give it up. This choice was even easier than the first. "I want my memories back."

Kaia twisted a strand of hair over one of her fingers. "You and Prince Brannick are connected now. If your memories return, his might return as well."

"Would that be so bad?" Elora's words came out strained.

With a gulp, Kaia stepped forward. "The prince's escape from Fairfrost was his first real victory. He *must* believe he did that on his own or he will lose all his confidence."

Elora turned away with a huff. "He might not lose all of it."

"Do you want to take that chance right now?" Kaia put her hands on her hips. "He is on the verge of overthrowing High Queen Alessandra. Do you want to take that chance now when something so important to Faerie is at stake?"

Biting her bottom lip, Elora turned her eyes downward. "We can do it afterward then, but my stance has not changed." She looked up again, even more determined than ever. "I want my memories back."

Brannick popped his head around the corner, glancing between Elora and Kaia a few times. "Did you say *memories?*"

CHAPTER

34

In a castle filled with dangerous snowflakes and creatures made of thorns, Elora never expected to be more afraid of an overheard conversation. How much had Brannick heard? Did he know she had helped him escape Fairfrost Palace and that both of them had since lost those memories?

Based on the ease with which he held himself, it didn't seem likely. He had probably only heard the last sentence or two and only knew that Elora had memories she wanted back.

Either way, his eyebrows drew more tightly together the longer the silence stretched around them.

At last, Kaia swept a portion of emerald hair behind one shoulder. "My prince." She nodded. "Soren has gathered forces as you suggested. They will be ready when you need them."

He folded his arms over his chest. "You are changing the subject. Did you—"

Before he could ask another question, Elora pulled the crown out from behind her back. She held it out to him, which sucked every remaining word from his lips.

His eyes widened. "How…"

She quirked an eyebrow upward. "You could have told me you still needed it. I would have told you I knew exactly where it was."

Both of his arms fell to his sides while he continued to gaze at the crown. "How did you know I needed it?"

"Mostly because you never answered directly whenever the other rulers asked if you had it." She smirked as she handed to him. "I really am getting better at recognizing deception."

His eyes widened as he took the crown into his hands. It let off a shower of sage green sparks the moment he touched it.

The sight of them sent a silent sigh of relief to her lips. The crown had chosen him too. She gestured toward it. "We have everything we need now. We should get back and finalize our plans."

"Yes." The prince's eyes stared off as he carefully tucked the crown into his magical pocket. Blaz nudged his head against the prince's leg. The movement caused Brannick to shake his head. "The memories." He narrowed his eyes at Kaia. "We will discuss them later."

Kaia gave another nod. "Yes, my prince. Send word when you need Soren's forces. They will be ready for you."

He opened a door, and Elora followed after him.

When they returned to Quintus's home, Chloe and Grace sat in the kitchen with the others. Their faces had turned pale.

Chloe jumped up from her chair at the sight of her oldest sister. Her face was nearly as light as her blonde hair. She clasped her oldest sister's hand with both of hers. "Elora, you will stay here with Grace and me when the others try to overthrow High Queen Alessandra, right?"

"What?" Elora blinked before answering.

Tears welled in Grace's eyes as she too came forward to grab her sister's hand. Her chin trembled through each of her words. "It's going to be so dangerous."

"I…" Before her time in Fairfrost Palace, Elora would have laughed at their suggestion. She would have been more afraid of being cooped up than fighting in some battle. But now?

"You may stay here if you choose." Brannick did not look at her as he lowered himself into the nearest chair.

Apparently, that was all she needed. A choice. That was something she never gotten while Ansel and Queen Alessandra had her trapped.

Tugging her sisters close, Elora held them as tight as she could. "I will go with the others." Both of her sisters whimpered. "But I will be careful too."

Even while holding her sisters tight, she still saw the hint of a smile that passed over Brannick's lips at the sound of her words.

Her sisters didn't protest as she led them back to the table. They sat on either side of her, still each holding one of her hands.

Vesper's eyes sparked as he looked up at the rest of them. "We can ambush High Queen Alessandra in Noble Rose."

Everyone glanced toward him, and the spark in his eyes grew. "She has been traveling to different villages in Noble Rose, has she not? We should bring our forces and ambush her there. She has great power as High Queen of Faerie, but with enough of us, we should be able to overpower her."

Chewing her bottom lip, Lyren strummed her nails on the table. "That will not work. We have no idea which villages she has already visited and which she has not."

"The sprites know." Elora sat up straight even when the other fae looked at her like she had turned into a troll.

Quintus rolled his eyes before glancing back to his sketchpad. "They will not share their knowledge with us."

Elora smacked her palms against the table as she leaned forward. "The sprites want Queen Alessandra overthrown more than anyone. They *will* help us." She glanced toward the floating green lights above them. "If you know which village we should go to, please tell us as soon as you can."

Brannick rubbed his wolf behind the ears as he nodded toward her. The other fae continued to look at her like she had turned into a troll, but they didn't say anything about her speaking to the sprites.

Adjusting the sea flower in her hair, Lyren glanced toward Brannick. "I will gather the other rulers and bring them to Noble Rose while the rest of you capture the high queen."

Brannick sat forward. "We need every soldier we can obtain. Will Queen Noelani bring any of her forces to help us?"

Lyren's lips pressed together before she answered. "I will bring as many as she will spare."

He rubbed Blaz's ears a little harder than usual. "High Queen Alessandra's magic is great. We must act now before she grows even stronger, but we cannot underestimate her in this fight." The air grew still as he took in a breath. "She is High Queen of Faerie now. It will be more difficult than ever to defeat her."

Chloe jabbed her elbow into Quintus's side. Instead of acting surprised, he shushed her. Her eyes narrowed before she gave a deliberate clearing of her throat.

Sitting forward to get a better view of her middle sister, Grace gestured. "Chloe had an idea, but Quintus says it will never work."

With a nod, Chloe placed her hands delicately into her lap. "Iron is a fae weakness, right? And we have the high queen's talismans, don't we? Can't you use them against her?"

Quintus used the end of his pencil to scratch his head. "The talismans will harm us as much as they harm her."

Chloe raised an eyebrow. "And didn't you craft a device that would help with that?"

Eyes widened around the table, but Quintus only sank deeper into his chair. "It would never work."

Chloe's mouth pinched into a knot. "Why not?"

"It…" He trailed off. He scratched his head even faster with his pencil. Finally, he gulped. "It requires a mortal to carry it. If fae handle the device, the iron will destroy them." His jaw set as he glanced toward Chloe. "I did not think you would be willing to join the fight with us."

The little color remaining in Chloe's face drained. Now her skin turned even lighter than her hair. She slumped back into her chair. "Oh."

Both Lyren and Vesper looked at her like they wanted to change her mind, which Elora didn't like at all. She sat up straighter, drawing everyone's eyes toward her. "Maybe I could handle the device."

Quintus rolled his eyes as he stuffed his pencil back into his coat. "Iron still affects you, even if you cannot use your magic yet."

Unfortunately, she knew from experience that he spoke the truth about that.

The blue and gray in Vesper's eyes shined bright as he sat forward. "We might not need the talismans. The first few moments of an ambush are the most important."

Brannick nodded. "Vesper is right. The longer we take to capture High Queen Alessandra, the less chance we have of succeeding. We do not need any fancy devices. We will catch her off guard and then surround her with our forces and with as many enchantments as possible. She will likely have the power to break through them eventually, but if the other rulers are there, they can give power to the crown of Bitter Thorn before she has a chance to escape."

Vesper bounced on his chair, his eyes growing wild. "Finally, a chance for some real fun."

"Elora." Brannick spoke her name loud enough for everyone to hear, but it was still clear that he said it just for her. He tipped his head toward the doorway. "I need to speak with you."

She followed after him without question while the others continued to discuss the specifics of their plans. The prince opened the door to the second room in the house, the one he and Quintus had been sleeping in.

He shut the door once she entered the room. Blaz settled onto the ground next to Elora, lowering his head onto her foot.

Brannick reached into his pocket and pulled out the crown. He only glanced at it for a moment before pushing it back into his pocket once again.

"Oh." Elora reached into her own pocket and pulled out the crystal with Brannick's essence. "You must need this."

He glanced at it for only a moment before closing her fingers over it. "Faerie led you to that crystal. It is yours now."

Her head cocked to the side. "Will you leave the front of the crown empty then?"

286

"No." He dug his hand into his pocket once again. "A stone must sit in the crown in order to use it properly, but I had another idea."

Just as he finished speaking, he pulled a clear crystal from his pocket. It sparkled in the light as it sat on his palm. "You asked if it is possible to open a door to a person instead of a place."

"Is it?" She stared at the crystal as she asked.

"I do not know for sure, but if a strong connection exists between two fae, it might be enough to know that fae's location. The door must still open to a place, but the connection would make it possible to always know the correct place."

Her eyes finally left the crystal to look at the prince. The colors in his eyes swirled even faster than usual. "Can you create such a connection?"

He gestured toward the sage green crystal in her hand. "You hold a piece of my essence. With magic, you could use it to sense the location of the rest of my essence."

She pressed a hand to her mouth as her jaw dropped. Though the crystal had always felt special, it gave off an even stronger energy now.

Gulping, Brannick glanced down at the ground. "I thought it might be fitting if I carry a piece of your essence as well."

Elora took a step back. Every hair on the back of her neck stood on end. "You need to extract my essence?" She swallowed and lowered her voice. "Just like the gemstones Ansel made with my blood."

Brannick's face twisted as he turned away. Blaz gave a short growl that matched the prince's scowl. Brannick shook his head. "Those gemstones only hold a shadow of your essence.

Such barbaric methods are unnecessary to gather your true essence."

Closing his hand over the clear crystal, he dropped his hand to his side. "But I will not do it if you do not wish me to."

His eyes convinced her more than anything. They always did. They swirled and pulsed and showed every color and none at all. They were as beautiful as they had ever been, but they spoke of more than just beauty. He would not use her.

With a nod, she stepped closer to him. "Do it."

He brushed a hand across her cheek with a smile and then held the clear crystal out once again. A rush of wind blew around them. His lips moved as he muttered under his breath. Every few moments, his eyes would flutter closed, but then they would snap open once again.

She watched him so steadily she didn't even realize when he had finished. He nodded down at his palm. "It is even more beautiful than I expected."

He held the crystal out to her. It *did* look beautiful, but while she held his crystal in her own palm, that was hardly the first thing she noticed. She had examined Brannick's crystal many times, so she was very familiar with its sage green color and raw cut. Her favorite part was the thin stripe of purple along the top edge.

Knowing the shape and color so well only made her crystal that much more remarkable. The purple color had a softness to it, which complemented the raw cut. Along the top edge, it had a thin stripe of green. Sage green. It looked like the exact opposite of Brannick's crystal.

When she glanced up, she caught his eyes. Instinctively, she knew he had already realized the same thing. Her mouth tipped upward as she placed a hand over his chest. "Your heart is tied to mine."

It seemed appropriate to repeat the prince's own words when he had first discovered she had his crystal. He nodded, confirming that the shape and color of her crystal meant exactly what she thought it meant.

He took her hand and brought it to his lips. He took a deep breath before he spoke. "I will not let you get hurt." His eyes closed as he kissed each of her fingers. "You must vow that you will keep yourself safe."

Stepping even closer, she looked up through her eyelashes at him. "And what if something happens to you? What am I supposed to do then?"

His face only hardened. "You are strong and courageous and perfectly capable of taking care of yourself." He gave her hand a gentle squeeze. "But that will not stop me from protecting you, especially from *her*."

Elora gulped.

Brannick pulled her closer still. "Vow that you will keep yourself safe, or I may trap you inside your room again."

She glanced into his eyes but still couldn't decide if he was serious or not. "Fine." Her eyes narrowed. "I vow I will keep myself safe, but I will still protect you as best as I can."

Before he could respond, a glowing green light with a pink sparkle inside flew toward them. Soon, Tansy hovered right in front of them. Her limbs looked stronger now. "We know exactly what village you should go to."

Elora glanced toward Brannick. He was thinking the same thing as her.

It would all begin when night fell.

CHAPTER

35

More frost lined the cobblestone streets of Noble Rose than it had on their previous visit. Elora gripped her sword, finally gaining strength from it the way she always had. No sounds drifted from the quaint brick houses around her.

Brannick had convinced the fae to leave their homes. He instructed them not to return until day dawned. They could only hope the fae would listen. And that it would be safe by then.

Glowing green wings fluttered next to Elora's ear. Tansy kept lifting herself higher, but she would always lower herself again until she landed on Elora's shoulder. "The high queen will be here soon," the little sprite whispered. "All sprites will leave once she gets here, but we will stay until then."

After the pain they had endured in Fairfrost, Elora understood why the sprites refused to stay for the fight. Still, part of her knew their presence would be missed.

Elora's sisters had arranged her hair in two braids that hung over each of her shoulders. They said it would keep her safe because then her hair wouldn't fly into her face while fighting. Whether that was true or not, it did feel like a piece of her sisters was with her. Ribbons from her mother's old skirt tied the two braids off.

They had also helped her pick out the leather pants and fitted leather shirt she wore. Brannick had imbued the leather with magic that made the fabric as strong as steel armor. Paired with her iron sword that could injure fae just by touching them, she had never felt more powerful. Still, it didn't take away her fear.

Brannick glanced toward her. The swirling and pulsing colors in his eyes mesmerized her as they often had before. His essence had never been stronger.

Raising both hands high above his head, a green and gold enchantment shot from his fingertips. The shimmery magic rained down on them, melting away the fear that filled the air. When it finished cleansing the air around them, it gathered into a large canopy that started high above their heads. It dropped down far outside the small village where they stood, creating a large dome around them.

He glanced toward her again after he had finished. His eyes were duller now. He took a deep breath, but it did nothing for the gray swirling in his eyes. The enchantment had cost him, exactly as they knew it would. But they couldn't very well overthrow Queen Alessandra while they cowered in fear.

On Elora's other side, Vesper bounced on the balls of his feet. His fingers twitched at his side, waiting for action. He wore a ward necklace made specially for this fight. Brannick had imbued it with strong magic that allowed Vesper to be in his own court, even though he had been banished from it. He had worn a similar ward that allowed him to attend the tournament in Noble Rose during the final phase of testing. The magic inside it would only last until day dawned.

Behind them, Quintus and Soren stood at the front of a small army. The gnome had gathered and trained many fae of Bitter Thorn so they would be ready for this moment.

Lyren hadn't arrived yet, but it would be better if she got there later anyway. They didn't want her and the other rulers to appear until after the ambush.

Brannick closed his eyes as he waved his hands through the air. When he finished, everyone around them turned invisible.

Elora curled her fingers around her sword hilt. *Breathe.* Why did she have to keep reminding herself to breathe? And why did the air feel so thick?

Icy air danced across her cheeks, but she still felt too hot. Or was it cold?

Waiting did strange things to the mind.

Her knees bounced, eager to move. It was difficult to keep them still.

Breathe.

She had forgotten again.

Even with the reminder, her breaths were still too shallow. How much longer?

Brannick took her hand, squeezing it gently before he faced forward again.

That tiny gesture turned out to be all she needed. Her heart continued to thump wildly, but why shouldn't it? They were about to attack the most powerful fae in Faerie, after all.

Fear coursed through her veins in churning waves. But maybe that just proved how brave she really was.

Her sisters always called her brave, but was it really courage if she never felt fear? It certainly felt different now. Fear gripped her tighter than she gripped her own sword. But she stood ready to fight anyway.

Her eyes flicked to where Brannick stood invisible before she faced forward again. Now she had something to fight for.

When a sparkling white tunnel appeared on the cobblestone steps, a chorus of sucked in breaths erupted around her. She might have internally scolded them if she hadn't sucked in a breath too. But they couldn't afford to make such noise again. The glamour keeping them invisible did nothing for sound. Their ambush would never work properly if Queen Alessandra heard them before they attacked.

The queen stepped onto the cobblestone with her head held high. Even as she brushed a wrinkle from her brocade dress, Elora began creeping forward. They all did.

With each step, they moved with as much silence as possible. Just a little bit closer.

Elora was close enough to tackle the queen now, but she didn't. They had to wait for the queen's door to close.

It did only a moment later. Queen Alessandra tipped her nose in the air. "I command—"

So many fae jumped forward, Elora couldn't tell exactly who had joined her in tackling the queen.

With a shriek, Queen Alessandra sent a shimmery enchantment from her fingertips. With her other hand, she blasted a golden enchantment toward them.

The wind knocked out of Elora as she fell onto her back. The other fae around her let out grunts as they too slammed onto the cobblestone streets. At the same moment, their glamours fell away.

Elora had already seen Queen Alessandra remove a glamour of invisibility, but a part of her had hoped they might keep theirs a little bit longer.

Ice formed around the queen's fingertips as she pulled her arm back, ready to blast another enchantment toward them.

But while she focused on the group in front of her, she didn't notice the group of fae behind her. They leapt forward, crashing into her just as Elora and the others had only a moment earlier.

Another shriek pealed from the queen's throat as she blasted them with the same enchantments as before. While her back was turned, Elora and those around her charged toward the queen once again.

When the queen sent an enchantment toward them a second time, they all scattered. Elora used her wings to fly high enough to avoid the blast.

The air felt empty without the sprites floating above. She hadn't even noticed when they flew away. Flying downward, she drew her sword for attack.

The queen continued to send enchantments toward anyone who attacked her, but with fae coming from all sides, she couldn't stop them all from closing in.

Things were going exactly as they planned.

Vesper finally moved close enough to ram a shoulder into the queen's stomach.

Her breath came out in a hard puff as she landed on her back. When the queen raised a hand to attack Vesper, Elora sliced her sword across the queen's wrist.

It was the best strike she could manage from her angle, but it was enough.

Queen Alessandra hissed as smoke sizzled out from the cut made from Elora's iron sword. Her eyes flew upward, glaring at the wings that kept Elora just out of reach. "*You*." The queen clenched her teeth. "I will kill you."

Using her wings, Elora darted down until she was almost within the queen's grasp. Just when Queen Alessandra reached for her, Elora flew back and out of her reach.

The distraction had worked exactly as they intended. While Queen Alessandra focused on Elora, she did not notice that Brannick had pulled long roots and vines from the nearby gardens. The plants twisted around the queen, holding her arms in place at her sides.

"Lyren." Brannick shouted over his shoulder while he continued to use plants to hold the queen down.

Elora folded her wings into her back as she frowned. "She is not here yet."

With a shriek, Queen Alessandra snapped the bonds around her. Before she could wave her hands, Brannick wrapped more vines around her limbs.

Even bound, she managed to send a blast of iridescent white from her fingertips. Elora's wings popped out again to raise herself away from the enchantment. Brannick shot his own enchantment forward to block the blast from hitting him or Blaz.

The other fae around him were not as lucky. The iridescence slammed into their chests, forcing them backward.

Blaz growled as he closed in on the queen. He snapped his fangs, trying to catch one of her legs. She darted away fast enough to avoid him, but it gave Brannick enough time to wrap more vines around her.

"Prince Brannick." Lyren's voice had never sounded so sweet. Her black curls billowed behind as she gestured to her side. "The rulers are here."

He managed a short nod, but his hands were busy waving and pushing to send even more vines to entrap the high queen.

Queen Noelani held her blue javelin high as she approached the prince. "Do you have the crown?"

With one hand still twisting the vines tighter, Brannick used the other to fish the crown from his pocket.

King Jackory touched a hand to his own crown. He shook his head at the sight of the writhing vines around Queen Alessandra. "Why must these things always be so messy?"

Approaching on her tiptoes, Queen Nerissa held onto the thick braid that fell to her knees. Her eyes flicked up toward the feather that adorned her jewel-encrusted crown. Maybe it was the light, but her shoulders seemed to be shuddering. She ducked behind Queen Noelani and King Jackory, staying just out of sight of the high queen.

Queen Alessandra glanced over them before letting out her loudest shriek yet. "I am High Queen of Faerie." She shoved one hand out of the twisting vines surrounding her. "You will not defeat me so easily."

That one hand was all she needed. With a tiny wave, she opened a door and shouted into it. "Send me reinforcements at once." Her mouth curled into a grin. "And bring the trolls."

CHAPTER

36

The sparkling white of Queen Alessandra's door had never looked so ominous. Elora stomped toward it, already holding her sword high. The door gave them a distinct advantage. Only one, or possibly two, fae could step through the door at a time. That meant Brannick's forces could defeat Queen Alessandra's forces one by one.

Elora arrived at the door alongside Vesper. He wielded a mace with sharp points coming off at all different angles.

The prince continued to use his magic to bind Queen Alessandra.

Over a dozen Bitter Thorn fae stood with Vesper and Elora. A dozen. And they only had to fight off one fae at a time.

Why wasn't that more reassuring?

Tension wracked through Elora when the first shadow appeared in Queen Alessandra's door. Vesper bounced even faster on his heels, breathing in beat with the movement. Everyone around them raised their weapons. Elora was no different. Years of practice allowed her to lift her sword without much effort.

Whatever fae stepped out to greet them would be met with a collection of spears, javelins, and blades. No fae could defeat all that at once.

But a mountainous creature with green-tinged skin lumbered through the door and onto the frosty ground of Noble Rose. The troll held an axe high above his head for only a moment before he swiped it toward the fae in front of him.

Elora's wings pulled her upward at once, but even she had difficulty getting away before the blade could slice her. Cries erupted from those who hadn't been so quick. A growl burst from deep in the troll's throat, which sounded more like a gargle than anything. It bared its yellow teeth and swiped again.

Expecting the attack now, Elora flitted over the heads of those who stood up to the troll. Her sword pointed downward, straight at the creature's head. She knew from experience that her sword could not pierce the thick skin of a troll, but the iron in it would still cause injury.

She pressed the point of her sword into the top of its head. Even with the iron in it, the troll continued to swing its axe and attack without abandon. After several moments, a sizzle of steam finally appeared beneath her blade.

The creature let out a gargling growl once again. Its axe swung toward her feet. She flew high enough to avoid the strike, but the movement brought her sword away from the troll's head. Now it could attack without any problem.

Behind her, Brannick let out a pained hiss. She jerked her head toward him, already flying closer.

Queen Alessandra had freed one of her arms from Brannick's vines and used it to send glittering whips across the prince's back.

Using all the momentum her wings could provide, Elora zoomed down. Her sword aimed straight for the queen's heart. If she died, they might not even need to give more power to Brannick's crown.

But of course, Queen Alessandra sensed Elora's approach just at the right moment. She whipped around and sent a blast of sparkles toward Elora. They glinted in the light with breathtaking beauty, but they also cut into her skin like barbed needles.

Still, Elora aimed as sure as she could manage. Her sword only sliced a gash into the queen's shoulder, but at least it had struck something. The wound sizzled and popped as the iron in her blade tore into the queen's skin.

The beads coming down the front of the queen's crown slapped against her forehead as she sent more of the needle-like sparkles toward Elora.

Despite her counterattack, the damage had been done. The injury had distracted her just enough that Brannick tightened vines over the queen's arms once again.

Such a victory might have been sweeter if it ended there. But of course it didn't. Doors popped up all around their small battle. Fae with white roses tucked into their tunics and dresses stepped out of the doors that had appeared. Worse, guards in white brocade began pouring out of Queen Alessandra's door.

Even with her arms tied down, the queen managed to wave her hand slightly. The movement caused her door to grow larger. It widened to almost the size of one of the quaint houses on the street.

Now, a dozen guards could step out of the door at once.

Sucking in a breath, Elora glanced toward the prince. His eyes had never been so wide. He gulped. "Get the rulers. We must finish this now."

It would have been better to *not* enact the rest of their plan while they were in the middle of battle, but they didn't have much choice now.

Elora flew higher off the ground to get a better vantage point. Queen Noelani and Lyren fought side by side. Their javelins smacked and jabbed at every fae before them.

Queen Noelani's javelin shuddered as she slammed it against a fae with a white rose tucked into her dress. The attack caused the rose to drop onto the cobblestone street with a plop. The fae blinked at the fallen rose before turning her eyes back toward Queen Noelani. The fae's eyes widened. She took a step back with both hands raised. "I do not wish to fight you."

The queen of Swiftsea cocked a head at the strange behavior, but Elora simply let out a breath of relief. It could be helpful to know that removing the roses took away the fae's desire to do anything for Queen Alessandra.

But once the fae turned and saw the high queen in danger, she lifted her weapon again. It may have been outside her control. After all, the fae had vowed to protect the high queen, and vows in Faerie could not be broken.

Elora quickly flew as close to them as she dared without risking injury. After catching Queen Noelani's eye, Elora gestured toward the prince.

"We need you to give power to the crown now."

The queen of Swiftsea sent one last jab of her weapon to knock back the fae in front of her and then she ran toward

Brannick. Before she got there, a cluster of guards in white brocade surrounded her.

Beating her wings faster, Elora tried to swoop in to help. Someone grabbed her by the ankle and yanked her to the ground. The bone-breaking grip told her a troll had done it. She barely had time to put her wings away before her back slammed against frosty grass.

A troll with a yellowing tunic stood over her. Its bushy hair looked more like a clump of briars than hair. The troll held a hand to her shoulders, pushing Elora into the ground. "Know you."

Elora understood the words, but they sounded eerily similar to hacking coughs. The troll sneered, showing off a set of dark yellow teeth. "Fought you before." It pushed her deeper into the ground. "You killed brother."

"What?" It took almost all the breath Elora had left in her body to force the word out. She had never killed a troll before.

But then she remembered. Kaia claimed she *had* killed a troll when she rescued Brannick from Fairfrost. Her shoulders shook as she tried to free herself from the creature's grasp. She really needed those memories back.

When the shaking did nothing, she lifted her sword instead. The troll raised its curved axe, but she pressed the blade of her sword against the creature's arm. The troll blinked at her sword a few times before the iron began its destruction. Soon, steam sizzled off the troll's skin in a curling wisp.

It let out a gurgle, or maybe it was supposed to be a scream. When the troll backed away, Elora jumped from the ground and continued to press her blade against its skin. It finally moved away quick enough to avoid her blade.

Accepting the victory, she popped out her wings and lifted herself into the air once again. Brannick continued to struggle in his fight against Queen Alessandra. Even with Blaz's help, they only barely kept her from escaping at every moment. Queen Noelani of Swiftsea still had a group of Fairfrost fae surrounding her. King Jackory stood at the very edge of the fight, only lifting his own weapon when someone attacked him personally.

Queen Nerissa of Dustdune must have been hiding, because Elora couldn't find her anywhere. If she was going to get the other rulers anywhere near Brannick, she needed help.

She scanned the fight again and flew down near Queen Alessandra's enormous door.

"Vesper!" She shouted his name, but she couldn't see him anywhere. That thought twisted inside her, but at least if something had happened to him, she would be able to see him. Her chest tightened as she scanned the area again.

"Quintus?" Even he was nowhere to be seen. They wouldn't have abandoned the prince, but if they weren't here, had they been taken unwillingly? She gulped.

"Elora." The name was whisper-shouted from a nearby garden, but it wasn't the whisper or the shout that had tangled her insides.

Chloe. Chloe had said her name. Chloe, who insisted she wasn't brave and even begged Elora not to fight. Chloe was here? In the middle of everything?

"Get in this garden." The words came whisper-shouted once more, but Elora still couldn't see her sister anywhere. Regardless, she flew toward the garden as fast as she could.

CHAPTER 37

A melting layer of frost covered the gate that surrounded the garden. Dripping icicles encased the wilting flowers. A cobblestone path cut through the manicured bushes. Elora saw nothing but the garden in front of her.

"Chloe?" She whispered in a low voice.

"I'm right here."

The sound came from right next to Elora. She jumped at the sound of it but still couldn't see anything but flowers. Then it dawned on her. "Are you glamoured to be invisible?"

A scoff erupted that clearly came from Chloe's mouth. "Yes, obviously. Do you think I would have come here otherwise?"

At least that brought a measure of comfort.

"I'm here too."

Elora's blood ran cold at the sound of her youngest sister's voice. "Grace?" She swallowed and glanced over her shoulder at the raging battle only a few steps away. "Who brought you here?"

"It doesn't matter now, does it?" Chloe said.

"Yes, it does." Elora folded her arms over her chest, hoping she was looking at least somewhat in the direction her sisters stood. But then, she heard a twig snap behind her. It sounded in the opposite direction from which her sisters' voices came. Her hand formed a fist as she punched at the air.

Instead of air, her fist made contact with a shoulder.

"Ow."

Elora narrowed her eyes at the invisible fae in front of her. "Quintus."

"We needed a mortal." He spoke defensively, but at least a smidgeon of guilt lined the words.

She slammed her hands onto her hips, shooting the deathliest glare she could manage. "So, you decided to bring *both* of my sisters to the middle of a battle?" Even in a whisper, she was surprised at how ruthless her voice came out.

"I asked Quintus to bring me." Grace's young voice sounded even more vulnerable among the clashing weapons nearby.

When Chloe spoke again, her words came out strained. "Then I felt awful about staying behind, so I decided I should come too."

Elora pinched the bridge of her nose as she let out a heavy sigh. "You will pay for this, Quintus."

"If you blame him, you must blame me as well." Vesper spoke from somewhere near Chloe. Having a conversation with invisible people was not the most enjoyable thing Elora had ever done.

She glared toward where she hoped Vesper stood. "This is too dangerous for them."

Without warning, Vesper appeared. The wild need for adventure was completely snuffed from his features. Only desperation filled his face now. He jerked his head toward the battle. "You know we have already lost this fight." His chin dropped to his chest. "We needed a new plan."

Flinching, Elora glanced over her shoulder. Queen Alessandra had freed one of her hands again. She sent enchantments and blasts that Brannick only narrowly avoided. Swarms of Fairfrost and Noble Rose fae surrounded the soldiers Soren had gathered. A handful of trolls dotted the landscape, wreaking havoc everywhere they went.

She let out a huff. "Fine." The whisper probably came out too quiet for anyone to hear. Taking a deep breath, she turned back to her fae brother. "Who is glamouring them to be invisible and how can you ensure they *stay* invisible?"

"No one is glamouring Chloe and me." Grace appeared right in front of Vesper. She held her dress out in front of her and gestured to the stone sitting on top of it. "We both have stones from Prince Brannick, remember?"

She went to pluck the stone that sat on her dress, but she turned invisible as soon as she touched it.

Chloe spoke from nearby. "As long as we touch the stones, they keep us invisible."

"Exactly," Grace said. "And if that fae, Ansel, is near us, we will automatically turn invisible, even without the stones."

Elora's throat thickened at the mention of him. "Good." Her voice didn't come out as even as she had intended, but it was too late to worry about that now. Ansel better not show up.

She gripped her sword hilt so tight her fingers ached. Fear slithered into her chest where it settled like a writhing knot. She wasn't ready to face him again.

Not yet.

It took three attempts before she could swallow down the lump in her throat. "Where is the device that Quintus crafted? How do we use it?"

Chloe touched a hand to her older sister's arm before she answered. "Don't you worry about that. We have the talismans, and we have the device. We know what to do. Right now, we just have to get close enough to High Queen Alessandra to use them."

"We're going to do it together."

Grace sounded far too chipper for something that could very well spell out their doom. Since the fear had already settled inside Elora's chest, it only grew bigger now. The battle raged louder while she stood, but her feet felt like iron too heavy to lift. She gulped. "Are you sure I cannot do it instead?"

A snort filled the air that obviously came from Chloe. "I'm pretty sure Prince Brannick would rip us all to shreds if we let you attempt it. Besides, Quintus is adamant that it *will* harm you."

"We can do this, Elora."

Why did Grace have to sound so sure?

Chloe's voice lowered. "Just stay near us while we walk through the battle and fight off anyone who gets too close to us."

Gripping her sword hilt tighter, Elora nodded. "Where do you need me to go?"

For the first time since the conversation started, Quintus appeared. He nodded toward the fight. "Lead them to High

Queen Alessandra. They know how to place the device so that it will hurt only the high queen but not Prince Brannick."

"And then what?" Hopefully no one noticed the strain in Elora's voice.

Chloe gave the answer. "Then we'll run back to the garden as quickly as we can, and one of you will take us back to Quintus's house."

Elora drew her sword and pointed ahead. She didn't like not being able to see her sisters, but at least no one else could see them either.

"Ready?" Grace asked.

"No," Chloe responded with a squeak. "Let's do this."

The wings popped out of Elora's back, and she lifted herself into the air to hover just above the ground. Vesper and Quintus were both visible now. They moved toward the fight slowly. Looking closely, Elora could barely make out her sisters' footsteps in the frost just ahead of where Vesper and Quintus walked.

It only took one fae who barely crossed in front of the sisters to make Chloe gasp. Elora wanted to smack her forehead, but that probably would have only brought more attention to the fact that a gasp had just erupted from nowhere. Chloe needed to learn how to keep her mouth shut while invisible.

When the fae turned to glance at where the gasp had come from, Elora gasped. Hopefully the fae would assume the first gasp had come from her as well. She swung her sword hard enough that the fae stepped back.

Letting her wings lower toward the fae, Elora swiped her sword even harder. The fae stumbled back and turned to find an easier target.

Almost as soon as that fae left, another fae passed in front of them, and Chloe gasped again. Elora tried to cover it by grunting as loud as she could. Again, she swung her sword as hard as she could.

Maybe it was because her actions didn't seem to put Queen Alessandra at direct risk, but Elora easily fought off any fae who crossed their path. Even with Chloe's ill-timed gasps, they moved toward the high queen even faster than Elora expected.

Her suspicions were confirmed when a fae with a white rose caught a small scratch from Elora's sword. The fae stumbled backward and muttered under his breath, "She is not hurting the high queen. There is no need to fight her."

Soon enough, they had moved close enough to Queen Alessandra and Brannick that the prince nodded in Elora's direction. She would have loved to join in his fight. Her iron sword could have inflicted plenty of damage.

But she knew it was more important to keep her sisters safe and let them do their work.

She knew the exact moment they finished placing the device wherever it needed to be. Queen Alessandra stopped in the middle of waving her hand only to double over from within the vines surrounding her. She let out a scream and curled her hands into fists.

Brannick raised an eyebrow at the sight. He turned and glanced toward Elora.

Flapping her wings, she lowered herself near enough to whisper to her sisters. It came out just loud enough for the prince to hear as well. "Get back to the garden as fast as you can."

He glanced at the empty air between them, but then his eyebrows jumped upward. He understood. Without another word, he turned back to the high queen and began twisting more vines around her.

Queen Alessandra continued to scream as Elora guided her sisters back to the garden. They moved even faster than they had on the way there. Chloe continued to gasp at inopportune moments, but Elora simply grunted to cover it up.

When they only had a few steps to go, the troll who had attacked Elora earlier lumbered toward them. The creature swiped the air, trying to yank Elora down by the ankle as it had done before. She had to fly high above to avoid the troll's grasp.

She spun her sword around in a circle and glared at the troll. In a flash, she darted downward, ready to hold her blade against the troll's shoulder. The iron only made contact with the creature's skin for a few moments before it backed away with a glare.

Elora turned toward the garden just in time to see a flying axe strike Quintus's leg. A growl erupted from his throat as he tore the weapon from his leg.

Chloe screamed.

An entire group of fae jerked their heads toward the sound. Elora immediately screamed louder, and hoped it sounded enough like her sister's scream that the fae would assume the first scream had come from her as well.

She hovered just over the ground and swung her sword to fight off as many fae as she could. She just had to give her sisters enough time to get to the garden. They were nearly there.

After a sharp spin, Elora jabbed the nearest fae. The blade only glanced across the fae's skin, but the sizzling steam it caused sent the fae running. It only took two more injuries for the other fae to decide fighting against an opponent with an iron sword was not worth it.

The continued screams coming from Queen Alessandra indicated they weren't the only ones dealing with iron. Her talismans were clearly hurting her.

As Elora swung her sword at the only remaining fae, a flicker brought her eyes upward.

Grace's red hair flashed in the dusky light. Her eyes widened as she jerked her head down. She surveyed the ground with stilted motions.

She had lost her stone.

Elora shoved away the fae before her.

Grace stood just outside the garden in full view of anyone who bothered to look her way. Her bottom lip quivered as she continued to search the ground.

Elora sprinted toward her youngest sister. Why didn't she just jump into the garden and behind the cottage? This was no time to search for a stone.

With eyes widening each moment, Grace frantically searched the ground. But then she vanished.

She had not found the stone. Elora was certain of it. Her body never bent to retrieve it. The fear in her eyes never relaxed. So, if she hadn't found the stone, why had she suddenly turned invisible?

The answer pierced Elora through every nerve she had. Hadn't her sisters just explained? Only one thing would make them turn invisible automatically.

Her breath hitched as she turned around slowly. A rocky gray door had just opened beside her. The owner of it had just stepped out.

Ansel.

CHAPTER

38

I ce crept into Elora's shoulders, but her hands were the ones that shivered. She felt thin drips of blood sliding down her neck, but it had to be her imagination. *Right?* Even though she stood on a cobblestone path in an outdoor space, the air suffocated her.

Chains wrapped tight around her arms, pinning them down, but they weren't real.

They weren't real.

She lifted her sword into the air just to remind herself that no chains shackled her now. It didn't matter. Once Ansel's mouth twisted into a smile, she was back in those chains, back in Fairfrost Palace, with no way to escape. Why did her imagination have to be so vivid? Why could she feel something that wasn't even there?

The only reason she knew it was in her head was because she still had her arm lifted high. She could still see the rolling hills of Noble Rose surrounding her. And the blood that dripped down her neck wasn't warm like it should have been. It was ice cold and tingling.

Ansel took a step toward her. "It is a good thing I have spies in Fairfrost Palace, or I never would have known to find you here."

She gulped. She would have taken a step back if her legs would move. But they wouldn't. "Get away from me."

His disgusting smile grew more wicked. "The prince will not win this fight. If you are here when it ends, High Queen Alessandra will kill you." He leaned closer. "Come with me, and you can live."

A shaky breath shuddered through her. "I would *not* live if I came with you. Not really."

Delight danced in his yellow eyes. "You belong to me. I will have you eventually."

Her arm moved automatically when he stepped toward her. Muscle memory became her greatest friend in that moment because it jabbed her sword at him when she could not. He dodged it easily. The single strike was all she could manage before her entire chest constricted into a tight knot.

She couldn't breathe.

With one look, he seemed to understand how much power he held over her. Why wouldn't her sword move now? His hand reached out, and everything inside her turned to ice.

She tried to step out of his reach. She begged herself to turn and run away. But she stood still, as if frozen to the frosty cobblestone beneath her feet.

As she had guessed, she wasn't ready to face him.

His hand stretched out, ready to touch her cheek. When his fingers were only a breath away, a golden enchantment slammed into Ansel's chest. He flew onto his back, coughing hard once he hit the cobblestone.

A blur of black fur passed between them and Blaz pounced onto Ansel's chest. Another golden enchantment hit the fae, carefully avoiding Blaz. The wolf chomped his fangs down on Ansel's torso. The golden enchantment around him transformed into knife-like branches that stabbed all over his body.

With a shriek, Ansel jumped to his feet. He shoved the wolf away, but Blaz just charged him again. When his teeth clamped down on Ansel's leg, a mace flew through the air. The dagger-like points struck the fae in the back of his shoulder. A wave of small rocks came from the garden, but their thrower was unseen. Chloe possibly.

Ansel tried to kick Blaz in the face, but the wolf caught his foot in his mouth instead. It took several yanks to free himself. The sharpened branches grew more aggressive, stabbing more and more critical areas in his body. The rocks from the garden continued to shower him, which probably only exacerbated the pain from the mace that still stuck in his shoulder.

He flashed his teeth before opening a door. His eyes narrowed at Elora. "This is not over." With rocks smattering against his back, he darted into his door and disappeared.

Elora let out a heavy breath, finally able to breathe again. She glanced over her shoulder toward the prince.

Brannick used one hand to keep the vines around Queen Alessandra in place, but he had obviously sent the two golden enchantments that knocked Ansel off his feet. He let out his own sigh of relief once she met his gaze.

Breathing in deeply, she dropped to her knees and wrapped her arms around Blaz. "You saved me again," she said into his fur.

He nuzzled close to her before he darted off toward Brannick once again.

The knot in her chest continued to loosen as she stepped toward the garden. She couldn't see Grace anywhere. Maybe she had found her stone, or maybe she had simply hidden behind the cottage. Either way, Elora needed to know for sure that both of her sisters were safe before she joined the fight again.

She would face Ansel again someday. Part of her knew it was inevitable. But she wasn't ready to truly face him yet.

Her feet trudged over the path. She still carried the weight of fear in her chest when an enormous hand wrapped her around the middle and lifted her off her feet. Sucking in a breath, she turned her blade and pressed the flat side of it against the green-tinged arm that held her.

The same troll from before shook its twiggy hair as it glared at her. Clenching her jaw, she pushed her blade even harder against the creature's skin.

Steam sizzled out from under the blade, which caused the troll to growl. It squeezed her tighter around the middle, but she didn't move her sword away.

Letting out a guttural scream, the troll tried to shake her enough to move the sword. When that failed, the troll bit into her arm. The injury stung and burned, but Elora kept her weapon tight against the troll's skin.

Finally, it dropped her onto the cobblestone. Holding the iron-burned arm in one hand, the troll retreated. Gurgles and spits spewed from its mouth with every step.

Her arm continued to burn where the creature had bitten her, but it didn't stop her from rushing into the garden. She would try to clean the wound, but only once her sisters were safe.

Tumbling through the little gate, she cradled her arm and peeked around the side of the cottage.

Both Chloe and Grace were visible now. Vesper and Quintus stood on either side of them. The mace Vesper had been using earlier was missing.

Sucking in a gasp, Chloe grabbed her oldest sister's arm and pulled it closer to her face. "Where did you get this wound?"

A grunt spilled from Elora's mouth before she answered. "A stupid troll bit me."

Chloe's eyebrows flew up to her blonde hair. "It *bit* you? This is a troll bite?"

"Yes." Elora squeezed her fist, hoping it might eradicate some of the burning sensation.

A glint appeared in Chloe's eye as she turned to their youngest sister.

Grace bit her bottom lip, looking far less excited. "What about the atmosphere?"

Tremors shook through Elora's limbs, dropping her to her knees.

That glint in Chloe's eye only grew. "It was dusk then and it is dusk now. This is perfect."

Quintus lifted an eyebrow. "Perfect? Your sister's arm is deeply injured. Even for a fae, that will take great energy to heal."

After blinking, Elora's eyes refused to open again. She sank deeper into the frosty grass beneath her.

"Are you still awake?" At least Vesper sounded worried.

315

She didn't answer him.

"But we aren't in the right court." Grace's voice seemed to blur at the edges.

Chloe's answer sounded muffled, and the words faded even more. "That doesn't matter. I have to send… need…offering."

Maybe Chloe had spoken without pauses, but Elora only heard half the words. Now the voices around her turned to mumbles. She tried to open her eyes again, but too much weight filled them.

Had she fallen asleep? An acidic scent filled her nose.

With a jerk, her eyes snapped open. She couldn't sit up completely, but her head tilted upward, at least.

Kaia waved a white feather over the wound in Elora's arm.

Kaia? No, that couldn't be right. The dryad couldn't go that far away from her tree. Already, striations covered her dark skin, making it look more like bark. Her emerald hair turned stringy.

"Tree." Elora had an entire sentence in her mind, but apparently only one word wanted to come out.

Kaia offered a gentle smile before she turned back to the wound. "I only have a moment, but I can finish by then."

The dryad rubbed a grainy, berry-red mixture over the troll bite. The burning sensation vanished at once. Elora's head felt clearer already.

Pushing deeper into the wound, Kaia massaged the area. When she wiped away the berry-red mixture, not even a scar remained where the troll bite had once been.

When Elora tried to sit up this time, she succeeded without much effort. Questions bubbled inside her throat, but she swallowed them down when the dryad held something toward her.

A tiny clay pot painted with purple flowers sat on Kaia's palm. She pushed it toward Elora. "Drink this."

Familiarity tickled at the back of Elora's mind. She took the tiny pot. Instead of drinking its contents, she examined the little flowers.

"Drink it." The words held more urgency this time. Her brown skin turned more bark-like as she gave an eager nod.

After blinking once, Elora tipped the clay pot back and swallowed the spicy liquid inside it.

Even before the liquid finished pouring down her throat, memories came flooding back. The memories she had once lost were hers again. She remembered seeing Kaia back in the mortal realm. She had thought it was a dream.

But then the dryad took her to Fairfrost, and nothing had ever felt so real. She remembered everything.

The bearskin rug.

The troll bite.

Brannick.

Her lips curled upward. He had been so audacious. He had been so fun.

Chloe dropped to her knees. "Did it work?"

The emerald hair on Kaia turned into thick branches.

"Yes." Elora couldn't help but smile.

A heavy sigh of relief burst from Kaia's bark-like lips. She jumped to her feet and disappeared through a door in almost the same breath.

It took a few deep breaths before Elora got to her feet again. Ansel's presence had shaken her more than she cared to admit. But he was gone now, and a fight awaited.

When she moved toward it, Grace pulled her arm back.

"Don't go." Grace's eyes shimmered as she gulped. "What if you get hurt again?"

The question had merit considering the injury Elora had recently obtained. Elora glanced over her shoulder at Quintus. "I need you to take them back to your home. Will you do that?"

He nodded.

Her eyes narrowed. "Stay there with them. Make sure they are safe."

"I will."

Vesper sidled up to her, glancing at her through the side of his eye. "Who will make sure that you are safe?"

She chuckled. "I vowed that I would keep myself safe. Besides, I have spent far too long considering all the way things could go wrong." She quirked her mouth upward. "It is time to have some fun instead."

CHAPTER 39

After watching her sisters disappear through a door with Quintus, she moved to return to the fight. Her steps were lighter now. The fear Ansel had planted within her did not fade, but something new hung alongside it. The spirit of adventure.

Her lips formed a small smile as she swept out of the garden. Vesper continued to stare at her. "You should have gone back to Bitter Thorn with your sisters."

She smirked at him. "Where would be the adventure in that?"

He chuckled. "Your safety is of more concern to me at the moment. I am not overly impressed with how you have kept yourself safe so far."

Lifting herself off the ground with her wings, her smile continued to grow. "See if you can keep up with me, then."

The wild light in his eyes that had been extinguished earlier flitted back again. She scanned the area, noting that Brannick had Queen Alessandra taken care of. She kept freeing a hand every now and again, but he would tighten vines over it almost as quickly.

Now they just had to take care of the queen's forces. She had trolls, guards, and fae of Noble Rose. The most dangerous of those three was pretty obvious. The trolls.

Despite Brannick's hold over the queen, his forces fought with less vigor than before. Their faces were drained. Their eyes dull.

No matter how the prince held his captive, the rest of his forces fought like had already lost. They needed a boost in morale if anything was to change.

Hovering downward until her feet touched the cobblestone, she raised an eyebrow at Vesper. "Have you ever jumped onto a troll's back?"

He shook the curls off his forehead before responding. "That does not sound like something they would like."

"Oh, they hate it." She paired the words with a devious grin. "That makes it all the more fun."

She used a combination of jumping and flying to propel herself upward. She landed hard onto the nearest troll's back. The creature let out a gurgling scream as it threw a fist back to hit her. Her head ducked to the side to avoid the blow. Next, she drew her sword and held it tight against the troll's neck.

The creature flailed, but she continued to hold her iron sword against its skin. It stumbled on its feet, moving closer to the prince. With the iron still held tight against its neck, she caught the prince's eye.

The colors in his eyes had gone dull. Blaz panted heavily each time he leapt forward to keep the queen from escaping. Both of them glanced up at Elora with too much weariness.

She offered a cheerful wave to them both. "Lovely evening, isn't it?"

Stiffened features overtook Brannick's face as he cocked his head to the side.

The troll lumbered all around. It shook and jerked its body, attempting to throw Elora off its back. Holding her sword even tighter to the troll's sizzling skin, she grinned. "Who knew a ride on a troll could be so thrilling?"

A crack in the prince's features finally appeared. He didn't quite smile, but his expression turned lighter at least.

Another troll came pounding past them. It ran with surprising speed while also jerking its body in every direction. Vesper held it tight around the throat, the rest of his body flying behind. The troll moved too fast for him to hold on with his knees or legs.

Despite that, his grin matched Elora's. He tipped his head toward her and the prince. "If you get your troll really angry, it makes for an even bouncier ride."

Brannick chuckled. When he twisted another vine to hold Queen Alessandra down, he moved more gracefully than he had a moment ago.

Vesper's troll had moved far enough away that Elora had to shout for her brother to hear her. "Excellent advice." Using one hand to hold her sword in place, she formed her other hand into a fist.

Maybe her hand didn't have has much killing power as her sword, but it still had to do something to the troll's weak spot. She slammed her fist directly under the creature's arm. The hit alone probably wouldn't have been enough to topple the troll,

321

but since she had an iron sword against its throat, the troll immediately dropped to its knees and then to its stomach.

The troll continued to release ice-cold breaths, but it seemed to be unconscious.

Even with vines holding her down, Queen Alessandra managed to let out a blood-curdling shriek. Her ice blue eyes narrowed to tight slits, directed straight at Elora. "I will tear you limb from limb. When I am finished with—"

Her words cut off abruptly when Elora threw a ball of snow straight into the queen's mouth. Bending at the waist, Elora gathered more frost from the grassy hill she stood on.

Queen Alessandra sputtered as she spit the ice from her mouth.

With another smirk, Elora held her newest ball of frost up for all to see. "You were saying?"

From across the distance between them, Brannick flashed a brilliant smile toward Elora. His grin looked almost as carefree as it had when she rescued him from Fairfrost Palace. His hand waved in a circle, and a door appeared a short way away.

He waved his hand again, which caused a length of vines to lift from the ground and tighten to a straight line. The moment he finished, a troll stumbled right into the tightened vine. It tripped forward. The creature grunted as it fell into Brannick's door.

With another wave of the hand, the door disappeared. Brannick raised an eyebrow. "I thought the trolls might enjoy the scenery more if they went back to Fairfrost." His lips lowered in a mock pout. "They look ever so upset being here."

Elora chuckled as she leapt onto another troll's back. It flailed and screamed, but it couldn't wrest her away any better than the other had.

Vesper's troll came lumbering back toward them. He continued to grip it around the neck. Even though his curls blew in the wind, he looked more delighted than ever. "What a brilliant idea, Prince Brannick." He waved his hand, which opened a door directly in front of his troll. "I am sure the trolls would prefer a spot deep in the ice forest of Fairfrost." He adjusted his grip until he held the troll by the shoulders. "Somewhere far from the palace."

Pushing himself away, Vesper kicked the troll through his door, where it immediately disappeared. He managed to close the door just in time that he didn't fall through it as well.

All around them, the faces of Brannick's soldiers brightened. Soon, they were fighting with near smiles on their lips. Vesper and Elora continued to shove trolls through doors until only the unconscious one remained.

The clash of weapons continued to ring all around them, but the tide had changed. The queen's forces were not winning anymore.

Of course, Elora counted the victory a moment too soon.

Queen Alessandra screamed so loud, it echoed across the rolling hills. "I am High Queen of Faerie!" The bonds around her snapped as she ripped both of her arms free. Leaping backward, she pulled a single purple gemstone from her pocket.

After squeezing it tight in her hand, a flash of purple light burst out from her grip. The light shot outward, knocking every fae to their backs. Even Brannick.

A crack sounded at the queen's feet. A thick box covered in geometric designs appeared, but then a fire flashed around it. Whatever device Quintus had crafted to house the talismans, it was now destroyed. Based on how Queen Alessandra acted now, the talismans must have been destroyed as well.

It took a hard breath before Elora could leap to her feet again. She moved just fast enough to see shards of iridescent ice form around Queen Alessandra's fist. When she punched her fist forward, the ice broke away and shot forward, right toward Elora.

Her fingers held tight to her sword hilt. The shards of ice moved too fast to leap away in time, but maybe her sword could block them.

"Watch out!"

Vesper slammed into Elora from the side, toppling her to the ground. A single shard of ice pierced him straight through the chest.

Her heart leapt into her throat as she got to her knees. Chaos reigned around them once again, but she was too focused on her fae brother notice anything else.

By the time she reached for the ice shard, it seemed to burrow deeper into Vesper's chest until nothing remained. Or had it melted?

Her eyes narrowed as she reached for him.

He rubbed his chest with his knuckles. The shard of ice had pierced him right in the heart, but he didn't seem injured in any way.

"I…" His knuckles continued to work across his chest as he sat up. "I think I am fine."

"Fine?" She helped him to his feet. "A shard of ice pierced your heart. What will that do to you?"

He shrugged. "I do not know. But it does not hurt anymore."

The iridescent flash of light continued to move outward, but without warning, it changed direction and moved back toward the queen. She caught the light in her hand. Her smile did not bode well.

Then they felt it. After Queen Alessandra's other attacks, they should have realized she would manipulate them again at the first opportunity. The emotion cut deep, dropping Elora to her knees.

Sadness, grief, pain. The exact name of the emotion didn't matter. What mattered was that every fae in the area dropped to their knees and grabbed their chests.

Elora soaked in the grief. She welcomed it without any hesitation. Fear had affected her more than the other attacks because of what Ansel had done to her, but grief? She almost laughed to herself. If the queen wanted to overwhelm her, she shouldn't have used the emotion Elora had the most experience with.

At her side, Vesper rocked himself back and forth. His face was stricken. "What if I die before I can ever see my Cosette again?"

Elora grabbed him by the shoulders. "Listen to me. Queen Alessandra can make you feel a certain way, but she cannot choose where you direct that emotion. You just need to direct it toward something productive."

Tears welled in his eyes as he blinked up at her. "What if I never get to see my youngest baby grow up?"

Shaking her head, she turned away. She didn't have time to force Vesper into the right frame of mind. It might be easier to convince someone else anyway.

She moved toward Brannick. He was huddled in a ball only a small distance away from Queen Alessandra. Blaz nudged him with his nose. He didn't move. Besides the queen, everyone else was still on the ground. Most of them moaned or cried. The emotion hadn't affected Queen Alessandra, but it had taken out her own forces along with the prince's.

"Brannick." Elora called out to him, but he didn't move. Queen Alessandra, however, jerked her head in Elora's direction, so she released her wings and flew upward to avoid any blasts the queen might send.

Luckily, she sent none. Perhaps using the gemstone had temporarily drained her of energy.

Reaching into her pocket, Elora wrapped her fingers around the sage green crystal in her pocket. If she understood essence correctly, holding it and thinking of Brannick's true nature wouldn't be enough. He would also have to reach out to her essence in order to get help.

But he claimed the crystal gave her a connection to him. Maybe she didn't have complete access to her magic yet, but she *had* used it twice already. Maybe she could use just a little of it. Closing her eyes, she tried to sense the connection. Or Brannick. Or *anything*.

At least it was easier to think of Brannick's true self now that she had her memories back. He had been so carefree then. She would have given anything to restore that part of his personality.

Her thoughts were so focused, she almost didn't notice Brannick get to his feet. He kept his hand on Blaz's head and sucked in a deep breath. The queen took a step back.

He waved both arms wide and shot out a golden enchantment. It rippled through the air like leaves caught in the wind. The enchantment curled and circled until it had touched everyone in the crowd. The grief in Elora's chest melted away once it touched her. But that wasn't all that melted away. The frost on the grass, the ice wilting the flowers, all of it turned to water and sank into the soil.

Queen Alessandra flashed her teeth and waved her own arms. Her iridescent enchantment returned. It knocked into

Elora with the same force as before, bringing grief back in a wave. Once again, frost and ice stretched over the landscape around them.

Brannick set his feet and lifted his arms to wave them once again.

While he worked, Elora scanned the area around them. Lyren sat in a heap. Her blue javelin lay at her feet. Lyren shook her head at it, which tumbled her black curls. "The decay." She dug her fingers into her hair. "What if it is *my* fault?" Her voice lowered. "I never told anyone what happened when I was a child."

Brannick's golden enchantment filled the air again. Queen Noelani sat nearby. She plucked her own javelin off the ground and jabbed it toward a guard in white brocade.

The iridescent enchantment returned, slicing grief deep once again. The Swiftsea queen's face twisted.

Elora turned toward the guard in white. "Queen Alessandra has stolen the life you should have had when she tricked you into entering a bargain with her."

A tear slipped from the guard's eyes. He stared back without saying a word. When a golden enchantment filled the air and melted the frost again, the expression on the guard's face didn't change.

Elora leaned toward him. "You must help us defeat her. Is there any loophole that will allow you and the other guards to leave this place?"

The guard blinked back at her. The iridescent enchantment returned, causing him to bury his face in his hands. After a moment, he looked up. His face still looked stricken and pained, but he looked determined too. "One of our longstanding commands is to keep Fairfrost Palace safe. If we knew it was being attacked, we would have to leave this place to go defend it."

An idea brewed in the back of Elora's mind, but apparently, the Swiftsea queen thought of an idea first. Queen Noelani held her javelin high. "Swiftsea fae, I order you to leave this place and attack Fairfrost Palace."

There was a momentary pause, and then a golden enchantment danced through the air. Soon, doors began opening as Swiftsea fae stepped through them. But it didn't stop there. Queen Alessandra's own guards began opening doors. Even the fae of Noble Rose must have been compelled to protect the queen's palace, because they started disappearing through doors as well.

Would Queen Alessandra call them back?

Elora jerked around to see.

The high queen opened her mouth, but Brannick whipped a vine toward her. It knocked her off her feet with almost no effort at all. Apparently, using the gemstone *had* weakened her after all.

The fight ended so quickly it almost didn't feel real. Brannick continued twisting vines, finally holding Queen Alessandra so tight that she couldn't free herself.

Only a handful of fae remained. The Swiftsea fae, Noble Rose fae, the high queen's guards, and even most of Brannick's soldiers were gone. King Jackory stepped forward, brushing a layer of frost away from his sleeve. Queen Nerissa of Dustdune appeared suddenly, removing the glamour that had been hiding her.

Vesper stood. He continued to rub his chest as he moved to Elora's side.

The fight was over. They had Queen Alessandra at their mercy. The other rulers were there to give power to Brannick's crown.

But only one thing filled Elora's mind. Her hand still wrapped tight around the crystal in her pocket. It gave off energy the way it always did. But a new energy sparked as well.

Her hands, her fingers, they tingled unlike anything she had ever felt before.

Magic.

It brewed inside her. It wasn't there yet, but it was coming. She was sure of it.

CHAPTER 40

Vines floated overhead, each one carefully twisting around Queen Alessandra. Elora felt a little guilty for thinking it, but she wished Brannick would have pulled the vines even tighter. Instead, he carefully situated them to bind the high queen's limbs tight. He even bound vines over her mouth to keep her from speaking. The vines twisted tight enough to keep her completely still but not enough to injure her.

When Elora stepped toward them, King Jackory stared at her through the side of his eye. The king turned to the Dustdune queen, who was too busy fiddling with her golden hair ornaments to notice.

Clearing his throat, he gestured toward Queen Alessandra. "Now that the high queen is bound, the rest of this should be done with only the rulers."

Queen Nerissa dropped her hands away from her hair ornaments and snapped her head up. "I agree."

Brannick folded his arms over his chest.

Holding her blue javelin tight, Queen Noelani shrugged. "I have to agree as well."

Even after setting his jaw and glaring at the three of them, their expressions didn't budge. Finally, Brannick let out a burst of air. He turned toward the gnome with the long white beard at the edge of the cobblestone street. "Soren, take the soldiers back to Bitter Thorn. I will find you when this is over, and we can retrieve the other soldiers who are now in Fairfrost."

Soren's brown hat bounced as he gave a nod.

At Elora's side, Vesper shrugged. He waved a hand to open a door and then nudged Elora toward it.

She scowled at him. "*I* am not leaving."

Her words caused King Jackory to shoot a pointed glance in Brannick's direction. The prince shot his own glare back, but he stepped toward Elora anyway.

"You may go, Vesper." The prince gestured toward the misty door beside them. "I will open a door for her."

Vesper raised an eyebrow high into his curls before disappearing through his door.

Brannick had stepped close enough to take Elora's hand. The other rulers stared at the pair of them until the prince glared at them. Now they all looked away.

Before she knew what was happening, Brannick had dipped her backward and caught her lips in a fiery kiss. It lasted only a moment, but it sent her heart racing all the same.

When he pulled her up straight again, his eyes said the moment had ended far too soon for his liking. His arm settled into the small of her back as he trailed a finger across her lips. "I did not actually have anything to say." He smirked.

Heat burned into her cheeks as she bit her bottom lip. "I do not want to leave you right now. I want to stay until it is over."

Stroking her jaw, he offered a carefree shrug. "The high queen is captured. What could go wrong now?"

It didn't matter how carelessly he spoke the words, they still sounded ominous. But the other rulers didn't seem likely to change their minds.

When Brannick waved a hand and opened a door, she stomped toward it, huffing as much as possible. Just before she reached the swirling tunnel, a small stone on the ground caught her eye.

Grace's stone. The stone could turn Elora invisible, and the other rulers would never know she was even there.

She continued to stomp and huff. Just before stepping into Brannick's door, she bent and snatched the stone off the ground. She turned invisible at the exact moment she would have stepped into the door.

Except she didn't step into the door at all. She stepped to the side instead.

Brannick cast a suspicious gaze in her direction. Did he realize she hadn't actually gone through the door? At least the other rulers had been too focused on the high queen to even look at Elora as she pretended to go through the door.

Queen Nerissa ran her fingers through her thick, dark hair. "She is gone. We need to finish this."

Brannick gazed for another moment before closing his door. He reached into his pocket and pulled out the crown of Bitter Thorn. The obsidian glinted even in the dusky light.

The other rulers' eyes widened at the sight of the crown. Queen Noelani touched a hand to her seashell necklace. "What about the stone for the front of the crown?"

Tapping his pocket, Brannick nodded. "I have a stone. I will put it in after we are finished."

Without another word, Queen Noelani turned her hands in circles. Foamy blue sparkles shot from her fingertips and moved straight for the crown. The branches and obsidian absorbed the magic. Soon, blue sparkles moved along every edge of the crown as the tines grew taller and more intricate. Eventually, the sparkles died away, but the crown retained its height and added splendor.

Brannick moved the crown closer to Queen Alessandra. Though bound by the vines, her crown still sat perfectly on her head. The prince held his crown next to hers, as if comparing their heights. Queen Alessandra's still stood taller.

He let out a sigh and turned to King Jackory.

The king of Mistmount puffed out his chest. "It is time to reveal my request."

Brannick flinched at those words, which perfectly matched the flinch that shook through his wolf.

"And my request," Queen Nerissa added. She glanced up at the feather swaying at the front of her turban crown. She gulped. "King Jackory and I have the same request."

With a nod, King Jackory folded his arms over his chest. "You must close the portal to the mortal realm. We want Faerie cut off from all emotions as it once was."

Queen Alessandra tried to jerk free of her bonds, but the vines held her still.

Brannick raised a single eyebrow. "Excuse me?"

The king of Mistmount puffed his chest out again. "You have seen how High Queen Alessandra has manipulated our emotions." He pounded a fist to his chest. "You have experienced it too. Do you not see how dangerous it is to have emotions in Faerie?"

Queen Noelani gripped her javelin tight as she took a step forward. "We have had them for so long now, it might be more dangerous to lose them again."

Plucking a golden ornament from her hair, Queen Nerissa scoffed. "More dangerous than what High Queen Alessandra did this evening?" She gulped as she placed a hand over her heart. "I have never felt so broken."

The crown in Brannick's hand shook but only because his hands did. "You will not give power to my crown otherwise?"

King Jackory set his jaw. "Our bargain is set. If you close the portal, I must give power to your crown. If you do not, the bargain is broken, and I will give you nothing."

Brannick stared long enough to show he considered it.

A knot formed in Elora's gut. He was actually considering it.

But...

He couldn't. He couldn't do it. Didn't he think their love was worth it?

When Queen Nerissa stomped her foot, it shook the feather in her crown. "Do you want High Queen Alessandra to continue to manipulate us?"

"No." Brannick's answer came fast. Too fast.

King Jackory's eyebrows pinched together, showing more emotion than ever. "You are meant to be High King. Everyone in Faerie knows it. Just close the portal and take your rightful title."

Brannick's hand lifted into the air. Blaz's ears perked as he glanced up.

He was going to do it. He was going to close the portal. Everything Elora had fought so hard for would be gone with the wave of his hand.

A lump settled high in her throat. It refused to be swallowed down. How could she blame him? He *was* meant to be High King. He did deserve it.

What was she compared to that?

Queen Nerissa huffed, frustrated by Brannick's hesitation. She squished her mouth into a knot. "What could matter more to you than claiming your rightful title?"

His head turned slowly to face her. Once he met her eyes, his hand dropped to his side. "I will not close the portal."

Her eyebrows flew toward her crown as she took a step back. "What?"

The prince stood taller now. His face was set. "We fae are different now." His lips twitched upward. "But different is not always bad."

King Jackory clenched his jaw. "You will let High Queen Alessandra continue to terrorize us?"

"No." Brannick reached into his pocket and drew out the sword he had used while training with Elora. He pointed it toward the high queen. "There is another way."

Queen Noelani gasped as she lifted her javelin off the ground. "You are going to *kill* her? The High Queen of Faerie?"

He positioned the sword carefully for a killing strike. "I will do what I must to save us."

When he swung his blade, a metallic clang rang out just before he hit his mark. Things had moved in a blur. Elora couldn't tell what had happened until Brannick's sword stopped.

Queen Noelani's javelin stopped his sword, but it wasn't her who wielded it. The queen of Dustdune held the blue weapon with her features hardened. She must have stolen it from Queen Noelani.

The feather in her crown fluttered as Queen Nerissa shoved Brannick's sword to the ground. Her eyebrows lowered. "You should have closed the portal when you had the chance."

At the sound of those words, figures began appearing all around their small group. The soldiers wore long orange tunics and held short daggers as weapons. They had been glamoured to be invisible, but soldier after soldier came into view now.

The other rulers were greatly outnumbered.

CHAPTER

41

Every muscle in Elora's body froze. She tried to run. Her mind told her feet to lift and sprint toward Brannick. She urged her legs to propel her forward. They would not. It felt nothing like when fear had rendered her immobile. The force keeping her frozen now was far more powerful than fear.

It was magic.

Faerie itself held her in place. She tried to drop the stone that kept her invisible. She tried again to run forward to offer aid to Brannick. She even tried to scream. But she couldn't.

No matter what angle or action she tried, her body stayed frozen in place. She knew why. Brannick had begged her to make the vow that she would keep herself safe, and like a fool, she had. When the troll had injured her, she had done everything in her power to stay safe and get away as quickly as she could.

But now? Deep in her heart, she knew that any action would lead to her death. And so she didn't move at all.

She couldn't.

Her vow forced her to stay still and silent even when her heart pleaded for action.

The Dustdune soldiers continued to appear all around them. They marched forward and clapped chains around Brannick. He fought valiantly against them, but there were too many. And he had no reinforcements.

King Jackory and even Queen Noelani vanished through doors once they realized they had no chance to win the fight. Brannick snarled and gnashed but the soldiers still closed in on him. The golden color of the chains around him looked familiar. They looked exactly like the chains Queen Alessandra had wrapped both him and Elora in while they were in Fairfrost Palace. There must have been something inside of them that suppressed Brannick's magic.

Tipping her head to the side, Queen Nerissa addressed her soldiers. "Unbind the high queen."

The Dustdune soldiers followed her orders. Elora continued to urge herself to run, to scream. *Anything*.

But she did nothing. The Fairfrost queen had more power than ever.

The moment High Queen Alessandra was released from her bonds, she smacked a hand across Queen Nerissa's cheek. The blow came with so much force that it knocked the Dustdune queen off her feet.

High Queen Alessandra towered over her as she flashed her teeth. "You tried to betray me. I will not forget that."

Sucking in short breath, Queen Nerissa got to her knees. Her gaze stayed on the ground. "You still won in the end. What difference does it make now?"

With her head still tilted downward, Queen Nerissa lifted the jewel-encrusted crown off her head. She held it out toward the high queen. "I give up my claim to Dustdune. It is yours to rule."

High Queen Alessandra snatched the crown from Queen Nerissa's hands. She glared down at her as she unceremoniously placed the crown on her own head. The moment the silk touched her light brown curls, sparks of orange light burst off the crown.

Even with the white Fairfrost crown still on her head, the Dustdune crown bound itself to High Queen Alessandra. Once it finished, she plucked it off her head and stuffed it into her pocket. Its power must have transferred into the Fairfrost crown because now the white crown stood even taller than before.

When she turned on Brannick, Blaz was nowhere to be seen. He must have been using his glamour to hide himself, but High Queen Alessandra didn't seem to notice. Her face twisted into a sneer. "Everyone knows Bitter Thorn has the most magic of any court." Her nose wrinkled at the prince. "How else could you be so powerful even without ever wearing a crown?"

At those words, her gaze turned downward at the crown in Brannick's hand. She eyed it with the surety that she'd be able to pluck it from him easily now that he was bound. Her lips curled upward. "I have sought power over your court even before I met you. Indeed, that is the reason I worked so hard to meet you in the first place. I thought love would be the best way to win my prize, but I should have known, love is too fickle."

A wild gleam flickered in her eyes as she ripped the crown of Bitter Thorn away from the prince. Reaching into a pocket, she pulled out a turquoise stone Elora recognized at once.

Elora had given High Queen Alessandra that stone herself. The high queen thought it was the crystal that had once sat in the front of the crown. It wasn't.

Waving a hand, High Queen Alessandra sent the turquoise stone into the center of the crown. "I am queen of Fairfrost, Noble Rose, and Dustdune. I will soon be queen of Swiftsea and Mistmount too. I am even High Queen of Faerie. But no title will ever taste more delicious than this."

The stone moved into place in the front of the crown. Elora's breath hitched. Maybe the crown wouldn't work for her. Maybe it would refuse to bond to the high queen because she had used the wrong crystal.

But of course, it wasn't meant to be.

High Queen Alessandra placed the crown on her head, and it immediately set off large showers of green and brown sparks. Energy danced in the air as the crown bonded to her head. The high queen stood taller, her face more twisted than ever.

"I am Queen of Bitter Thorn." She followed the words with a wicked laugh.

Waving one hand, she moved the chains that held Brannick. He lifted off the ground even though his feet did not move. She opened a door and glanced back at him. "You will not escape my palace again. You are going to help me find the source of the creation magic in Bitter Thorn. I will steal it and then I will have more power than Faerie itself."

Without another word, she used her magic to take her and the prince through her door.

They were gone.

Elora still couldn't move.

The Dustdune soldiers disappeared through doors of their own. Elora tried to run, to move, to scream. She couldn't, not until every single Dustdune soldier had left.

All at once, Elora collapsed into a heap. She screamed and punched the earth, but it didn't change anything. Alessandra was Queen of Bitter Thorn.

Brannick was captured again.

The little magic that had been dancing at Elora's fingertips had vanished. She glanced up, and her stomach sank. No glowing lights, which meant no sprites to send a message.

She was alone.

Taking a deep breath, she forced herself to her feet. Her fingers gripped her sword hilt, hoping to draw some comfort from it. She had to get back to Bitter Thorn to find the others. Then they could start planning Brannick's rescue.

She gulped. But with no magic, she couldn't open her own door. And with no sprites, she couldn't send for anyone who could.

That meant she only had one way to get back to Bitter Thorn. Her jaw set as she popped the wings from her back.

She would just have to fly.

ACKNOWLEDGEMENTS

As always, I must begin by expressing my gratitude to you, the reader. This book has some dark moments. It took a lot out of me to write those. But that's the great thing about books. When we see our favorite characters going through dark moments, and then overcoming them, it helps us overcome the dark moments in our own lives.

It is my hope that Elora's journey throughout this book will help you discover the strength you have inside you.

If you enjoyed the book, please consider leaving a review for it on goodreads or on the retailer where you bought it. Your review could help a fellow reader discover this series!

I must also thank my amazing cover designer, Angel Leya. I feel that each book cover is better than the last in this series. The crown on this cover is truly magnificent.

I was able to work with two incredible editors while writing this book. Deborah Spencer, thank you for always understanding my vision and helping me get the book where it needed to be. Justin Greer, thank you for your expertise with line edits. As always, you help me so much.

My dear author friends, Queens of the Quill, deserve every thanks in the world. You ladies have been here for me through so many things. I was grateful to rely on you while dealing with several life issues. Thank you to Abby J. Reed, Alison Ingleby, Charlie N. Holmberg, Clarissa Gosling, Hanna Sandvig, Joanna Reeder, Kristin J. Dawson, Rose Garcia, Stacey Trombley, Tessonja Odette, and Valia Lind!

Of course, I must end by expressing gratitude for the best and most amazing man ever. Thank you to my husband for standing by me through everything. My heart is tied to yours.

ABOUT THE AUTHOR

Kay L Moody is proud to be a young adult fantasy author. Her books feature exciting plots with a few magical elements. They have lots of adventure, compelling characters, and sweet romantic sub-plots. Most of her books have a dystopian flair. They include a variety of technology levels and lots of diversity.

Kay lives in the western United States with her husband and four sons. She enjoys summertime, learning new things, and doing her nails with fancy nail art.

MORE FROM KAY L MOODY

The competition could save her life… but only if she wins.

A divided empire. Manipulation of the elements. Torn between duty and freedom, Talise must learn that clinging to the past might destroy her future.

If you love royalty, romance, and intrigue, and elemental magic this addicting fantasy series is a must read.

THE ELEMENTS OF KAMDARIA

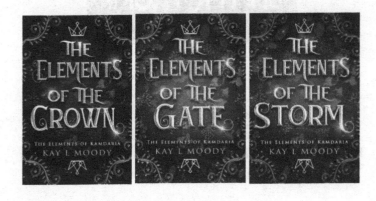

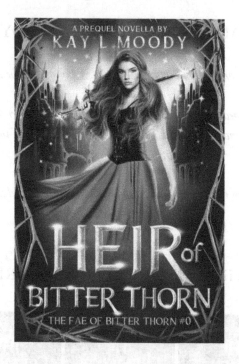

Visit kaylmoody.com/bitter for the complete prequel

Heir of Bitter Thorn is a prequel to The Fae of Bitter Thorn.
Discover how Elora got the mysterious scar on her hand,
how Prince Brannick escaped Fairfrost, and why the two of
them don't remember their first meeting.

ELORA NEVER felt more alive than when a sword swung
toward her body.

This one aimed for her heart, but she parried the blow. As
always, her sword acted as a shield as much as a weapon. The

two blades clashed midair. It took her a moment to regain a ready stance.

In the precious second she lost, her opponent managed to sneak in another strike. The lethal point of his sword kissed her bare arm on its way to her heart. It was too bad for him that she knew the move well.

Her steady footing gave just the right angle to slide her blade against his until the tops of their hilts clanged. With a great shove, she pushed the sword away from herself.

Her opponent stumbled backward for three steps and then landed on the dry, cracked dirt of the clearing where they fought. Faced with his defeat, Elora's father let out a chuckle as he smoothed wispy brown strands back over his balding spots. His silver eyes shined as he reached for the leather-wrapped hilt of his sword.

"I don't know how much more I can teach you, Elora." Hearing his gentle voice always jarred a bit with the ferocity of his sword fighting. He let out another soft chuckle and shielded his eyes from the sun, looking toward his forge.

The little clearing in the woods had always been the perfect spot for sparring. It sat close enough to his forge for her father to see when a customer approached. And even though their little cottage stood nearby, the clearing was far enough away that Elora's mother wouldn't see her fighting—in a dress and corset, yes, but *without* the long-sleeved under slip she was *supposed* to wear at all times.

The tight corset only barely limited her movements now that she was used to fighting with it. But the under slip that covered her arms always got in the way when she had to move fast. Fighting without it always went smoother.

Her father had sheathed his sword. He stroked her cheek with his knuckle, wearing a smile that always made her feel proud. "I think you're better than me now."

The words came with a biting reminder. Her blade sang as she slammed it into its sheath. "I'll never get to fight in the tournaments as long as I'm a woman, though. How do I know how good I really am if I'm not even allowed to fight?"

Her father managed to stop himself from wincing at her words. Maybe he'd been practicing. Apparently, he didn't want to start a fight. He leaned up against a tree filled with leaves fluttering in the gentle wind. "You don't need to fight. I won hundreds of tournaments in my day, and you can beat me. That should tell you exactly how good you are."

That was all her sword fighting was allowed to be. A hobby. Something to pass the time, like needlework or poem writing. A woman could have a talent for others to applaud and admire, but it could never be something she earned money from.

Besides that, beating her father now didn't mean as much as it used to. As a child, she loved sitting on her mother's lap and ogling as her father easily defeated every sword fighter he went up against. But he was an old man now, with three daughters to provide for and only a forge in an out-of-the-way village to do it with.

He hadn't even ordered a new shipment of ore for several weeks.

From the corner of her eye, she noticed a flash of movement. Her head jerked toward it but only found the same tree that had always been there. After narrowing her eyes for a moment, she turned back to her father.

With a handkerchief embroidered by her mother, he dabbed at the sweat on his forehead. "I have something for you."

He must have been in a very good mood if he limited his lecture to those three sentences. Now he reached for the leather bag that usually held his business letters and a few of his favorite forging tools.

From out of the bag, he pulled a soft leather-bound book. The pages all poked out at different angles; a haphazard length of string seemed to hold the whole thing together. His silvery eyes brightened again as he pushed the book toward her. "It's from my friends who still work at the castle."

Her stomach danced a jig as soon as she touched the book. Her fingers buzzed as she struggled to open the buckle that held it closed. When the pages fell open in her hands, a gasp of sheer delight escaped her.

Visit kaylmoody.com/bitter for the complete prequel

CPSIA information can be obtained
at www.ICGtesting.com
Printed in the USA
LVHW041701070521
686776LV00002B/226